THE LAND BEYOND

THE DARK CORNER UNIVERSE
BOOK 8

DAVID W. ADAMS

ISBN:
978-1-916582-25-5 [Paperback]
978-1-916582-26-2 [eBook]
978-1-916582-27-9 [Hardcover]

Copyright © 2023 David W Adams. All rights reserved.

This book is a work of fiction. Names, characters, places, and incidents are either the product of the authors imagination or are used fictitiously or in reference. Any resemblance to persons living, dead or undead, or locales are purely coincidental.

No parts of this book may be reproduced or used in any manner without written permission of the copyright owner except for the use of quotations in book reviews.

ECHO ON PUBLICATIONS

CONTENTS

Note From The Author   v

Prologue   1
Chapter 1   5
Chapter 2   19
Chapter 3   29
Chapter 4   39
Chapter 5   47
Chapter 6   55
Chapter 7   59
Chapter 8   67
Chapter 9   71
Chapter 10   77
Chapter 11   83
Chapter 12   89
Chapter 13   99
Chapter 14   105
Chapter 15   111
Chapter 16   117
Chapter 17   123
Chapter 18   131
Chapter 19   137
Chapter 20   143
Chapter 21   147
Chapter 22   153
Chapter 23   157
Chapter 24   163
Chapter 25   171
Chapter 26   177
Chapter 27   183
Chapter 28   189
Chapter 29   193

Chapter 30	197
Chapter 31	203
Chapter 32	207
Chapter 33	215
Chapter 34	221
Chapter 35	225
Chapter 36	229
Chapter 37	231
Chapter 38	233
Chapter 39	239
Chapter 40	245
Epilogue	251

ADDITIONAL CONTENT

The Road Not Taken	259
Afterword	265
About the Author	271

NOTE FROM THE AUTHOR

Firstly, I would like to thank you for picking up a copy of this revised, reformatted, and brand spanking new version of a *Dark Corner* book. I will never take that for granted and appreciate each and every one of you for doing so.

Let's cut to the chase.

This is not the first version of these books, as some of you may know. However, being an independent author comes with limitations, and for me at least, a great deal of impatience. When I wrote the original *Dark Corner* book, it was in the midst of the Coronavirus Pandemic, and the UK was in its first official lockdown. Go nowhere, do nothing, see nobody.

Basically my life in a nutshell, if you exclude going to work.

But I learned one day in my miserable and bland meandering through the days, that self-publishing had been on the rise while I looked the other way dreaming of having the time and money to be able to potentially have a crack at finally getting all of the stories out of my head. But better than that, was when I discovered there was a way to do it for FREE!

I was warned by several forums and articles that KDP, although

Note From The Author

an excellent resource compared to the previous nothingness, was also full of issues, pitfalls, and Amazon's usual greedy ways. You will make no money, nobody will see your book if you have less than 50 reviews, and nobody reads horror these days anyway.

Sadly, I must admit, that I was tempted to chuck the briefly stirred ambition of mine in the bin, and carry on going to work everyday during an outbreak so people could buy their 'essential' bathroom paint or Sharpie marker pens.

But it was my wife who encouraged me to continue. She had always written both poetry and fan fictions, but had never felt comfortable with the idea of the world reading her work. She was, however, incredibly persuasive, and after I reworked a story I started writing 20 years previously into what became the first story, *The White Dress*, I got bit by the bug. Over the course of 2020, I wrote ten short stories varying in severity, but overall quite reserved for horror, and resolved to get them published come what may.

Sadly, I couldn't afford an editor or proofreader, and my wife was also working full time and so simply didn't have the time to read for me. And so I decided to publish through a previously unknown, to me at least, website called My Bestseller. They were based in the Netherlands, and required you to buy an ISBN number or publish without one. However, while they offered expanded distribution, this did not include Amazon. I also discovered after purchasing an ISBN for that original version of the book, that it came at a reduced cost for one reason. The code was registered to the website. Which meant exclusivity.

Bollocks.

Exclusivity and not even on Amazon? No this would simply not do. I did however, make it work for a while, and in the course of three months sold a whopping two copies. I bought more than that myself!

Then came the time to explore KDP properly. I had published

Note From The Author

the book on My Bestseller without ever proofreading or editing it. I figured nobody was going to read it so didn't really worry about it. But one day, when writing the stories for the second book, *Return to the Dark Corner*, I went back to examine plot points that could be expanded.

Shit.

Errors, grammar issues, typos everywhere and more worryingly, plot holes. But it wasn't too late! Barely anybody had read it so I could fix it! That's when I revised the book, and published through KDP, which came with free ISBNs! Jackpot I thought! But you must remember I was incredibly naïve and undereducated in this area. Exclusivity was a requirement again, but I didn't care. It was Amazon! Everyone uses Amazon! I even got suckered into Kindle Unlimited with the promise of more royalties. They really do know how to con you into things!

Anyway, since then, the *Dark Corner* series has grown and grown, even into producing several pieces of merchandise for the series such as posters and keyrings. The series concludes in the 13th book, a number I chose because I figured it fitting for something that began as a horror series primarily, although it became so much more!

And when the opportunity came along to work with Christian Francis to redesign, reformat and relaunch the series with a new uniform and polished look, I jumped at the chance. Christian put the shine to my stories that I had always hoped to achieve, and even redesigned the covers for me to give it a true 'series' look. I will be forever grateful for his generosity, hard work, and friendship, and am honored for these versions of my works to fall under the banner of Echo On Publishing.

So here we are, entering the *Dark Corner* once again. But I don't do things lightly. These are not simply redesigns of the exact same work. Oh no. My conscience wouldn't allow that! So every single book has an extra short story included to further expand this

Note From The Author

varied, fascinating and horrific universe. Consider it my gift of thanks to you all for sticking with me, encouraging me not to give up, and pushing me to do better.

As always, I encourage you to be kind, be healthy, and stay safe.

And thank you.

David W. Adams
28th November 2023

I've chosen to dedicate this book to everyone involved with Flare Peer Support.

Thank you for the friendship and support you have shown me in the short time we have known each other.

These characters are inspired by you.

PROLOGUE

In the wake of their desperate flight, the ominous snarls drew ever closer behind them, a haunting symphony of menace that eclipsed even their own laboured gasps. Petri's fear-stricken gaze darted backward, and his eyes widened with dread. The writhing black smoke seemed to gain momentum, a tempest of malevolence. His heart thundered within him, a deafening cacophony, drowning out the sounds of their frantic panting and breathless strides. Pushing himself to the limit, Petri's feet trampled the meadow's tender flora, releasing a soft symphony of lament from crushed grass and blossoms. Berg towered above him, and urged him to run faster, but Petri's reserves were depleted, and his strength had all but evaporated. Berg, being taller and able to take bigger strides, began to move ahead and leave Petri behind.

"Wait! Berg, don't leave me!"

He cried out, pleading with Berg not to abandon him, but his calls fell on deaf ears. The imposing gates of the Fifth Kingdom loomed ahead, an elusive sanctuary that Berg relentlessly pursued. He kept his focus on those huge stone archways, for fear that if he looked back he would never reach them.

"Wait!"

Petri's desperate cries echoed futilely once more, his appeals proving fruitless as the merciless tendrils of darkness closed in on him. His frail form was ensnared, lifted off the ground like a forsaken twig carried on the foot far from its forest. Petri was now in the maelstrom's grip. The shadows converged around him, fixated on their hapless quarry. As Berg approached the gates, he dared to glance back, just in time to witness the horror that unfolded. From within the shroud of smog, a sinister figure manifested – a malevolent wolf-like spectre with crimson eyes that pierced the abyss. Its jaws, lined with menacing fangs, struck like lightning, wrenching Petri's head from his anguished form. The echoes of his torment were no longer audible, silenced by the cruel grip of death. Veins bulging upon his pallid visage, Petri's final moments of agony etched themselves into Berg's mind.

A surge of pain and shock coursed through Berg as he grappled with his first encounter with mortality. Not only that, but the loss of his best friend, his brother in all but name. They had played in these meadows for almost ten years, never venturing further than the wildflowers and always returning together. But not this time. His heart pounded vehemently against his chest, and he shuddered with revulsion. The predatory entity, after a cold, disdainful glance, shifted its focus, then coalesced back into a swirling mass, retreating through the meadow, carrying Petri's remains along with it.

Frozen for a fleeting moment, Berg eventually managed to command his legs forward. Against his instinct, he felt compelled to return to the site of the atrocity, to confront the macabre reality that now haunted him. Was it real? Or had he conjured this monstrous nightmare in his mind? But there it was. A searing brand etched upon the Earth – an imprinted trail snaking like a malevolent serpent, leading back to the far reaches of the horizon where their ill-fated journey had commenced. In that singular moment, Berg questioned why they had even travelled to such a place. Everyone knew if one ventured out from the gates of the Fifth Kingdom on the West side, you dared not stray more than thirty minutes walk away. And for why? Teenage curiosity because the adults had instructed them not to do so. Impudence of the innocent mind. But of course Berg's mind was no longer innocent. Death was a forever tenant.

Panic then gripped Berg once more, and he fled back towards the gates, his legs ablaze with pain, his chest pierced by agonising stabs. Collapsing onto the cobblestones beyond the gates, he was discovered by a concerned family who rushed to his aid. They were typical residents of the Fifth Kingdom, and wore tattered and soiled clothes, but they were good people. Honest and caring. The treatment they were given in this place was not brutal but it was harsh.

"Are you alright, my young friend?" the father enquired with genuine worry.

Berg shook his head frantically, attempting to find his voice amidst his breathlessness and terror stricken mind.

"The..."

The wife had now attracted the attention of members of the King's Guard, who advised her to take her children away.

"What is it?" the father implored, eager to understand.

Summoning the strength to speak at last, Berg breathed deeply and finally uttered the chilling truth.

"The void... the void has opened."

1

The dim lights struggled to pierce the thick darkness that surrounded Josh in this damp and desolate building. The cruel conditions gnawed at him, a constant reminder of the crushing poverty endured by the forgotten souls seeking solace within these walls. Yet amidst these shadows, a glimmer of hope and compassion permeated the air, for this was a place of love and kindness, despite its dismal façade. The soup kitchen, which had stood for four decades, had never witnessed such an influx of desperate souls as it did now. A veil of denial shrouded the government and local authorities of Wealdstone, attempting to cloak the chilling reality that had taken root over the past decade. But the truth could no longer be denied, at least not to the residents living here. For the monsters lurking in the shadows were real, and their presence left a trail of destruction and despair in their wake.

With the destruction of much of this town, courtesy of the now infamous Jasmine's visit, the soup kitchen's visitors surged by an unimaginable five-hundred-percent. As if the pain of the not-so-distant-past wasn't enough, a second recent supernatural clash had further ravaged the town. Even Crossroads, a settlement far from the heart of the turmoil, felt the tremors of battle. The few who had flocked there clinging to Monarch's offered aid had found themselves bound in reluctant servitude, and following his defeat, found themselves bereft of the very support they had sought there. Many of them had travelled with the maniacal demon seeking refuge in his sanctuary for reasons as simple as the warmth of a hearth and a morsel of sustenance. Not everyone who sought such comfort could be condemned as monsters. The so-called heroes, like Kathryn Silverton and her ilk, may have fought evil with grandeur, but their legacy left shattered lives in their wake, forgotten by those who celebrated their valour.

When the town was rebuilt after the Pain Wraith attack, housing became even more unaffordable than it had previously, without the rises in the cost of living passed on by the suited privileged few in Washington. This made life difficult even for those who considered themselves to be out of reach of poverty. Not the Silvertons though. They were given a shiny new house on the site of their former headquarters. In fact, it had been prioritised over the needs of the townsfolk who were truly struggling.

It was one of the main reasons that Josh volunteered here. He was burdened by his own loss, driven by the faint memories of his father's untimely death during the attack on Main Street. The exact details were blurry to him as if his mind was trying to bury them due to the intense grief. Even though it was only four years later, he struggled to form a clear image of his father in his mind. Two of his cousins had been enjoying a drink at Sisko's and were too snatched away by the unforgiving hand of fate. While others idolised the so-called heroes, Joshua Shaw scorned them, dreaming of possessing magical powers but tethered by the weight of reality.

"Evening Josh, nice to see you here again!"

A familiar face brought Josh back from his reverie. It was his favourite visitor to the kitchen.

"Hey Alan, how's it going?" Josh responded, attempting to find

Chapter 1

solace in the old man's bright smile, but the pain in his eyes betrayed the hardships he faced.

Alan, who had lost everything – home, wife, and job in a cruel twist of fate – clung to his unyielding spirit. Despite his hardships, he radiated a resilient hope that contrasted with the darkness of their circumstances.

"I'm doing pretty good young man, thank you for asking. Might even have the prospect of a job interview on Friday!"

Josh smiled, but deep down he knew the world's cold realities would likely extinguish that glimmer of hope. The few jobs that were available were going to the younger applicants. They were cheaper, disposable and easily replaceable. Despite his amazing outlook on life, Alan was still a sixty year old homeless black man. Even in the twenty-first century, somebody like that would always be at the back of the queue. Nobody had any humanity left in them anymore when it came to business and survival.

"That's great buddy, let me know how you get on."

Alan smiled and nodded at Josh as he collected his mashed potatoes and walked away, but not before his usual tip of the hat to the girl on the end of the serving row. Josh smiled to himself as he was reminded that even at sixty, Alan was still thinking of himself as a ladies man. Chantel had always indulged Alan. He was never inappropriate and was always the perfect gentleman, and she was still fairly new in town, carrying scars of her own. Josh had admired her since her arrival almost a year ago. Not in a romantic sense, but in the sense that she too had suffered trauma, and yet seemed to be facing it with determined resolve and an open mind.

They had spoken a handful of times, and he had thought how her scientific background seemed futile in a place like Wealdstone, devoid of opportunities for such knowledge. But her unwavering determination and open heart gave him genuine cheer. She had even been taking up extra work towards new topics including bioengineering which Josh felt fascinated by despite knowing absolutely nothing on the subject. Again, his thoughts were interrupted by the supervisor, Polly, tapping him on the shoulder.

"Hey Josh, that's your shift done for the night, you can head off now."

Josh smiled.

"That's okay Polly, I'm happy to do another hour or so. I don't have plans tonight."

Her smile faded, and directed his eyes to the containers of food in front of him, or more precisely the lack of it.

"Oh. I see."

Polly nodded sadly.

"Supplies have been cut again. This afternoon's truck was diverted to Trinity Bay. What possible emergency they can have over there I do NOT know, but either way, the next one isn't coming until Monday."

Josh's heart ached at that statement. It was only Wednesday. That would mean the people who relied on this place would now not have food provided to them for four days. He exchanged knowing glances with Polly. They both knew what that would mean, and they both knew there wasn't much that either one of them could do about it.

"We'll keep the doors open 24/7 for them to have somewhere warm to sit or sleep. And who knows, somebody might come through for us."

Polly's enthusiasm was laced with undertones of doubt and uncertainty. The people of Wealdstone had been so consumed by fear that they now held on to whatever they had and were loathed to part with a single box of cereal let alone money or joints of meat. Josh nodded once more, and slid his apron over his head, hanging it on the hook behind him. As he made his way to the door, Alan waved at him, a huge smile on his face.

"I'll remember you when I get back to the top of the corporate ladder Josh!"

Chapter 1

Josh chuckled and waved back, but as he exited into the cold sharp night air, and out of the view of the people inside, his smile vanished. Deep within him burned a passion, a determination to make a difference, despite the odds stacked against him. In a world where darkness prevailed, he aspired to be a beacon of light and hope for those who had lost everything to the lurking shadows of the night and bolts of lightning struck down by evil entities. But in truth, Josh wasn't in that much of a better position himself. He was working part-time in an imported candy store, with a second job in a coffee shop and was only making enough to cover his rent, utilities and a tiny amount of disposable income. He always used some of that money to bring fresh fruit and vegetables to the kitchen, but saved a tiny amount of it once a month for his passion project.

As Josh reached the end of the row of dilapidated housing, with its pawn shops and forgotten dreams, he caught sight of the familiar neon glow above the comic book store. The name always made Josh smile, being a huge comic and sci-fi fan. Final Frontier had become a haven for his comic book and sci-fi obsessions. Here he could escape the bleakness of the modern world and immerse himself in fantastic realms. But before indulging in his passion, Josh faced the harsh reality of his own financial situation. Checking his banking app on the cracked screen of his smartphone, he discovered a meagre sum of fifty dollars remaining after paying rent and utilities. With the soup kitchen facing such a shortage, he knew that every dollar mattered. Resolved to make at least some amount of difference, he decided to allocate forty dollars to his favourite store, and use the other ten to head down to the local discount food warehouse for essentials to aid the kitchen.

The door to this particular store did not jingle with the sound of a bell, but with the opening riff from the *Indiana Jones* theme. The volume, as usual, startled him, but he greeted Dalton with a warm smile.

"Hey Josh, how is the next big screen adaptation coming?" Dalton asked from behind the counter.

"Hey buddy, yeah not too bad. Been spending more time at the kitchen and trying to pick up a few extra hours at work, so I haven't had much time to move it forward yet. How's things in here?"

Josh reached for the latest issue of his favourite comic, *Doctor Strange*. His carefree attitude toward comic books clashed with the delicate handling expected of collectors. For him, the magic lay in immersing himself entirely in the stories, devouring their very essence. Dalton found amusement in his friend's enthusiastic approach and offered encouragement for his creative endeavours.

"To be honest, you're the first person I've seen since noon. Spent most of the day figuring out how much all this is worth."

That caught Josh's attention.

"Is it really that bad?" he asked, his face resembling that of a boy who has been told his favourite dog is going 'off to the farm.'

Dalton nodded reluctantly. His long greying hair was both a sign of his stress and of his true age, which despite his chosen outfits was much older than he felt.

"Had a final notice for the electricity bill this morning. They've offered me a payment plan though, so I'm not too worried about that. It's the rent."

Josh's face began to move towards an angrier demeanour. There were a few untouched by the devastation and destruction in this town and rather than share what they were blessed with to help out their fellow townspeople, they chose to profit and dominate those below them on the food chain. Dalton's landlord was one of the untouched.

"He put it up again?"

Dalton nodded once more.

"Raised it by another hundred dollars a week. At this rate, I'll be gone by the end of the month."

Chapter 1

For the next ten minutes or so, Josh and Dalton discussed the misery and depression surrounding the town and a brief five minutes looking over Josh's own graphic novel that he had been working on. He took great pride in describing the unusual powers of his superhero, which up until this point, had not been revealed to his friend.

"Well, that's certainly a new one, I've not heard of that anywhere else before."

Josh shrugged his shoulders and held his hands apart indicating that was exactly the point.

"You can't tell me it's not cool though right? Having the ability to take electricity and reconstitute it into any other form of matter? Literally drag power from a bedside lamp in the middle of the night and turn it into a glass of water? It's genius."

Dalton found it hard to argue with that and gave Josh a high five. In truth, it was a hero Josh had seen in his mind for years and years and the creation was so vivid that he saw himself doing those exact things, almost as if he *knew* how to do them. Another five minutes went by, and Josh said goodnight to his friend, wished him luck and exited through the door, again jumping at the loudness of the jingle. He removed his rucksack and opened up the main compartment, stuffing his new purchases inside along with his own creation, before he zipped it back up. He swung the bag over his shoulder, and charged forward, straight into Chantel.

"Oh god, Chantel I'm so sorry," exclaimed Josh as he knelt down to pick up her books that had been spilled in the impact.

"That's okay, don't worry about it. They're not mine anyway, they're Grace's."

Something about her French accent just made Josh pay more attention to everything she said. It made him feel like more of an adult to have a European friend. Grace, however, was somebody that Josh was very much afraid of. He had heard of her enhanced abilities and on the few occasions he had seen her, she had looked ready to snap somebody in two. Still, he could tell with the fondness Chantel spoke about her, that she cared for her deeply. Maybe one day he could find somebody that thought that way about him. Although after Chantel had a prolonged stay in hospital less than a year ago, Grace seemed to be around less and less.

"Interesting collection she has. Didn't figure her as much of a reader."

Chantel's brown eyes sparkled in the light of the street lamp, and she leaned slightly to one side.

"She is becoming more cultured in her retirement, I'll have you know."

The two of them giggled, but Josh suspected it was at different things. She was perhaps laughing at the suggestion she can make Grace more cultured, and he was laughing at the thought of a twenty-five year old retiring. In truth, he sensed the relationship Chantel and Grace had was not what his French friend would have liked.

"You heading in here?" Josh asked her, pointing at the comic books in the window.

"Yeah, American graphic novels just have more colour and optimism about them. Well, most of them. I'm trying to make myself switch off from the science most days. Otherwise if I think about what I left behind in Paris too much, I'll slip back into the rabbit hole."

Josh's smile narrowed. He had remembered the day he found out her origin story, and exactly what she had lost before she came to Wealdstone.

"Well, Dalton's got some new ones on the front rack, so go nuts. He could do with the business."

Chantel nodded, gave him a brief hug and went inside. She too jumped at the *Indy* theme and Josh chuckled to himself, before starting his walk home. The wind had died down, and most of the

Chapter 1

streets were empty. As he turned the corner onto his own avenue, he noticed all of the streetlights were out. He let out a deep sigh.

"Not again."

This was the fourth week in a row the lights had failed. Contractors were busy putting the finishing touches onto the new and improved cineplex over at the Silverton Shopping District.

Again.

There were no workers left to tend to the small but important things. It was far more important to knock down and rebuild a cinema for the third time in a decade. It brings money in, and streetlights don't. Except it didn't bring money in. Blockbuster movies had flopped continuously year on year since 2023, but lavish construction projects always caught the eye of potential investors.

The problem with Ingram Avenue, was that either side of the street was lined with forest, which blocked out any moonlight unless the moon happened to be directly above. Josh knew he had a torch, and fumbled in the darkness to find it. He felt the plastic clip on the back of the torch, and unhooked it from his rucksack, but as he lifted it up, his fingers slipped and he dropped it, the sound of it clattering to the floor echoing around the empty street.

"Shit. That better not be broken."

He leaned down, and ran his hands over the broken asphalt trying not to focus on the disgusting materials his fingers were now running over. A few cigarette butts later, and something squishy he didn't want to think about, he found the plastic rectangle which encompassed the torch, and he stood back up to his full height and flicked the button.

"Woah!" he exclaimed jumping back. "Where the hell did you come from?"

Before him sat a cat, its fur the colour of flame, bathed in the radiance of the torch's light. The cat's eyes locked with his holding an almost human-like gaze. As Josh attempted to move forward, the cat remained unmoved, seemingly obstructing his path.

"Do you mind? I have a house to find," Josh implored with a mixture of frustration and curiosity, half expecting a response.

The cat, however, had its own agenda, and after refusing to move twice more, gestured with its head toward the forest. Josh stopped and looked at the cat. There was something all too familiar about the animal, that Josh simply could not identify. It repeated the same movement and began to meow, gesturing towards the trees.

"What is it?" he asked, feeling slightly foolish that he was talking to a cat in the middle of the street.

The cat repeated the noise and motioned for a third time, and then began to walk towards the trees. When it noticed Josh was not behind it anymore, it paused, looked over its shoulder and meowed again. This peculiar encounter began to evoke a strange fascination within Josh, as if some otherworldly force beckoned him to follow. Unable to resist, he gave in to the explicable pull, running his hand through his curly hair in resignation.

"Guess we're doing this then," he mumbled as he set forth into the dark embrace of the forest, "but this is always the start of some horror movie where they run toward danger, so if I die, I'm blaming you, furball."

When the cat saw him moving in its direction, the feline continued down the side of the street and into the tree line. Josh tried to shine the light straight in front of them, but the uneven ground made it hard for him to remain steady. He tripped over a rock and landed on his knees, the sound of wet mud sploshing beneath him making him groan. Almost in response, the cat turned back to him, and meowed sarcastically, and even in the darkness, he could have sworn the cat rolled its eyes at him. After a few moments, he looked behind him and saw that they had already travelled far from his street, and yet the cat continued on its path.

Chapter 1

"Hey, cat, where are we going?" he asked, narrowly avoiding a large puddle.

The cat ignored him, but appeared to be slowing down as it approached a large clearing. The light from the torch began to flicker, and within seconds, the battery was dead.

"Great."

He heard the cat meow once more, and when he looked up from the now defunct torch, he was surprised to see the cat sat in the middle of the clearing, bathed in a green light. Josh's mouth began to open involuntarily as he tried to grasp what he was seeing. The cat meowed again, and Josh slowly moved towards the phenomenon.

Directly in front of him was what appeared to be a doorway. Only there was no door, and no structure to speak of. A thin almost neon green line traced itself along and down on two sides mimicking the shape of a door, and although the space in between was empty, the air felt charged with energy.

"What is this?" he whispered to himself, his mind reeling with countless questions.

Josh wasn't sure if he was asking himself or the cat, or some unseen higher power. But he couldn't stop moving forwards, drawn to the mystical glowing frame. Suddenly, the cat sprung to its feet, and leapt through the doorway. Josh gasped as he watched the animal vanish into thin air. The only trace of the movement was the apparent rippling in the space between the door frame, like the aftershocks from a stone thrown into a lake.

In a state of disbelief, his mind running wild, Josh circled the doorframe of light, he walked around the back, and then back to the front. It almost felt as though a breeze was coming through from the other side of wherever this phenomenon led.

"There is no way," he mumbled to himself, looking the doorway up and down. "Absolutely not. Not a chance."

But the curiosity within him was burning like fire, his heart pounding with anticipation. His imagination was running rampant inside his mind, and he felt his arm raise towards the doorway, and he closed his eyes, clamping them so tightly, that his face wrinkled around them. He gritted his teeth, and tensed up every part of his body. He opened his mouth, took a very large breath, clenched his teeth once more, and stepped through the doorway.

Immediately, the world shifted around him. He felt his head spinning, and his skin tingled. But it only lasted a couple of seconds at most, before it was replaced with a blast of cool air, and a spray of water, and the sensation of falling. Josh threw his eyes open to find himself stepping off the top of an incredibly large waterfall. He tried to arrest his momentum but it was too late. He tumbled forwards, somersaulting multiple times as he plummeted down through the spray, the water and wind plastering his hair to his head and soaking his clothes. As he approached the base of the waterfall, he closed his eyes once again, and took the biggest breath he could. The waterfall was so vast that the impact of Josh's body into the water made almost no extra sound. Had somebody been walking by, apart from the faint sound of his screams mingled with the roar of the water, they wouldn't have known anything was amiss.

That is of course, presuming anyone *could* walk by. This was a far different place to the forest surrounding Ingram Avenue. The water itself was of a deep turquoise colour and seemed to shimmer rather than glisten in the sunlight, as if glitter had been spread into the river. The sun in question was high in the sky, and a small rainbow was cast between the spray of the falls and the nearest trees. At the base of the falls, there was a small rocky beach, surrounded by trees similar in height to those of the forest Josh had just left, but the wood was maple coloured, and the leaves a vibrant shade of purple, each spreading out at six points, rounded at their tips.

Josh managed to haul himself onto the edge of the pebbled

Chapter 1

beach, gasping for breath. Somehow he had managed to keep his rucksack attached to his back, but water was pouring out of the bottom of the fabric. A few coughs later, and he discarded the bag beside him, and rolled onto his back staring up at the sky, his chest heaving.

The sound of the water roaring not far away was muffled slightly in his ears by the presence of the same water. Josh reached up, his arms aching and attempted to bang the water out of each ear, before squeezing his curly beard between his fingers in an effort to lighten the load on his face. After a few moments, he pulled himself forward into a seated position, and began to look around.

"What in the f...,"

Meow.

Josh snapped his head around, and sat behind him licking its front left paw, was the ginger cat which had started this trip. Rage began to build in him, and he found the strength to push himself to his feet and he began to stomp towards the cat.

"YOU!" he bellowed.

The cat did not move, and simply continued to clean its paws.

"Where the hell have you brought me?!?" he shouted again. "What the hell was that?"

He pointed at the waterfall, and as he turned to look, there did not appear to be any evidence of a doorway at the top, just more trees. When he turned back, the cat was gone.

Josh moved his head left to right rapidly, searching for the animal, but found nothing. The trail of water that he had been leading was beginning to slow, and he felt a little lighter, but his mind was still buzzing with the effects of his transportation to what was clearly far from where he had started.

As he took a couple of steps forward, again searching for the cat, an arm swung out from behind a large yellow bush, and met Josh right in the centre of his chest, winding him and knocking him back to the ground with a thud. As he shook his head to clear his vision, a glimmer caught his eye, and caused him to blink quickly several times. When he did manage to focus his face became one of fear. A sharp point was now sticking in his throat, and as his eyes followed the line which led to it, he realised he was staring down the business end of a broadsword.

And at the other end of the sword, towering above him, was a man with shoulder length wavy hair, and sporting a medieval style goatee beard, peppered with blonde and grey. His clothing, or more like armour, was of a greenish hue, and appeared to be covered in scales of some sort. The metal did not shine in the way the sword did and seemed to move independently of the wearer.

The man pressed the point to Josh's throat with slightly more pressure, and leaned his face in.

"Just how did you break into this realm?"

2

The glass shattered against the gilded stone walls of the ancient chapel, and the dark crimson of the spilled merlot cascaded downward, staining the masonry like blood. In the aftermath of his fit of frustration, Chan stormed out of the courtyard, seeking solace in the nearby meadow.

"Why is this so difficult?" he seethed, his emotions a tempest of anger and sadness, his brow furrowed in deep contemplation. This was not the first setback he had encountered, and the unyielding desire to recapture the indomitable fire that had surged within him during his time in Wealdstone only intensified his inner turmoil. Unfortunately, he had so far not managed to recreate that all-consuming fire anywhere but in his own frustrations.

"You must calm yourself, my young friend."

The reassuring voice of Nybor, his wise mentor and friend, gently pierced the storm of emotions. Her tone was a soothing balm to his wounded spirit, but even then, Chan could not seem to unclench his fists.

"But I should be able to do this, Nybor! I have the desire, clearly as we saw in the human realm, I am capable, and I have the wisdom of your guidance. Why can I not replicate what happened?"

As Nybor approached her distraught student, her tall and stoic figure exuded an aura of wisdom and tranquillity. Her long white hair cascaded like a river of moonlight, and despite her sympathy for Chan, a lingering fear remained within her. For Chan had changed since his visit into the human world. His arrogance, impatience, and frustration had grown exponentially, almost as if the burning within him unleashed a hidden personality.

It was also true that she had not gotten over the definitive death of her father, Dorn and still felt the weight of responsibility for his actions, the memories haunted her thoughts constantly. Dorn had been one of the seekers who sought out and released the Yellow Demons, malevolent beings driven by hunger, power and destruction. They inhabited the bodies of those who sought them out, wreaking havoc and suffering. Their release was part of a sinister plot by one of these such demons, called Monarch. This particular creature was hell-bent on merging the gateways between worlds and subjugating all realms under his rule.

The unique elements in the Crossroads area of the human town of Wealdstone had certain geometric properties when exposed to the right level of energy, which drew these gateways closer together. Ultimately, Monarch's plan had been to sacrifice the energy of the humans and entities he had become aware of, to achieve the aforementioned goal.

The pivotal battle in Wealdstone, where the brave group of humans, Pain Wraiths and Blue Spirits were joined by Nybor and Chan, had seen the young apprentice evolve into a Fire Demon – an entity of immense power thought to be extinct. The once-powerful Fire Demons had succumbed to infighting and civil war, ultimately leading to their downfall. Some had wanted to be benevolent, some wished to be dominant. In the end, they all

Chapter 2

perished and the magic which created their powers in the first place died out.

At least that was what people *believed* had happened.

And yet here was Chan, a Fire Demon reborn with untapped potential. In a fateful confrontation with Monarch, his power surged like a blazing inferno, before being struck down. Since then, Chan had struggled and subsequently failed, to recreate the extraordinary might he had once wielded. Nybor had been tireless in her efforts to help him rediscover those dormant powers, albeit under strict guidelines, through meditation and conjuring techniques. Still, success proved elusive."I think perhaps it's best if you head home for the day," Nybor suggested, although she was cutting the session short for fear that Chan's anger may actually lead to the very thing he was trying to achieve.

But his frustration only deepened, his yearning for that incredible power fuelled his determination.

"I need to feel this again, Nybor," he declared, his voice a mix of determination and desperation. "It was incredible and with those powers, I can help people in ways beyond their imagination."

Nybor's smile masked her underlying concern for Chan's eagerness to help others – a rarity in a world plagued by distrust and suspicion. She reached out, placing a comforting hand on his shoulder, her voice tinged with both affection and caution.

"Chan, we must tread carefully. Your emergence as a Fire Demon is a phenomenon unseen for over a thousand years. In this tumultuous world, such power may unsettle and terrify people, particularly at the sudden emergence of such an ancient bloodline. We must keep your abilities a secret, at least for now."

Though Chan's frustrations abated slightly, his youthful impatience still gnawed at him. At just ninety-nine years old, he had discovered a power he could never have imagined, and now he yearned to explore and share these new found abilities with the world.

"What about Annie? Everybody knows about her, and she isn't even here anymore!" he protested.

Nybor shook her head, her expression stern, clearly failing to impart the urgency of the matter into her young protégé.

"Chan, you fail to grasp the impact of a Blue Spirit's appearance. The events of that day have sent ripples of fear across the realms. People talk, but not in gratitude. They are suspicious, and afraid of what might be lurking in the shadows."

Confused, Chan's frown deepened.

"But Annie helped us save everyone. Surely they can see the good in that?"

Nybor chuckled gently. The innocence of youth.

"That would be too easy wouldn't it? The people of this world do not think like that. This world has been scarred by wars and destruction throughout its history, long before your species even existed. People find it hard to trust anything that appears too good to be true. The deeds of our Blue Spirit friend are met with suspicion, not gratitude."

Chan did not like the way these events were being portrayed, but if he was truthful with himself, he had noticed it too. Murmuring in the streets, and occasional side eye from passers-by in his direction, simply for being a part of it. If they knew about him, what reaction would he receive? Resigned, he closed his eyes, taking a deep breath to quell some of these emotions. He nodded in acknowledgement of Nybor's counsel, grateful for her guidance. Bowing to his mentor, he left the meadow, making his way towards the nearby village of Seven, his heart burdened by the weight of secrecy once more.

Nybor, too, carried a heavy burden – of unsettling events and brewing unease. The appearance of outsiders from other realms disturbed her, as the mystical gateways, meant to be rarely used if ever, had seen a surge in activity. The guardians, the Green Dragons, were supposed to ensure their controlled use, but

Chapter 2

Monarch's careless lies and false breadcrumb trails to create distractions, had seen their number dwindle. The resurgence of the Phantom Wraiths had been utilised by the Yellow Demon to slay many of the guardians of the doorways to further his plans. The irony was that Phantom Wraiths did not need the doorways to move between realms and it was simply a strategic act of violence.

Taking a deep breath, Nybor turned and walked back towards the entrance to the chapel, where she retrieved her staff from its resting place against the second archway to the right of the door. With a swift flick of the staff, the bottle and the contents were lifted from the floor and the surface of the stone wall, reassembling themselves and landing gently on the table Chan had snatched it from, as if nothing had happened.

As she walked along the pathway outside the chapel towards the castle, Nybor thought how grateful she was that thankfully that threat of the Phantom Wraiths had not appeared since, but Nybor could not shake the sense that it was simply a matter of time. She had devoted seventy-five years of her one-hundred-twenty-five year service to leading the Order of the White Falcons, and she had never been questioned about her loyalty to the realm, or her duties.

Not once.

Her family's history with the Yellow Demons had only strengthened her resolve to protect her realm. But lately, the King had requested several meetings with her surrounding her recent activities, and involvement with the humans, particularly Annie. She had taken the decision not to confide in the King about Chan's emerging abilities. He was already cautious of her involvement with a Blue Spirit, and did not want to test him further.

Annie had been a strong ally in the battle against Monarch, and Nybor found she often missed her. Unfortunately their paths would likely never cross again. Upon their return to Beyond, Nybor had ordered the remaining Green Dragons, to mask the doorways with a powerful binding spell. The doorways were to be hidden on both sides to prevent detection and any possible threat to Beyond. However, an ominous shift in behaviours across the First Kingdom – the realm's wealthiest and most influential city - and into the royal castle, had heightened her unease.

Nybor had done nothing in her life that wasn't geared towards safeguarding her home and the people within it. But she felt a resistance building. Almost as if the air was shifting and she was beginning to fall onto the wrong side of a battle that had not yet surfaced. In just over a thousand years, she had done both terrible and wondrous things to protect Beyond. Some she would very much like to forget. And yet somehow, she was sensing that it would not be enough. Behaviours within the people of Beyond, were shifting towards a more militant feel. Everyone was starting to look after themselves, and no one else. There was no sharing, no love towards others, and no generosity at all. The human expression 'rats leaving a sinking ship' kept playing on her mind. There were a few human expressions Nybor had picked up in her short time in the human realm, and of course with hidden prior knowledge unknown to many. She thought back to the bottle of something called tequila that one of the other humans, Kathryn, had given her. She looked forward to a glass of that when she returned home that evening.

A larger gust of wind came in from her right, and as she turned her head, her eyes fell upon the incredible spectacle of another White Falcon coming in to land on the walkway. LeVar was her most trusted Falcon, a beacon of unwavering loyalty and strength, and had fought by her side since the day she joined the Order. The first thing she had done upon becoming leader, was to make him her First. The role brought great honour to those who were bestowed with the title. LeVar was in command of the Falcons any time Nybor was incapacitated or unavailable, and was unwavering in his duty. Despite this, Nybor was still the only White Falcon

Chapter 2

permitted to commune with royalty. Something that irked LeVar greatly.

Nybor couldn't help but smile as she saw his wings fold away and his long white hair dancing in the breeze as he walked. Unlike Nybor, LeVar did not wield a staff to channel his magic. He had chosen a pair of white metal daggers. Each handle was topped with a bone carving of a falcon, and the metal itself was forged from the Fallen Mountains. However, her smile soon began to fade, as it became clear from the expression on his face, that LeVar was not here with good news.

"My lady," he said in his deep booming voice, as he bowed before rising back to his full height of seven feet. "I bring you disturbing news from the Fifth Kingdom."

Concern washed over Nybor once again, not that it ever truly left her these days. She had never seen her First so agitated. Even his customary inquiry about her day was absent, emphasising the gravity of his report. Urging him to continue, she sought to brace herself for whatever grim tidings awaited.

"I can tell the news disturbs you, old friend. Please continue."

LeVar nodded.

"There was an incident in the meadow beyond the Kingdom walls. A boy was attacked and killed by what the surviving friend of his described as a 'smoke creature.' He barely escaped to the confines of the city, but on further examination, there were scorch marks in the grass."

Nybor's heart sank, and her stomach began to swirl. The familiarities of this description triggered painful memories within her. Events buried deep began to resurface, veering very close to secrets she wished to keep hidden, secrets which haunted her. Her mind raced but she needed to hear what she already knew.

"And the trail of these scorch marks? They lead all the way back there?" she asked.

LeVar nodded.

25

"To the boundary of the void, my lady."

Turning away, Nybor leaned against the stone railings before her, her gaze searching the horizon for solace but finding none. This incident must not reach the public's ears. Panic would spread like wildfire, surpassing the fear caused by a mere Fire Demon's presence. The burden of secrets continued to weigh heavily on her, the list of which was beginning to expand far too rapidly. She returned her gaze to LeVar.

"How many know of this?" she asked LeVar, fearing the worst.

"The surviving boy, Berg. He is an orphan and had gone exploring with his friend. But he did relay the story to several of the Kings Guard and at least two families we know of who helped him to safety."

This was not good. In the Fifth Kingdom, word travelled fast. Where in the First and Second Kingdoms, people kept things to themselves, and chose not to gossip for fear they would be implicated in something, in the lower Kingdoms, gossip was rampant.

"Who do we have stationed near the Fifth at the moment?"

LeVar thought for a moment, before shaking his head.

"Negligible Falcons, my lady. I believe only Eva, Gregor and Skye."

Nybor nodded. They were some of her finest. Skye had grown up with her and they had at one point become best friends. However, events in Nybor's past meant they had grown apart until Skye was inducted into the White Falcons fifty years prior. But the important thing was they could be trusted.

"Get a message to them and inform them that nobody is to leave the Fifth Kingdom within the next twenty-four hours. No ravens are to be sent. This must be contained."

LeVar nodded, assuring her that he understood. With an unspoken bond, he trusted her implicitly, and she trusted him to execute her commands efficiently. He moved to turn away.

Chapter 2

"And LeVar?"

He paused and looked back over his shoulder.

"The first sign of trouble, I want you out of there and calling for reinforcements. Do you understand?"

He nodded, and a small smile began to form in the corner of his mouth. His affection for Nybor had never been romantic, but their bond was one of incredible strength. He took her word as law, and never questioned it. As Nybor watched on, her friend soared up into the sky, his wings briefly blocking out the light of the sun, before he disappeared into the distance.

Now, however, she had an unpleasant task ahead of her. It was time to visit the King. She loathed speaking to him under any circumstances, and was still dubious about how he attained the throne in the first place, but this could not wait. Thoughts of this smoke creature and its implications lingered as she clutched a rather unique piece of jewellery.

The necklace was of a unique design. The main part of the jewellery consisted of a silver diamond shape forged of metal, with engravings along the edges of an ancient language no longer spoken. Set within that diamond, was a black oval jewel. And it was this jewel that her fingers were pressing against. With a deep breath, she steeled herself, clutching her staff, and marched toward the castle. Dark times lay ahead, and she had to confront them head-on. But the people of Beyond had no idea just how dark those times would be.

3

The surreal situation refused to settle in Josh's mind. He couldn't shake the notion that he might have just tripped over a curb, hit his head, and now found himself dreaming or hallucinating. Yet the excitement brewing within him hinted at the possibility that this might be real – a scene straight out of his own stories or fan fictions. The despair and miserable reality of his recent life seemed a distant memory in this strange realm. A feeling of *familiarity*.

However, what convinced Josh that this was in fact reality, wasn't the scent of blossoms of the purple trees surrounding him, or the sound, the crisp and pristine sound of the water behind him. No, it was the fact that he was now sat huddled up on the dirt ground in just his underwear, staring at his clothes drying above a campfire on a makeshift contraption with branches and sticks as construction materials.

Behind the fire, the man with the wavy hair sat on a large moss covered rock, staring at Josh with a puzzled expression, running his left hand through his facial hair repeatedly. His mind was clearly attempting to figure out a mystical riddle of some sort. After what felt like an eternity, he broke his silence.

"So you have no idea where you are?"

The question implied he had received a previous reply but following the introduction of the man's sword against his throat, Josh had rather embarrassingly, passed out.

"What makes you think that I ever did?" Josh replied with more bravado than he had intended.

The man tilted his head suggesting a fair point had been made. He then picked up Josh's rucksack, which he had taken from him earlier, and a small pile of items resting nearby. Holding the bag aloft, he gestured toward Josh.

"I plucked this off your back when you decided to check out earlier."

Embarrassment flushed Josh's cheeks, but he remained quiet, sensing there was more to come from the man..

"Some stuff had fallen out, so I wandered over to the waterline and found a few other bits and pieces. And I have to say, they did bring back memories."

It was then that Josh noticed a smile forming on the face of the man as if a memory had indeed been awakened within him. Then he noticed that the object causing this, was one of the comic books Josh had bought from Final Frontier.

"Memories?" he managed to get out. "You mean, you're not *from* here either?"

The man put the comic book down on top of a second rock to help it dry out faster. It was joined by not only the others in its company, but Josh's own creation, which he was relieved to see had survived, albeit a little damp.

"No. I was a different man back then, but like you, I am human."

Josh was stunned by this revelation. Despite his bizarre

Chapter 3

surroundings, the realisation that this seemingly mystical man was, in fact, just another person, mystified him.

"Okay, two things," Josh started, growing more comfortable in this man's company. "First, how did you get here, and second... what's with the costume?"

The man appeared slightly irked by the suggestion that he was wearing a costume, but composed himself before responding.

"My name is... was... Tommy. I used to work in the *Starbucks* in Wealdstone."

A gasp escaped Josh's lips which he quickly regretted, but settled back down to listen intently.

"Then about six weeks after I started the job, a guy came into the store. It'd been a bad day, awkward customers trying to tell me a flat white and a latte are the same thing, and I was basically a shoestring away from telling them where they could shove their job. And this guy, just had something about him. He said he was working on reopening the historical western settlement on the edge of the town and he was looking for people to help. I said sure, my dad had been in construction, so I had some knowledge. The man's name... was Monarch."

Josh's blood ran cold, and his goosebumps developed their own goosebumps. That name was now synonymous with the misery that had plagued Wealdstone recently. This did not go unnoticed by Tommy.

"I can see that name triggers you as much as it does most people. But at the time, I believed him, and I threw in my apron and walked out of that door with him and all the way to the settlement. When we got there, there were others milling around doing various things like stocking up the old general store, and unboarding the windows of the houses. But something felt a little off. The air seemed... thicker somehow, like an energy was floating around everyone and everything. And the one thing that stuck out for me was that nobody was speaking. Nobody looked happy, and most of them were wearing clothes from Peasants 'R Us. It became very clear, very quickly, that I was not going to be allowed to leave."

Josh hung on to every word, captivated by Tommy's account. It was difficult to listen to the tale of Monarch because Josh had seen first-hand what it had done to people, but he felt it was important to know more.

"Did you know what he was then, or was it just suspicion?" he asked.

Tommy shook his head.

"Not at first, but it didn't take long. Somebody, a woman, spotted one of the doorways emerging the first night I was there. Monarch had his henchmen drag them away. He had a cabin away from the settlement with electricity where he would interrogate and torture people. Next thing I knew, the woman had been thrown through the doorway and it vanished. Over the next few weeks, we saw what Monarch truly was. He displayed his powers on few occasions but each was memorable. Burned into the back of people's minds with the same intensity of those golden eyes. Then I met Grace."

Another flinch from Josh, and another thing that Tommy noticed, raising his eyebrows slightly. Josh responded this time.

"I know *of* her. I'm friends with her best friend. Or girlfriend. I'm not really sure what's going on there, but either way, yeah I know who you're talking about. She's retired now apparently."

Tommy let out a wild chuckle that caught Josh off guard.

"She certainly wasn't retired when I met her. She'd noticed people leaving town and not returning, and she'd noticed the revitalisation of Crossroads and decided to try and investigate. She was the one who talked me into trying to escape, convinced that Monarch was formulating something worse than a cult. Some world ending shit. So I ran. They caught me, and they threw me through one of the doorways. I landed here, and when I couldn't

Chapter 3

figure out how to go back, I started trying to explore. I didn't realise the doorway was still open. It's one of the few that still had its Guardian."

The cool breeze made Josh shiver a little, and Tommy noticed. He quickly checked the makeshift clothes dryer and handed Josh his now dry garments. As Josh gratefully reassembled himself, he sought some clarification.

"The Guardians, aren't they the beings that Monarch tricked the Phantom thing into killing?"

Tommy nodded sombrely.

"Phantom Wraiths. Yeah. He spread word that he had a secret way of traversing between realms in case he needed a distraction. He was all about the performance. Of course he had nothing, but it worked. He managed to escape and the Wraiths in their anger massacred almost all of the guardians."

This aspect confused Josh slightly.

"Why would they need something to move between realms if they had done just that in order to find it?"

Tommy shrugged his shoulders, causing his armour to make a scraping noise against the rock as he did so.

"We never found out. To be honest, I prefer not to think about it. I expect they wanted to be the only ones to move freely and wanted to destroy any object capable of giving that gift to others. But once I was told that there was indeed a way back, I decided to take it. En route, I saw a family being hijacked by mercenaries. They had a young child with them, and I stepped in to help. It was only afterwards that I realised they were the family of the then King. They told me that the Guardian of the gateway was dying and wished to live out his final days as a mortal, and offered me the chance to take over. I thought long and hard about it. Who missed me back home, what I really had there, and I decided that the people of this place were so welcoming and kind to me that I would take them up on their offer.

That was five hundred and three years ago."

Josh let out an audible sounds that resembled someone getting their nose tweaked, and his face contorted into the pinnacle of confusion.

"I'm sorry, how many years ago?"

Tommy chuckled again. It seemed his guard was beginning to lower the longer he spent around Josh.

"Time moves differently in Beyond. You can leave the human world on a Monday, and by Friday a century has passed here. Or sometimes, longer. Or shorter. Time isn't exactly linear here. So we count by the sunrises and sunsets. I no longer age because of the powers I have been endowed with."

"So... you're like five hundred years old?"

"Actually I like to think of myself as still forty-two. Unless you wanna tell me I look five hundred?"

Unwilling to take up that particular invitation, Josh's eyes wandered toward Tommy's sword. Tommy noticing the shift in Josh's demeanour, asked a question of his own.

"Your turn young man. How did you get here?"

Tommy's voice returned to a more stern timbre and his eyes bore into Josh's. Josh hesitated before replying.

"This is gonna sound weird."

Tommy snorted.

"What part of what I just told you sounded perfectly normal?" he asked.

That was very true. Josh decided to just roll with it.

"So I was on my way home after my volunteer job, picked up the comics you see over there, and when I got to my street all the lights were out. And then this cat…"

Tommy held up his hand and interrupted him.

"Cat?" he asked, suddenly with a heightened level of anxiety.

"Yeah, it was like a gingery colour, and it seemed to be, I

Chapter 3

dunno, like leading me with purpose. I don't even know why I followed it."

Tommy ran a palm over his face much like that of a disappointed parent when their child was told not to do something, and then did it anyway. His change in mannerisms peaked Josh's curiosity.

"This cat, did it... speak to you?"

Josh thought about it for a moment or two before replying.

"Not with words, but something about its eyes felt like they bore into my mind and I could almost hear it telling me to follow it, telling me I had to go where it led me."

Tommy stood quickly with a muttering of 'for fuck's sake' under his breath. The sudden action caught Josh off guard and he too stood, confused by the whole response.

"Tommy, what's wrong?" he asked.

Tommy sheathed his sword, and threw up a hood on the back of a cloak that Josh had not noticed until now. As he did so, his eyes closed tightly, and Josh saw Tommy muttering words quietly. When Tommy opened his eyes once more, they were glowing emerald green, and his cloak began to move independently without assistance from the wind.

Without warning, a shockwave burst forward from Tommy's chest and shot through Josh, knocking him to the ground, and continuing on across the water's surface and up the waterfall. An enormous explosion of green filled the area at the top of the drop and the doorway outline was visible once more, but only briefly. As Josh watched on, it appeared to collapse. The three sides of the frame broke apart, and cascaded down the waterfall, disintegrating as they hit the water.

And then all fell silent once more.

When Josh turned to look back at Tommy, he had returned to his previous state, hazel eyes, no flowing cloak, and he stood upright.

35

"What the hell was that?" Josh exclaimed.

Tommy strolled forwards and placed his hands on Josh's shoulders.

"There is only one cat who has traversed this gateway, and he was ordered never to do so again."

"Erm... okay. This cat is not a normal cat I take it?"

Josh's levels of confusion were only heightening. How bad could a cat be? Especially given the powers he had just witnessed Tommy utilising.

Tommy cleared his throat, and looked around the immediate area.

"Not exactly. He's a pain in the fucking ass is what he is. Always has been, treacherous little shit."

Josh, still attempting to grasp the situation and make sense of it continued with the questions that were seemingly throwing up little in the way of answers.

"Forgive me, but you are talking about this cat like it's a person."

Tommy looked up at Josh and nodded.

"That was not a cat. That was a Mimic. Or Changeling they like to be called"

"Changeling? Like... *Deep Space Nine?*"

Another knowing chuckle from Tommy, and Josh felt he understood the reference.

"Yeah, kinda. They're shapeshifters Josh. They reside in the Shadowlands, where most of them stay. *Most of them.*"

"But not this one?" Josh continued to press, still unsure he had heard Tommy correctly.

Tommy kicked dirt over the fire.

"That's right. This one just likes to cause trouble. And thanks to him, I'm now out of a job. Five hundred years and I'm back in the unemployment line. At least you'll be able to keep me company."

Chapter 3

"Woah, what? I'm trapped here?"

"I had to, it was the only way to contain the threat to Beyond!"

And then the unanswered question that was foremost at the front of his mind.

"Threat? What threat?"

Tommy's look never wavered.

"After what happened with Monarch, all of the gateways were disguised, made invisible to those on both sides. We Green Dragons are the guardians of the gateways, so we know the locations even if we cannot see them."

"But I saw it." Josh surmised. "And the cat did too."

"Yes. And that isn't supposed to happen."

Before Josh could say anything more, Tommy grabbed his arm and thrust him forwards into the trees. They moved with such speed that very quickly the only evidence they had been at the beach at all, was the branches that previously hung over the fire, and a small whisper of white smoke.

"Woah! Where are we going?" Josh yelled as he stumbled over loose rocks and shrubs.

"To the First Kingdom, to see an old friend."

Josh's boot caught the edge of a rock and he tumbled forward, sending up a cloud of dirt around him.

"And why are we doing that?" he asked as he stood and dusted himself down.

Tommy sighed loudly.

"Because, Joshua, if a human and a changeling can see a hidden doorway, that means others can too. And that either means you're super special and it's a one-off occurrence…"

Tommy trailed off and Josh had to bring him back.

"Or…"

Tommy looked directly into Josh's eyes.

"Or something is happening that threatens the very existence of this realm, and everyone in it. Including you."

There was no need for more words. Josh simply nodded and followed Tommy as he pressed ahead through the foliage, slicing branches away with a smaller dagger.

Behind them, peering between two bushes at the edge of the clearing, the ginger cat watched them disappear into the forest, its eyes glowing a soft yellow.

4

The entrance hall in the castle was the most unusual building in the entire world of Beyond. It stood as a stark contrast to the typical bright stone, stained glass, and golden adornments commonly found in castles. This castle was different, mysterious and dark.

The gates leading into the entrance chamber were made of gilded steel, aged yet still shining brightly when caught by the sunlight at the right angle. The chamber itself was an expanse of black. The floors were crafted from black marble, adorned with only thin veins of white running through them, and occasional flecks of long-stained red.

The walls were not carved from stone, but from rock and bone, adding to the eerie atmosphere. The architecture incorporated sharp points mimicking the blade of a sword, positioned high enough to not pose a threat to those who entered, but low enough to utilise if necessary. Above the entrance hall, a large glass dome rested, its glass tinted in plain red, which would bathe the rest of the interior in blood-red hues if not for the darkness that enveloped the space.

Nybor remembered the reason behind this unusual design. The First Kingdom was constructed around this castle, not the other way around. It had been here since the dawn of time in Beyond, risen from the very ground itself, and was a place dedicated to rulers. Specifically, the highest ruler in the realm – the King.

Only two individuals guarded the King at any given time – the Chief of Protection and the High Mage. Magic was accepted and celebrated, integrated into everyday life, but mages were treated differently, due to their previous allegiance during the war between Yellow Demons and Blue Spirits. Most mages had sided with the Demons during the war, but upon their defeat, later pledged loyalty to the King. However, people still viewed them with suspicion and considered the few of them who remained, untrustworthy.

Over two thousand mages had survived the war, but many had chosen to relinquish their powers for fear of prosecution for war crimes. It was a painful process to strip one of their magical abilities regardless of whether they were born with them, or were endowed the power. Their fear had been unfounded, however, as the King of the time had given them pardon if they accepted a new role in service of the royal family. Those who relinquished their powers were housed in the Fifth Kingdom and left to their own devices, no longer able to wield any form of magic.

Largox, the current High Mage, was a peculiar creation – a primate with a face and upper body resembling a great ape, but with lighter skin. His arms and legs had a more human-like design, and he towered over all known creatures in the realm, at over nine-feet tall. The Chief of Protection was a coveted role, previously held by the leader of the Order of White Falcons, following two and a half centuries of service in that role. However, following the war, the rules changed, and the King or Queen could choose their protector based on trust and relationship instead of solely their service to the Order.

Chapter 4

Nybor didn't want the role of Chief of Protection. After all, who would want to stand beside their brother everyday feeding him grapes and waving a sword in people's faces to intimidate them?

Despite the changes in ruling over the eligibility for the position, the Chief in sitting, was one of her own. Zumo had served the White Falcons for over four centuries, and was due to take over as Leader. However, after thwarting an unprovoked attack on the King, he was rewarded with the position. He was a wise old man, and a friend to Nybor. But he was beyond battle these days, and enjoyed the comfort the job provided.

"It is good to see you again, young friend."

Zumo's words were always soothing to her. His voice flowed like silk and comforted her even in her darkest times.

"And you, Zumo. Is he around?"

"Your brother? He is always around. Not much war to be fought these days. Besides, I fear he has grown too comfortable in that big black chair," Zumo replied, his words tinged with sarcasm and humour, eliciting a smile from Nybor.

"I need to speak to him. It's… urgent," she said, her expression serious as she conveyed the importance of her request.

Nybor stood at a crossroads, as she often had done in her past, torn between confiding in her friend Zumo, or keeping her worries to herself. Ever since Zumo had left the Order, she feared that even well intentioned individuals might unintentionally spread her concerns. With a determined glint in her eye, she added two words.

"In private."

Zumo's keen eyes caught the expression on Nybor's face, one that he had seen before in the past. Knowing better than to pry, he simply nodded and disappeared into the royal chamber where the grand throne resided.

Being the sister of the King of the realm was no easy life,

especially considering her family's troubled history. Her uncle had been poisoned by her own father, who then aligned himself with Monarch, nearly bringing about the destruction of not only their realm, but all others as well. Their family's actions had left them as perhaps the most untrusted royals in history.

Zumo reappeared between the grand doors and gestured for Nybor to enter.

"Here we go."

Her quiet murmur to herself still echoed around the vast empty space, and taking a deep breath, she walked up the five marble steps, the doors swinging open automatically upon detecting her presence. The castle seemed to possess a unique awareness, knowing when to open or close its doors. There were no people either side of them, it was simply part of the castle. It knew things. It had seen things.

"Ah, little sister."

King Eralf's booming voice echoed throughout the vast empty space as Nybor continued towards the throne. Despite the distance, Nybor heard her brother's words as if he were stood next to her ears.

"Your majesty," Nybor responded with a grudging bow before rising to her full posture.

Eralf chuckled heartily, a few drops of saliva escaping his mouth and landing in his thick black beard.

"Oh come now, Nybor. You don't have to stoop to pleasantries like that. Consider it a privilege of being related to your ruler."

Nybor couldn't help but bring up LeVar, her brother's old friend and her dear friend too.

"You know, that rule of yours still doesn't sit well with LeVar. You used to be friends, and he misses your musical concerts."

Eralf dismissed her concern with a wave of his hand.

"LeVar and I had completed our friendship long before I made

Chapter 4

my ruling. Besides, giving you the prestige of being the only Falcon to communicate with royalty gives more prominence to your position."

Nybor scoffed.

"It makes people think I got this role out of favouritism from my brother."

Eralf dismissed her suggestion, as she had of course gotten the position before Eralf became King. It was at this point that Nybor noticed the nine-foot primate, standing beside her brother. She had always avoided direct eye contact with him, but this time, she couldn't resist. Largox's eyes seemed like swirling portals, holding the secrets of the universe. They were captivating.

"Good morning Largox," she addressed the mage politely, though she continued trying to avoid meeting his gaze, afraid she might lose her purpose. It was of course impossible. She could only hope she did not forget the purpose of her visit.

"My lady," Largox responded curtly, his eyes continuing to shift with cosmic energy.

"Forgive me mage," Nybor said, gathering her courage, "but I did request to speak to my brother alone. It is a matter of great urgency."

Her directness caused a brief moment of tension, but she held her ground, hoping her brother would understand the gravity of her plea. Largox took two elegant steps forward, and knelt slightly to bring his face uncomfortably close to Nybor's. As he spoke, his breath permeated her nose, and she had great difficulty avoiding being swayed by the strawberry-like scent that emerged.

"We are already aware of the reason for your attendance this morning, my lady. The King has been fully briefed."

Largox returned to his full height and moved to stand against the wall behind the throne. Nybor's face twisted into a mixture of anger and confusion.

"You already know?" she exclaimed, her voice filled with more bluster than she should have displayed in front of a King, brother or not.

Eralf sighed and again waved his hand to dismiss her concerns.

"Two days ago, we received reports of people in the Fifth Kingdom spreading rumours of supernatural deaths. It is simply the disgruntled trying to cause unrest in order to climb the ladder of prosperity."

Nybor's eyes widened in horror.

"Are you serious?! A boy was killed by a creature from the Void, and you're dismissing it as mere rumours started by poor people to get richer? What the hell is the matter with you?!"

Before she could say more, Largox sent an orange flame towards her, knocking her off balance and sending her crashing down on one knee.

"We do not use *that* word here, my lady. You know better."

That word indeed, she thought. Largox returned to his motionless state, but she knew of the word he spoke. Eralf's face hardened, displaying none of its previous frivolity.

"The people in the Fifth Kingdom are troublemakers. They are bitter, dear sister, and they envy what we possess and they do not. If there had been a true attack, do you not think that your own Falcons would have borne witness to it?"

Steeling herself against the pain, Nybor strode forward with purpose.

"LeVar told me.."

"LeVar told you of the reports, Nybor. But none of the Falcons stationed there actually witnessed the event," Eralf interjected.

Nybor noticed Largox's subtle movements in her peripheral vision. She could take punishment, but even smaller strikes from the mage caused distinct pain throughout the body, so she backed down slightly.

"And the boy? His family? What of them?"

Chapter 4

Eralf pulled himself up from his chair. His robes and hair took a moment to part from the black bone of the throne, stuck to it by sweat. Clearly he had not moved in a while.

"The boy has no family, and those apparently supporting him have been reprimanded for spreading such an ugly and dangerous rumour, and life is returning to normal. And I suggest you leave it at that dear sister, or you yourself may face... consequences."

Zumo re-entered the room, torn by his inner conflicts but obligated to fulfil his duties. Regardless of his position, he was aware of unsolicited movement of troops and whispers in the night. Something more was going on, orchestrated by the King, but as yet leaving no evidence behind of illegal actions. Should Zumo find such proof, however, he would not hesitate to act. Nybor advanced until she was almost nose to nose with the King. Neither of them flinched.

"You threaten me, brother? Do you forget the secrets I keep?"

Eralf's eyes flickered as if haunted by the memories of those secrets. Pain. There was pain in his eyes. No, not pain. *Fear*.

He span away from her, and painted a smile back onto his face, strolled back to his throne, and fell onto it, reaching for a goblet of wine.

"You may return to your duties, Nybor. And think no more of the Fifth Kingdom. Zumo, please show my sister out."

Reluctantly, Zumo obeyed guiding Nybor out of the hall, and the doors closed behind them. Largox knelt beside the King and whispered into his ear.

"Do you believe she suspects, sire?"

Eralf swirled the blue liquid in his silver goblet, watching it slide back down the sides into the pool at the bottom.

"I am uncertain what she knows, Largox. But I know the secrets she keeps. And it concerns me deeply."

Largox nodded and took a deep breath.

"What are your intentions, sire?"

DAVID W. ADAMS

Eralf downed every drop of the blue wine and slammed the goblet on the arm of the throne. He ran his hands through his beard, before drawing them forwards and pursing them into points, meeting at each fingertip.

"Watch her closely."

5

The scenery surrounding them was a breathtaking wonder, captivating Josh's every sense. Each tree, plant, and shrub seemed to hold a unique charm, and the very sky itself painted a mesmerising canvas above them. Lost in awe, Josh stumbled and tripped over minor obstacles in the forest, not due to inexperience, but rather because he couldn't take his eyes from the captivating world around him.

"You know, I genuinely feel like I'm in an *IMAX* movie in this place," he exclaimed, still enthralled by the enchanting surroundings.

Tommy chuckled softly, a hint of sadness in his voice.

"Last *IMAX* I saw was *Bad Boys For Life*. Or was it *Terminator Dark Fate*? I don't even remember; it feels like a lifetime ago now."

Hearing the forlorn note in Tommy's words, Josh realised that his new companion bore the weight of solitude. Despite choosing to protect this realm, Tommy seemed to have no friends or comrades around him, and a sense of true isolation surrounded him. Empathy welled up within Josh, and he felt a connection with Tommy's loneliness.

"Do you miss home?" he asked, the question slipping out more directly than he had intended.

Tommy stopped and picked up an olive-coloured rock, seemingly lost in its beauty for a moment. He turned to face Josh, holding the rock aloft in his hands.

"This is a rock," Tommy said, his voice tinged with a sense of wonder. "It is solid and weighty and everything you would expect of a rock, except perhaps the colour. On Earth, a rock is just a rock. There are countless billions more like it. But here, every rock is unique, with beauty hidden within the stony exterior. A hard solid shell conceals a warm and nourishing interior."

With a purposeful gesture, Tommy bent down and shattered the rock against a stone boulder, and the rock cracked open to reveal fruit inside. Josh's eyes randomly flicked from the rock to Tommy back and forth trying to take it in.

"See?" he said, brushing his hands to remove fragmented pieces of the fruit. "I reflect on Earth often. But Beyond is my true home."

Tommy stood and continued forward. Intrigued, Josh reached for a piece of the fruit, but Tommy spoke back to him over his shoulder.

"I wouldn't eat that. Tastes like shit."

Josh chuckled and tossed the fruit aside, catching up to his armoured escort. There had been no further talk of the changeling which enraptured the Green Dragon when he had learned of Josh's entrance into Beyond, and Josh wanted to know more. Call it an inquisitive nature, but this is the way he had always been. It's part of what made his creations, his graphic novels, so deeply immersive. It was as if he could sense the energy within the hero contained in the pages.

The comic.

Chapter 5

Josh stopped and scrambled through his bag, and when he found his own piece of work, he pulled it from the rucksack and threw the bag to the ground. The thud of the impact caused Tommy to stop and investigate.

"What is it?" he asked.

Josh gave no answer but began leafing through the now wrinkled pages of his most recent work, searching for something. A desperate look of denial swamped his features, and he began shaking his head back and forth.

"No, I must be wrong. There's no way that could be true. My head must be messed up."

The page turning intensified. Concerned, Tommy moved closer towards him.

"Josh, what is it?"

Lost in confusion, Josh couldn't immediately answer, but he kept searching through the pages. Tommy noticed brief movement in the trees behind them, but his focus remained on Josh.

Suddenly, Josh found the page he was looking for, and dropped the book to the ground. He stepped back, running his fingers through his hair, pulling at the strands with confusion and angst. Tommy knelt to examine the page, his expression turning more serious. As he surveyed the image, his face fell. He looked up at Josh, who was still tugging at his hair in disbelief.

"When did you draw this?" asked Tommy sternly.

"Three months ago, after work at the coffee shop," Josh replied, his breathing steadying as he spoke. "But I swear, I had no idea. It just came into my head as part of the storyline! It's the companion for my character, my main character."

Tommy glanced at the pages once more, his face displaying a mix of emotions. The image depicted a curly-haired man in his mid-twenties, with a full yet trimmed curly beard, standing beside a waterfall next to a rucksack. And beside the hero's feet sat a

49

ginger cat. The revelation struck Tommy, and he looked up at Josh with a mixture of awe and concern.

"You've drawn a character from Beyond, someone who exists here – the changeling. How is that even possible?"

Before either of them had time to react, a large gust of wind billowed from behind Tommy, sending both him and Josh crashing to the ground, Tommy's sword flew out from its sheath and skidded away from him. The ground shook as three figures landed, sending vibrations along Tommy's armour, dust cascading through the air. Josh held his arm across his face to keep the sandy coloured fog out of his eyes. Maybe he was dreaming, he thought. This can't be real. The backlight of the sun was obscuring features, but the outline of the group was unmistakable. Tall. Wings. A white glow. Josh was now staring at three angels standing ahead of them.

Tommy lunged for his sword, but a foot blocked his path, preventing him from rising. As he rolled onto his back preparing to confront whatever was behind him, the wide end of a familiar staff pressed into his chest, its pressure penetrating even through his armour. Relief washed over him, and he relaxed slightly, as the voice swept across him.

"I thought you'd been training more, Green Dragon. Rather disappointed I so easily caught you unawares."

The staff retreated and was replaced by a friendly hand. Tommy smiled, gripped the wrist and accepted the lift to his feet. The face turned away from him and began issuing commands to the other two.

"I want this entire area sealed with a protective enchantment, and I want both of you to fly patrols along the perimeter. Proceed."

The orders received, the two other figures took to the sky, twirling objects so fast that they became blurs. Translucent pillars fell from the sky, embedding themselves in the ground. A shimmering net of white light fell upon them, forming an invisible dome around the area. Josh couldn't help but stare in astonishment

Chapter 5

at the display of angelic power. As he turned back to face Tommy, he locked eyes with the mysterious woman. Her long white hair cascaded gracefully down her back, and her armour bore delicate inscriptions on the shoulders and shin plates. She held a staff, four, maybe five feet in length, crafted from the same wood he had observed near the beach. Her face was youthful, but her eyes... her eyes radiated a wisdom beyond her years, along with a hidden depth of pain. Josh felt a peculiar connection to her, much like the bond he had with Tommy, but stronger. Much more recognition surrounding this woman. It was as if he could sense her emotions, her thoughts, her experiences. It was a sensation that bewildered him but had become strangely familiar since entering this realm. Tommy walked over to Josh, placing a reassuring hand on his shoulder. He turned and gestured towards the mysterious angel.

"Josh, this is the person we were travelling to see. May I introduce Nybor. She is Leader of the Order of White Falcons, protectors of the realm."

Nybor flashed a smile, and feigned a curtsy, playfully dismissing the formality of such an introduction.

"You're not in one of your Earth movies now, Tommy. No need for such elaborate introductions."

Tommy laughed, and Josh couldn't help but feel a growing trust in this formidable White Falcon. And as ridiculous a question as it may seem, he still felt the need to ask it.

"So... not an angel?" he asked hesitantly.

Both Nybor and Tommy chuckled, their laughter echoing in the air as the other two Falcons soared above them. Nybor stepped closer to Josh, not breaking her gaze once.

"No, Joshua. Not angels," she replied sweetly.

Tommy took the opportunity to inquire the reason for their company.

"So how did you know we were here? I mean we were on our way to the First, but nobody knew of that."

51

Nybor's face turned more serious, revealing the gravity of the situation.

"You destroyed a sacred gateway, Tommy. Repercussions of that were felt far and wide. You're lucky the King didn't notice. Ignorant bastard is probably still too busy drinking his fancy wine and eating grapes. When I sensed the tremor, I left immediately with two of my aides."

Tommy nodded and seemed to accept that response, knowing that the destruction of a gateway would inevitably have consequences. Still his quest for vital information outweighed the potential consequences. He did not entertain the fact he had never known a guardian to outlive their doorway.

"I had to destroy the gateway for a good reason, Nybor. Joshua here not only *saw* the gateway, but was led to it. By a cat."

Nybor's face fell immediately. Josh did not like the way people were reacting to his presence as if he was the prophet of doomsday. The expression on her face only deepened, and the weight of unspoken secrets and prophecies loomed heavily in the air. Her eyes flickered with a mix of concern and determination. She paced around, lost in her thoughts, until she turned back to Tommy, and grasped him with her free hand.

"Tommy, this is beginning to make sense to me a little more. Earlier today, I received reports that a boy in the Fifth Kingdom was killed by some kind of smoke creature. Scorches trailed along the meadow all the way back to the barrier at the edge of the Void. There are now fears that the barrier has begun to weaken."

The atmosphere around them shifted, and fear washed over Josh like an ominous tide. The once light mood now seemed encased in darkness, and the gravity of the situation was undeniable. This *was* a potential doomsday event.

"Excuse me?" he said clearing his throat before speaking. "What is the barrier? And why is it bad that it is weakening? And can someone please tell me how I knew what to draw in my comic book three months before I knew any of you even existed?"

His questions hung in the air, begging for answers. Nybor attempted to address them as concisely as she could without revealing all.

"The barrier Joshua, is what separates our realm, the realm of Beyond, from the Void. It is where the darkest souls travel after death or exorcism. There they are contained, mingling with each other, morphing into other beings. It is full of demons and darkness and evil. If the barrier is weakening, and any of that malevolence seeps through, it could spell the end of not only our world, but all others as well."

The weight of her words settled heavily on Josh's heart, leaving him speechless. But there was more to unfold.

"So its true then, Nybor. The barrier must be weakening and destabilising the magic of this place. That is how Josh was able to see the doorway, and the changeling was able to move through it too."

She nodded, her eyes locked onto Josh with a mixture of worry and conviction.

"Yes. While Joshua's arrival may have been the warning sign we needed against this danger, I fear it may have already begun."

Her words echoed in the clearing, leaving a haunting silence in their wake. Josh's mind raced, trying to grasp the enormity of what he had stumbled into. It was as if he had unknowingly stepped into a tale of epic proportions, a narrative beyond his wildest imagination. The cat, the strange feeling of familiarity and comfort he felt in this place, and towards Nybor. Was it all coincidence, or was there even more layers beneath the surface of this ever growing tension? His emotions continued to surge inside of him – fear, confusion, but also a strange sense of purpose. He couldn't ignore the synchronicity of his comic book. It was if his art had been a window into a world he had been destined to enter... or *remember*.

Seeing his reactions flickering across his face, Nybor's gaze softened, and she placed a reassuring hand on his shoulder.

"Do not fear Joshua, as there is still much we do not understand. Perhaps you were brought here for a reason. Whilst it is true we face unknown dangers ahead, we will find out the truth together."

Tommy nodded in agreement.

"We will face this together. We will find out the truth behind what is happening in the Fifth Kingdom and protect this world from whatever lies ahead."

As the trio stood there, united in purpose, Josh began to feel a newfound strength within him. He may not have asked for this role, but he knew that he couldn't turn away from it now. Destiny had seemingly chosen him, and he was determined to embrace it, not as a harbinger of doom, but as a force of hope. The adventure that lay ahead was far beyond anything he could have ever imagined or drawn in a comic book. But he was ready to step into the unknown and face whatever challenges awaited them.

6

The silence was deafening, and it echoed through the air like a haunting melody of loss and despair. The once vibrant city entrance now lay in ruins, a testament to the atrocity that had taken place here. LeVar, a usually valiant and fearless warrior, stood amidst the scorched marks at the gates, his chiselled face etched with concern and fear.

Multiple witnesses had seen the horrifying event unfold, but very few had survived its wrath. The onlookers who remained near the scene had been ordered to leave multiple times since the attack, but the true horror lay beyond the gates out in the meadows. LeVar's eyes surveyed the entrance to the Fifth Kingdom, a place that once boasted miles of unspoilt lushness, where sunlight danced on dewdrops and flowers bloomed in abundance. Now it was a desolate wasteland, a black, charred canvas stretching out as far as the eye could see. In the far distance, hidden beyond the sight of most in this world, LeVar witnessed ominous swirls of smoke and flashes of lightning clashing against an invisible wall. Each impact sent shivers throughout his entire being. Suddenly, a figure descended from the sky with breathtaking grace, before making a dramatic landing. Skye had returned from patrols.

"Report," LeVar commanded, his voice grave. This time, the casualties had been devastating, leaving little time for anything other than swift action.

"Seventy-five dead or missing so far, the entire meadow is destroyed all the way to the barrier. But..."

Skye hesitated, her usual directness giving way to concern. She was often admired for her ability to cut through the weeds of politics or contrived stories and get right to the point. This was yet another indication of the seriousness of the situation.

"What is it Syke?" LeVar asked, trying to comfort his comrade.

"There are... cracks," she finally revealed.

Dread washed over LeVar as he began to realise the implications.

"The creatures... they are breaching the barrier through these cracks?"

Skye nodded silently.

"Then time is against us. I must return to the First Kingdom and report this immediately. While we still have an advantage," LeVar spoke resolutely.

Skye couldn't fathom what advantage he could be referring to, considering the devastation they had witnessed. Seventy-five people were dead, seventy-six if you include the first young boy to lose his life. They were unaware of any power available to them to reseal the Void, should it fall into their realm, and yet LeVar spoke of advantage? Seemingly picking up on her concern, he offered his answer.

"The creatures, demons within the Void, may be sneaking through the cracks. But there is a crucial piece of information here. They keep returning."

Understanding jumped on Skye as she finally understood.

"So, they are not powerful enough to remain outside of the

Chapter 6

Void. That's why they keep snaking back. We have a chance to repel them if we act swiftly and bring in reinforcements."

LeVar nodded, but his tone grew sombre.

"However, I fear it will not be long before that advantage deserts us. The first attack was just one boy. The second, seventy-five. That level of increase would see the Fifth Kingdom destroyed with just five attacks."

The severity of that statement hit Skye like a physical blow from a hammer. He was right. A seven-hundred-fifty percent increase from one attack to the next would indeed leave Beyond with only four realms.

"Eva and Gregor are still attempting to contain the situation, but with the attack happening so openly, I fear it may be too late for any kind of reassurance to these people, and to contain the rumours from the other kingdoms."

LeVar had the utmost faith in his fellow brethren, but he too feared this time, there was no stopping word from reaching the rest of the realm.

"Keep a watchful eye on the barrier, and inform Eva and Gregor, they have full authority to provide whatever aid these people need. But we must maintain the protective barriers in place. Nobody leaves this kingdom until I return."

Skye nodded solemnly, and with a powerful flap of her wings, she soared into the sky, racing towards the far edge of the kingdom where disruptive chaos was unfolding between the surviving residents. LeVar took one last glance at the distant prison containing all the evil of all the realms, before turning away. He closed his eyes and drew his white daggers from his side. Crossing them against his chest, he muttered an incantation in an ancient tongue, and far above him, a cracking sound echoed, an opening surfacing in the protective barrier the White Falcons were renowned for. LeVar crouched slightly, then leapt with tremendous force, soaring through the gap in the sky, sheathing his weapons

57

before his wings even unfurled. In the blink of an eye, he was gone.

Unbeknownst to all, in the distance, with no watchful eyes upon the darkness, the sound similar to that of a gunshot rang out, and a bolt of black smoke shot through the air at unfathomable speed. As the hole in the protective shell sealed up, the slither of black slipped through.

The darkness was no longer contained, and now all the other kingdoms faced the looming threat of destruction. The fate of the entire realm hung in the balance, and the battle against the encroaching darkness had only just begun.

7

The forest continued to enchant Josh, and round every corner or twist of the dusty path they navigated, the symphony of sights, smells and sounds that seem to have sprung from the very essence of imagination itself. The radiant flora surrounding the bases of the trees, gave the ground surrounding them an almost ethereal glow. The trunks of the trees ahead were adorned with iridescent moss which was emitting a soft, silvery light. It really was like walking through a fairy tale. Even the ground Josh and the others walked on seemed to pulse beneath their feet, emanating a gentle energy that harmonised with the very rhythm of life. The soft flutter of unseen wings far above, created a delicate melody. Just hours before, Josh would have feared the approach of more enemies, or even allies, but right now, in this moment, it was as if the land and everything in it was pulsing through him, as if he could feel the energy everywhere in his veins.

During their brief trek through the forest, Tommy and Nybor had been in deep conversation regarding a meeting she had recently attended with the King. It sounded serious, and Josh tried to snap out of the allure of the forest and return at least his ears to the conversation beside him.

"So he really wouldn't listen to you? Your own brother?"

Tommy, his outrage palpable, couldn't fathom Eralf's descent into corruption since becoming the ruler of Beyond.

"I fear that the throne of the King has tainted what little remained of my brother's noble heart," Nybor lamented. "He has grown accustomed to the luxuries of power and refuses to heed reason."

As the conversation unfolded, Josh couldn't help but notice the familiar ring to this tale. It reminded him of stories he had seen in movies and television shows back home. It appeared that the trappings of power transcended the boundaries of mere fiction, and he couldn't resist uttering a cliched phrase.

"Power corrupts, but absolute power corrupts absolutely," he spoke with an extra boost of gravitas for dramatic effect.

Tommy gave him a 'really dude?' kind of look, but Nybor gave him a look of intrigue and a hint of surprise prompting a raised eyebrow from the White Falcon in their midst. Josh seemed to have gotten her attention.

"A wise, and true statement my friend," she replied. "And on such a note, we must return to the First Kingdom. It is imperative that we attempt to reason with my brother once more."

Tommy snorted.

Tommy snorted in disbelief.

"Do you really think he will listen to you, especially when you bring a human to his front door?"

"No, but at least then I can ignore him in good conscience," Nybor quipped, displaying a strength of character that Tommy had come to admire.

Nybor's wisdom had guided them since their journey to Crossroads, where they learned of the impending catastrophe threatening all realms. Her decisions were driven by honour and

Chapter 7

bravery, leading Toomy to hold her in high esteem. He had delved into her knowledge, learning the stories behind the Order of the White Falcons. They had only walked the perimeter of the clearing to ensure no hidden dangers lurked within their protective bubble, but the transport to the First Kingdom now came to the fore. However it was not he who broached the subject.

"You know that not all of us can fly, Nybor?" Josh hesitantly inquired, addressing the White Falcon directly for the first time.

Nybor smiled at his boldness, instantly setting Tommy on edge, expecting her to scold Josh for such informality. Instead, she admired the way he seemed to be growing in his surroundings. A memory hidden in the more pleasant areas of her mind began to surface, and she experienced a warm comfort amongst the fear that was to come.

"I am aware, Joshua," she acknowledged gracefully. "That is why I brought some of my other Falcons along for the journey. You shall travel with Soren. Tommy will be accompanied by Lursa."

Though Tommy nodded in acceptance, Josh felt a wave of trepidation. Nybor did not wait for his consent or comfort level to rise, she simply took to the skies, her wings spreading wide as her body twirled in the freedom of the air. Before Josh could take a breath, he found himself airborne, flying through the air at breakneck speed. Panic set in, and he squeezed his eyes shut as the ground suddenly rushed up to meet him. Then, as if by magic, the wild descent ceased, and Josh opened his eyes to find himself gliding smoothly through the air. Soren had him securely in her grasp, her wings propelling them forward. The exhilarating sensation replaced his fear with sheer elation, and he could not help but burst into joyous laughter. He felt the pulses from her wings beating along the entire length of his body.

"Hey!" came Tommy's voice from nearby, his hair billowing in the wind, clearly less comfortable with flying despite his dragon heritage. "Try to maintain some decorum, will ya?"

Laughing with glee, Josh attempted to control his unruly hair. Nybor was now a mere speck in the distance, her majestic wingspan marking her status. Josh couldn't help but wonder about her secrets and the questions that lingered in the depths of his mind, tucked away for a more appropriate time. As the journey continued throughout the enchanted skies of Beyond, the companions bond grew stronger, each Falcon entrusting themselves with their passenger, and the same sensations were fed back to them. Tommy was also deep in contemplation, if only to avoid the gargantuan drop that lay below him. He had never been a good flyer, even in his Earth days. He once boarded a flight to Manchester with the intention of seeing some Premier League Football, and before the plane even began to taxi towards the runway, he was scrambling at the door to be let out onto the tarmac. That little misadventure got him seven days in the county lockup. Any time since then, he took an Ambien. However, that was not a facility available to him any longer. His mind, however, attempted to distract him. The adventure which awaited him and the others, if Nybor's suspicions were correct, would test their courage, unravel ancient mysteries, and challenge their understanding of power, corruption, and the true meaning of sacrifice. Tommy was no fool. He knew Nybor harboured dark secrets. He had seen the look in her eyes each time she touched her mysterious necklace, and whenever she was asked about 'the days before.' Unfortunately, at this moment, that contemplation was shattered, as ahead of him, Tommy saw Nybor drop from the sky.

The landing was almost as abrupt as their take-off. One moment, Josh's gaze was fixated on the distance, where a foreboding black castle loomed on the horizon, and the next, his body thudded onto the ground, his organs feeling like they had

Chapter 7

been jolted out of place. Soren, who had broken his fall, groaned in pain upon the impact.

"What the hell was that!" exclaimed Tommy, wincing as he held his side and helped Lursa up with his free hand.

Emerging from the bushes, Nybor's face was etched with fury, her glowing white hair seeming even more radiant in her rage. Despite the pain in his legs, Josh found her appearance almost hypnotic.

"There is a ward in place around the First Kingdom," she said, and Josh recalled the concept of wards from his comics, where they were typically used to keep danger at bay.

"How is that possible?" asked Soren, now dusting herself off.

Nybor paced the ground, striking it with the base of her staff in frustration before the realisation struck her.

"Largox!" she seethed, and her companions could tell it was no ordinary foe she spoke of. "That filthy double crossing backstabbing... son of a bitch!"

Tommy and Josh exchanged impressed glances at Nybor's choice of words, acknowledging the fondness she seemed to have developed for human phrases in her short time on Earth.

"I'm assuming, this was not part of your knowledge, my lady," Lursa cautiously inquired, sensing that the topic may be sensitive. Nybor shot her a stern look, silently acknowledging the misstep in her question. Meanwhile, Soren and the others were visibly concerned, never having witnessed magic being wielded against their kind by royalty. The White Falcons were the realm's protectors and closest allies, making this a troubling revelation. But Nybor's reaction was far from over. Her rage swelled within her, and she let out a deafening scream, directing her staff at a nearby tree, causing it to explode. In the face of the unleashed power, Tommy and Josh sought cover as the tree disintegrated into a shower of wood splinters. A beam of light now penetrated the once-dense canopy. Nybor breathing heavily as she tried to calm herself, caught her breath and glanced around. While Tommy attempted to assess their location, Josh felt drawn to Nybor, an inexplicable familiarity compelling him to approach her. Static rose all around him, and he felt the hairs on his arm begin to rise. He reached out and placed a hand on her shoulder, surprising both himself and Nybor. In response, her fury seemed to dissipate as her eyes softened, and her breathing slowed. Tommy returning from his reconnaissance, witnessed the remarkable change, appearing perplexed.

"How did you do that, Josh?" he asked earnestly.

Josh shrugged, uncertain himself..

"I... I don't know. I just had a feeling that I could ease her emotions. It's as if it came naturally to me."

Nybor smiled, nodding at his response before addressing the group.

"Clearly our King wants us out of the loop, either because he is somehow involved in this malfeasance, or he is still in denial about the threat to our world. Sadly I fear the former is now all but confirmed."

Tommy had not taken his eyes off Josh, spotting a faint crackle of light beneath the young man's palm, though nobody else seemed to notice. 'This is how it starts,' he thought to himself, acutely aware that every threat to come into existence starts with an unknown secret. But for now, he kept his quiet. Josh was his friend and he would give both him, and Nybor, who had not shown any surprise by Josh's actions, the benefit of the doubt. For now. As Nybor considered their predicament, Tommy interjected with a pressing question.

"If either of those possibilities are true, how are we going to breach the First Kingdom's barrier? The rest of the Falcons are in there, we don't know the extent of this mage's power."

With an unexpected smile, Nybor seemed amused by the challenge ahead. Tommy's unease only deepened. She had a plan,

Chapter 7

and judging from her new smile appearing on a previously desolate face, it would not be conventional.

"Lursa. Soren. I want you to try and penetrate this barrier. It seems we in particular, have been banished. Find me a weakness," she commanded. Both Falcons responded in unison.

"Yes my lady."

With a nod from Nybor, the Falcons vanished on their mission, leaving behind her enigmatic smile.

"This isn't going to be fun is it?" Tommy asked wearily.

"What isn't?" Nybor retorted, the smile growing on her face. Josh felt like he was caught in the middle of an escalating argument between a married couple.

"Whatever is plastering that stupid grin all over your face," he snapped back.

"When was the last time you ventured into the Shadowlands, Green Dragon?" Nybor inquired with a mischievous glint in her eye.

Tommy's stomach dropped.

"Two hundred years ago. It made me sick to my stomach."

Her grin remained unyielding, and Tommy's expression soured.

"What are you suggesting?" he asked, a tinge of apprehension in his voice.

Nybor cast a glance at Josh and back to Tommy.

"I think it's time we took a little stroll to see a very shiny man I know."

8

The castle's grand hall was filled with an air of tension as LeVar stood before King Eralf. The absent look of concern on the King's face sent shivers down his spine. His heart raced with worry, uncertain of the true gravity of the situation.

"I do not understand, my King. What do you mean by banished?" LeVar questioned, trying to maintain his composure.

Only moments ago, he had returned to the castle gates, urgently demanding to speak with Nybor and the King. But instead, he found his commander absent, and none of the other White Falcons, including Chief Protector Zumo, were in sight.

"What I mean, LeVar, is that my sister chose to betray her orders and delved into matters beyond her jurisdiction. As a consequence, she has been temporarily banished from the kingdom until I deem it fitting to reinstate her." King Eralf's voice carried an undercurrent of uncertainty.

LeVar's gut churned with unease upon hearing these words. A dilemma rose within him – should he reveal his loyalty to Nybor, or should he prioritise his allegiance to the throne? Nybor had been his protector, his commander-in-chief, and his true loyalty lay with her. He hesitated, unsure how to proceed. Yet strangely, he realised he was able to communicate with the King without facing any resistance. A clear rule break by Eralf's own standards.

"May I say, sire, that I am surprised you permit me to speak to you in this manner. I believed it to be forbidden by royal decree?" LeVar cautiously remarked.

Eralf seemed momentarily panicked, but quickly regained his composure.

"You misunderstand, LeVar. The decree dictates that only the Leader of the Order may communicate with royalty," he stated with a feigned smile.

LeVar's eyes widened in astonishment. "You must be mistaken sire, I cannot..."

"Do you not fulfil the duties of your King? In Nybor's absence, you are second in command, are you not?" Eralf interrupted, a devious glint in his eyes.

LeVar nodded, still struggling to process the implications of the situation. King Eralf continued..

"Then I hereby bestow upon you the status of Leader of the Order of White Falcons. This shall be recorded in the official logs and codex of the First Kingdom. Congratulations... my friend."

At the King's command, Largox, the mage, stepped forward, his hands emanating beams of white light. The ethereal glow bridged the gap between the mage and the Falcon, enveloping LeVar's entire body. As the light subsided, LeVar's features had transformed entirely. He now stood taller, with a much broader wingspan, clad in a regal white and silver cloak. His daggers had been replaced by a tall staff, topped with a white bone frame that housed a mysterious obsidian gem. LeVar took a moment to look over himself. He was awestruck, trying to comprehend the extent of the changes. He felt the surge of newfound power coursing through his veins, and a sense of ecstasy washed over him. And there was something else. A small but deeply hidden drop of

Chapter 8

darkness. A drop which had not been there before. A drop which had been placed there by Largox.

"I expect you to serve the wishes of your King and pledge eternal loyalty to my cause. Whatever the demand, whatever the cost, you follow me to the ends of this world. Is that understood?"

A voice, unfamiliar yet resonant, emerged from within him.

"Yes my liege. Whatever the cost."

As the coronation concluded, LeVar found he had knelt to his King and was now propped up on one knee, gazing up at the throne. King Eralf's wicked grin returned, savouring the sight before him.

"Then arise, LeVar, Leader of the Order of White Falcons," Eralf proclaimed, his voice laced with satisfaction.

LeVar stood, now embodying the weight of his new title. A mix of exhilaration and trepidation coursed through him as he pledged his eternal loyalty to the King's cause. He knew that his life has been forever altered, and the destiny of the First Kingdom and therefore the entire realm, now rested heavily on his shoulders. The darkness now within him demanded dominance, but for now LeVar's true heart kept it suppressed. Only time would tell if LeVar would lead Beyond to glory... or damnation.

9

The path toward the Shadowlands was concealed with deliberate intent, not by overgrown vegetation, but by ingenious camouflage. Enormous drag marks and trails marked the route where massive boulders once sat, guiding their way. The companions moved in a single file, and Nybor frequently halted, leaping into the air to survey their surroundings for any threats. They had chosen to spend the night under a large tree canopy, Nybor and Tommy taking turns in watching for danger, but in truth nobody got much sleep. The foreign noises of the creatures within the woodland made sure of that. Josh's mind, however, was preoccupied with what had transpired in the clearing they had left behind the previous afternoon.

"Do not look so worried Joshua," Nybor addressed him, somehow sensing his concerns despite walking ahead. He shook his head in disbelief, but she couldn't see it.

"It isn't that," he replied, his voice tinged with resignation.

"Then what is it?" she inquired.

Struggling to articulate his feelings, Josh hesitated before speaking.

"When you were angry back there, I just... knew that I could calm you. I can't explain it. And then, I felt this tingle like... like..."

"Electricity," Tommy interjected from behind, startling them both. The group came to a halt, and Nybor turned to face Josh as he nodded.

"Yes, exactly. It was like I sent some sort of disruptive shock through you, and there was a feedback of sorts."

Nybor's gaze flickered back and forth across Josh, seemingly avoiding eye contact. Tommy narrowed his eyes, noticing her unease.

She knew something.

Tommy had always been aware that Nybor's age surpassed a millennium, granting her a wealth of knowledge that eluded him. Yet in recent years, he had detected changes in her behaviour – elusive responses to questions, fewer public appearances, a heightened sense of worry. The protector of the realm had never displayed fear before, but something was different now. However, the Shadowlands were no place for such inquiries. They were treacherous and unforgiving, and Tommy was unwilling to venture in without proper backup. Nybor offered a simple reassurance instead.

"Remember Joshua, you are in this realm now. There are things here beyond your understanding. Earth lacks the magic you see present in this world. Now let us press on."

With a motion, Nybor resumed leading the way, and the trio proceeded in silence for at least half a mile. Josh seeking a change of focus, began inquiring about their destination.

"How far outside of the First Kingdom were we, when we hit that barrier or whatever it was?" he asked.

"About a mile away."

"And how far from the First Kingdom is the Second?" Josh probed further.

Chapter 9

"Probably a day's ride. Why?"

Josh shrugged, trying to grasp the dimensions of the realm.

"Just trying to get a sense of how big this place is. Is it like a planet? Or is it another dimension altogether?"

Tommy chuckled, and even Nybor let out a small laugh. Josh felt frustration building, emboldening him to challenge them for the first time.

"Josh, Beyond is a realm, not a universe. There are no planets here. This is simply a place of existence. It's not like Earth, and the world isn't round," Tommy explained.

"More like... country shaped," Nybor added.

"C'mon, what's 'country shaped'? Which country? UK? Italy? Russia? How big is this place?" Josh prodded further using air quotes for added emphasis. Nybor remained unruffled by his sarcasm.

"There are five kingdoms in Beyond. The First Kingdom..."

"Yeah, yeah, Tommy told me all of that typical fantasy bullshit," Josh interrupted boldly. " I know the rich live in the First, and the dregs of society live in the Fifth. What I wanna know is how long would it take to get from one side to the other. You know, if it's country-shaped?"

Nybor did not take offence to his persistence and felt no harm in answering this question as it would not reveal more information than she needed to.

"From the gateway that the Green Dragon was guarding, at the very edge of the realm, to the edge of the Void, it would take a normal mortal twenty-eight days on horseback. Without stopping."

The realisation hit Josh like a thunderous wave – this place was anything but small. He tried to make sense of it by comparing it to the size of driving coast to coast across the US, a daunting journey that according to Google, took around forty-five hours. He recalled a titbit he had learned once – if you maintained a speed of fifty-five miles per hour and switched drivers periodically, you could

73

theoretically drive through all fifty states in around a hundred-and twenty-four hours. But mathematics wasn't his strong suit, and besides, he didn't even drive, so he had once again had to rely on Google's accuracy in the search engine's answers."We Falcons of course, can move much faster than that, but we are unable to carry the weight of another person for long. My second in command, LeVar will have taken only two days to travel to the Fifth Kingdom. I sincerely hope there has been no more occurrences."

Nybor's voice was laden with concern. Josh sensed that this topic might be a sore subject, but he had to ask. After all, through Tommy's actions, he was now stuck in this mystical realm.

"What exactly are you worried about Nybor?" he inquired.

There was a momentary silence, during which Josh observed her gaze darting from left to right, as if searching for the right words. He then noticed her left arm rising to touch something near her neckline – perhaps the unusual necklace he had noticed upon their first meeting.

"A return to darkness," she finally replied, her voice cracking slightly.

Before Josh could respond or pose further questions, Nybor quickened her pace, urging the others to follow suit. The Fallen Mountains ahead, marking the edge of their destination, seemed to darken ominously. Shadows began to creep up from the base, slowly ascending halfway up the mountainside. As he watched them, he could have sworn he saw something within those shadows. Then, in a fleeting moment, they blinked.

Eyes. He saw eyes.

As if in response to being detected, the shadows fell from the mountains with a speed that rivalled any avalanche, and once again, they were bathed in sunlight. A cold shiver ran down Josh's spine, and the snap of a twig to his left made them all stop and drop into a crouched defensive position. Nybor scanned the left side, while silently gesturing to Tommy to check out the other side.

Chapter 9

Slowly they moved toward the treeline, leaving Josh standing in the middle. Within a minute, his companions had vanished into the dense foliage.

And now, Josh was now completely alone.

The forest seemed to close in around him, and he couldn't shake off the feeling that something was watching him from the shadows. The stillness of the air only heightened his sense of isolation. Every rustle of leaves, every distant hoot of an unknown creature sent his heart racing. He gripped the hilt of a small knife Tommy had given him, that he had tucked into his belt, suddenly feeling a desperate need for some semblance of protection. He had no idea how to use a blade or weapon of any kind, but he felt better simply having it within reach.

Nybor and Tommy were gone, and he had no idea what lurked in the shadows beyond the treeline. The gravity of his situation weighed heavily on him. How had he ended up here? What did this world hold in store for him? Questions swirled in his mind, but for now there were no answers. Only fear. With a deep breath to steady himself, he took a step forward, delving further into the unknown, where adventure and danger awaited him. The sun dipped lower on the horizon, the day already almost at an end, casting long shadows that seemed to dance menacingly around him. Josh knew that time was of the essence. He had to find Nybor and Tommy, to reunite with his newfound companions, and face the enigmatic forces that were lurking in these lands. With each step, he ventured deeper into the forest, his heart pounding in his chest, and his mind determined to unravel the secrets of this captivating but treacherous world.

And then a twig snapped beside him. His heart almost leapt from his chest, he drew the knife and span in the direction of the noise, only for his wrist to be grabbed by a stronger and more powerful hand. He tried to wrestle free of their grip, not understanding what was going on.

"Joshua, it's me!"

The recognisable voice of Nybor's smooth tones deflated his fight or flight response immediately, and he dropped the knife into the grass, gasping for breath. As he turned away, hands on his knees, Nybor could see tiny sparks emanating from his fingertips, but quickly dissipating, as if they had not reached their peak. Moments later, Tommy stumbled from out of a large bush covered in crimson flowers.

"Anything?" he asked tentatively, but examining the focus on Nybor's face, and Josh's increased panting.

"Nothing," she replied. "But we are definitely being watched by someone... or *something*."

The three of them moved off together back towards the trail, Tommy collecting Josh's discarded knife along the way. Once on the path, they continued forward, Nybor making a mental note of how little defensive skills Josh was displaying, and it concerned her deeply. Unbeknownst to the trio, as the walked around one of the large boulders and out of sight, Largox's bulking form moved out of the shadows of a huge and imposing tree. His eyes glowed briefly, and he examined the path ahead of them. A swish of his hands and he was gone.

10

Eralf, clad in regal attire, paced restlessly within the dimly lit chambers of the castle he ruled. He had never been overly fond of the castle's design, always yearning for it to morph and bend to the whims of its occupier. In some ways it had accommodated his desires; he wasted no time in dispatching the previous ruler and remodelled this place to his liking. Yet the castle's dark and blackened structure remained unchangeable, a permanent scar etched into its very essence. A reminder of the days before.

As he roamed the room, thoughts of his sister, Nybor, clouded his mind. Once he had trusted her with unwavering loyalty, willing to lay down his life for her. That was a long time ago now, however. Now, she stood against him, failing to grasp the true vision he had for the five kingdoms of Beyond. And there was no doubt in his mind that she had known Eralf was planning something. It was why he had Largox place the tailor-made ward around the entire kingdom when she left. No more delays. Only Largox seemed to comprehend the grandeur of his plans. Elevating his former childhood friend LeVar to the position of Leader of the

Order, aided by Largox's slight darker influence during the ceremony, had been a calculated move to secure another ally. Yet a flicker of guilt lingered within him.

No, it wasn't remorse. He was too resolute for that. It was guilt, an acknowledgement that some of his actions had weighed heavily on his conscience. Though he knew that darkness threatened the realm, and he would be required by the people to act decisively, there was still a part of him that regretted the path he had chosen.

As King, he had achieved a position of great power, but it was not enough. Ambition surged within him, an insatiable hunger for more authority, more dominion. The desire consumed him, and he knew there was no turning back now. He had once been a servant under his sister's authority, crushed and suppressed, and now he was the most powerful man in the world. He would not go back to the way it was in the days before. In truth, he should have thanked Nybor. If it wasn't for actions in those days, he would not be standing where he was now. Most likely, he would have been killed. But this was his destiny now. The Fifth Kingdom, he mused, would soon meet its fate in the relentless embrace of the Sea of Eternity, as the Void opened fully. The loss of that kingdom seemed of little consequence to him, considering its citizens contributed nothing of value to his rule, only draining the kingdom's resources.

The Fourth Kingdom posed a more personal dilemma, for he had family who resided there. Actual family, not adopted like Nybor. He had wrestled with the decision, but it was overshadowed by his ultimate goal – a grand and decisive battle that would cement his supremacy. Those family members did not even know who he was to them. Nybor and her lackeys had taken care of that long ago. Conquering Beyond had only been the first step in the grand scheme. He, like his adopted sister, knew the secret of the realm – beyond that mysterious barrier lay the Void, where one last obstacle stood between him and that total dominion.

Chapter 10

Someone left to conquer.

The dark glint in his eyes revealed his hunger for ultimate power. Eralf was prepared to face any opposition that dared to stand in his path, even if it meant challenging the most formidable foe in the Void. More powerful than any wraith, spirit or mage. He would shape the destiny of Beyond, leaving a legacy that would resonate through the ages. But in doing so, he would descend into the abyss of darkness, forever altering the course of the realm he coveted. As the shadows deepened around him, Eralf's ambitions grew bolder, and the castle's ominous structure seemed to mirror the darkness within his heart. He suspected his sister's small band of allies were now on their way to thwart his grand plans, armed with courage, loyalty and the power of conviction. A storm of epic proportions was brewing, and the fate of Beyond was likely fated to hang in the balance. He knew she would not return to the First Kingdom. And he would see her at the final battle. And then, and only then would all of the dark history buried in the annals of time be revealed. Those memories of a long-forgotten era, shrouded in damnation and darkness which had been forcibly removed from the collective consciousness. Victory in the days before had come at a steep price, with many lives lost and much knowledge sacrificed, and yet he had survived against all odds.

However, Eralf's ambitions stretched far beyond mere survival. As the most powerful ruler in the realm, he had set his sights on total and complete conquest. The weight of a decision he had been forced to take that very morning, tugged at his conscience, though he knew a show of force was necessary to maintain his hold on power. A sudden knock at the door interrupted his thoughts.

"Enter," he commanded, his voice now firm and resolute. Largox, his trusted mage, stooped through the entrance, bowing in deference to his King.

"He is ready, my liege."

Largox stood aside, gesturing his King through the doorway.

As they walked through the castle's corridors, a knot tightened in Eralf's stomach. The task ahead weighed heavily on him, but he knew it was necessary to quell any dissent and reinforce his rule. It was the second time in as many minutes he had needed to remind himself of this fact. The wine cellar in which he and Largox now found themselves, had once belonged to a previous King, but now served as a grim prison for those who dared to defy Eralf, and an office of sorts for his mage. They entered the chamber, and there, hanging from the wall was the now former Chief Protector Zumo. The warrior had been captured and beaten, shackled in cuffs which repressed his abilities, and now stood as a symbol of defiance. Eralf wasted no time, addressing his former ally with cold authority, and accusation.

"Former Chief Protector Zumo. You are charged with treason against the crown. Due to your high status at my side, it is regretful that you have chosen this path. Do you have any words to speak in your favour?"

In response, Zumo spat blood at Eralf's feet, denouncing him as the true traitor.

"I have no words for you, Eralf. You are the one guilty of a crime. What you plan to do will kill us all. It is you who is the true monster, not that enemy which you seek beyond the Void. And it will destroy us all."

Eralf shifted his foot away from the glob of blood and spit and turned toward his mage, unfazed by this little speech. Largox nodded and moved forward, past his King, placing himself dead centre in front of Zumo. Behind the beast, King Eralf passed sentence.

"Due to your crime of treason, defiance in accepting your punishment in good grace, and your threat to the realm, I hereby sentence you to death."

Despite seemingly knowing his fate already, hearing the words out loud caused Zumo's eyes to flash with panic. Those of Largox

Chapter 10

however, flashed with an unsettling fire, and Zumo felt like he could sense... *enjoyment*.

The ground began to rumble, and the chains holding Zumo rattled without his movement. The hairs on Largox's face began to stand on the surface of his skin, and his eyes began to glow red. A blinding beam of white light shot from Largox's chest, engulfing the former Protector. The light spread across the warrior's body, causing his appearance to wither and change dramatically. His once white hair turned black, and then finally to a grey colour to match his clothes. But the affects were not just cosmetic. Zumo's hair became brittle, and his skin began to wrinkle and contort. *He was ageing*.

As the light subsided, Zumo had transformed into a frail and elderly man. The removal of his White Falcon magic had revealed his true age, and he struggled to draw breath, his body barely able to support him. Though Zumo hung almost lifeless from the wall, this would not be enough. No chances could be taken. Eralf walked past his mage who was now bringing himself back to his full height. He reached for his sword, and unsheathed it, bringing the point to the side of Zumo's desiccated face.

"Goodbye old friend."

As the sword sliced through Zumo's chest and the tip pierced his heart, the sound was not of metal slicing through flesh, but of something being pushed through paper. Skin crunching and ruffling, such was the condition of the body. Barely ten seconds later, Zumo hung dead from the wall, the remnants of a once powerful warrior now gone. However, there was no time to dwell on the death he had inflicted. Disturbing news reached him courtesy of a messenger who stumbled through the doorway, apologising for the intrusion.

"What is it?" Eralf asked, giving Largox a glance to ensure this boy would not see the light of another morning for his interruption.

"Nybor. She is with a human! They are heading for the Shadowlands."

Eralf felt the fire burning in his chest. A human? The only other human he had known of was the Green Dragon that guarded the now defunct gateway to their realm. But a second one? He glanced over to Largox once more, who of course was already fully aware of the presence of another human. He had, however, chosen to keep a watchful eye on the White Falcon and her associates in secret. His King would only get in the way of his own plans. Nevertheless, as the boy was dismissed, Largox decided to continue playing the ever loyal servant for this blundering fool.

"Your orders sire?"

Rage flared within Eralf, but he had come too far to let his emotions cloud his judgement. He knew Nybor had allies within the Shadowlands. He made his decision. One that he felt would come much later than it had, but his hand was forced by the circumstances he now faced. He turned to Largox, a sense of sadness creeping into his eyes, but gave the order, nonetheless.

"Kill her," he commanded, the weight of the words heavy in the air. It was the most difficult choice, but one he deemed unavoidable. She had forced his hand. As Eralf's commands were set into motion, he slumped into a nearby chair, alone in the prison cell of his own design, with only the dead for company.

11

Josh, Nybor and Tommy stood on a rickety wooden bridge, over a narrow point in the river below them, gazing at a peculiar sight – a line of trees with a gap in the centre. It was hardly a gothic and imposing entrance.

"This is the Shadowlands?" Josh asked, surprised and confused at the lack of grandeur.

His voice quivered with astonishment, reaching a higher pitch than he would've liked, betraying a hint of embarrassment. He of course had reason to be perplexed. Earlier on the mountainside, he had witnessed eerie shadows observing him. Now as they stood before the treeline, the forest appeared strangely peaceful, bright and welcoming. Small creatures scurried about, birds sang in the distance, and sunlight filtered through the leaves. It seemed harmless, but Josh knew based on what he had seen and felt so far, that this was probably a false impression.

"Do not mistake what your eyes show you, for the reality of the place," Nybor's voice cut through the air, dripping with coldness.

Tommy chimed in, his voice filled with unease.

"She ain't lyin kiddo. This place is vicious."

Still puzzled by their warnings, Josh observed the seemingly harmless surroundings and decided to move forward. Nybor called out to him, urging caution but he brushed off their suggestions, still angry following their earlier abandonment when they left him alone on the supposed dangerous path, forcing him to go into the woods after them.

"Joshua wait!" Nybor called.

He did stop and turn, but it was with callousness.

"Wait? What you mean like you both did an hour ago when you darted off and left me on my own in the middle of what you called a dangerous path? You mean that kind of wait?"

Neither Nybor nor Tommy could look him directly in the eye.

"It was simply a precautionary scout," Nybor offered. "We were only gone for a short time."

"FIFTEEN MINUTES!" Josh bellowed, his hands shaking. "I could have died in that time. And then I had to come look for you anyway! So forgive me if I take what you say to me with a pinch of salt right about now."

Determined, Josh continued forward, unaware of the darkness that awaited him beyond the treeline. As he crossed over, the world plunged into obsidian blackness, and an icy coldness enveloped him like a suffocating wave. His insides quivered with a bone-chilling sensation, leaving him breathless. When he emerged on the other side, he was met with a stark contrast to what he had seen from the bridge. It was a desolate wasteland of dead trees stripped bare of life and leaves, with no animals in sight and minimal sunlight. His senses overwhelmed, Josh rushed to a nearby dead bush and emptied the contents of his stomach, just as Nybor and Tommy entered the Shadowlands. Tommy had sympathy for Josh, having suffered similarly upon his first journey through the entrance.

"Yep. Same thing happened to me last time. Really don't like this place."

Chapter 11

To those with knowledge of the Shadowlands, they knew the place to be notorious for its eerie grey mist, and home to mythical beings such as witches, Blue Spirits, and the dreaded Yellow Demons, all of whom Nybor hoped to avoid in their quest to find her outsider. Her *shiny* man. She had recently been made aware of a rumour that there had been... disappearances here, from the two nearest kingdoms. Some had wandered in and not wandered out. These were of course unconfirmed reports, but she was at the peak of her guard, nevertheless. The man she was searching for, however, was not of this realm. He was very different, and possessed technology which she hoped might be of use in their quest, and in her experience, outsiders were more trustworthy than many of her own people. Josh recovered himself and was able to stand, wiping his mouth on his sleeve as he did so.

"What was that thing?" he asked, a slight pale tinge now coating his face.

"A portal barrier," replied Tommy. "The image you saw was actually of somewhere else in the forest. The portal brings you here, to the true Shadowlands."

Josh shook his head trying to shake the last of that cold feeling, as he noticed a trend in this world.

"You guys really love your barriers, huh? Think you've got the wrong idea about setting boundaries."

Tommy smiled and patted Josh on the back, before joining Nybor at her side.

"Do you know where your friend might be?" he asked.

"She shook her head.

"The shadows are not where they once were. Something has them spooked and they have shifted. The trees have also moved. I fear the situation may be more dire than we realised if the repercussions are being felt this far away."

Tommy had not fully listened to what his friend was saying to him, despite the darker tone in her voice. He was too busy looking at Josh. Looking at what he was doing.

"Uh, Josh, buddy, how are you doing that?"

Josh was unsure of what Tommy meant, until he followed his gaze down to his own hands. Each of Josh's hands was emitting a blue-white light, and below the light, a rock was twirling in the air. But the rock itself was no longer a rock. As the light moved over the stony surface, it broke apart and twisted into a flower, and then into one of the fruits Tommy had shown him earlier, and then back into a rock. Upon realising its presence, Josh jumped back, the effect stopped, and the rocks landed on the ground with a thump.

"What the fuck was I doing?!?!"

The panic began to take over, and he felt a knot in his chest, his muscles contracted, and he started to hyperventilate. Tommy ran over to him and tried to calm him down and regulate his breathing, but Nybor remained still. Her face had a look of resignation upon it, and as he managed to calm Josh down, Tommy noticed it. He couldn't ignore the way Nybor had been avoiding Josh's questions or giving deliberately vague answers, evading the truth lurking beneath the surface. He knew that now was the time to unravel the enigma that surrounded his new friend. Enough was enough.

"What's wrong with him Nybor? I know you know. I've seen the way you look at him, avoid his questions. We need to know," Tommy demanded, his voice carrying the weight of concern.

Nybor's nod was measured and deliberate, and she took a seat on a sizeable boulder, as if bracing herself to reveal those long-kept secrets.

"He is remembering," she said cryptically.

An interesting, if cryptic response.

"Remembering what?" Tommy inquired, eager to uncover the truth.

With a weary sigh, Nybor rubbed her eyes, the burden of her

Chapter 11

knowledge evident. It seemed that even one as wise as her was not immune to the toll of her hidden truths.

"Joshua is recalling his past, piece by piece, the memories of who he once was when he last walked these lands."

Tommy watched as Josh's face turned paler than the moonlight beginning to filter through the canopy, apparently following a missed sunset. A sickening feeling resurfaced in his stomach, though nothing remained to be expelled. Stammering and broken by this revelation, Josh managed to voice his confusion.

"I was here before?"

Nybor nodded solemnly, confirming the unthinkable.

"Joshua... you were born here."

The reveal of Josh's past hung heavy in the air, leaving a hushed silence to descend upon the trio. The implications of this were vast and unfathomable. Josh, a seemingly ordinary human from Earth, was now confronted with the truth of his origin, entwined with the very fabric of this enchanted land. Tommy was also mystified by these facts. Nybor had not confided in him that she knew of Josh before, nor had she given any indication that Josh was anything other than human up to this point. Was this the real reason he found the doorway back here? Did the changeling have a vested interest in him because it knew that he was of this land and not of Earth? While all of these questions and theories raced through both Josh and Tommy's minds, Nybor's voice broke the silence of confusion.

"Let's start at the beginning."

12

26 years ago in Beyond | 12 months ago in Wealdstone

"We can't go through that. It's too dangerous!"

"We don't have a choice! It's not safe here!"

The couple argued back and forth, shifting the dirt and leaves between their feet, pacing around the glowing doorway in the forest, which was beginning to glitch and shift, as if being affected by their argument. But she knew. Kathryn knew. It would not be safe here. Something was hunting them, she could feel it. She had felt it when she left Wealdstone a year ago, and she felt it even more now. Something was coming for her, and she suspected she knew what. *Or who.*

Jack leaned forward and gazed upon the green outline before them. They had not had a particularly good experience with these doorways, and they had been fairly certain they had all but vanished. That was until they received word from one of their friends, Annie, that some children had come across this one when playing. When one of those children tripped, their head had gone through the gap and saw what lay on the other side.

"There's no way I'm jumping over a waterfall," Jack said, still dead set against the idea.

"That's why we brought this," Kathryn replied, extracting a parachute from a duffel bag.

"Yeah, that's a great idea, a woman who is eight and a half months pregnant leaping over a waterfall and parachuting to safety. That won't endanger you or the baby at all!"

The emotions were now getting the better of Jack. He knew better than anyone that his family would not be safe here. As soon as they found out that Kathryn was pregnant, they had left the town looking for a quieter life. But all they had found were reminders that death followed them wherever they went. They knew Beyond was the only safe place for their child, and as much as it pained them to do it, he knew deep down that it was the right choice.

"If we do this, if we go through this doorway, you know we don't need to come back here. We could stay. Stay with our son."

His eyes were pleading but his heart knew the truth. They could stay in Beyond, but they'd be abandoning everyone else they cared about and leaving them to fend for themselves. Kathryn's niece, Grace, had warned her about the events at Moriarty Hospital, and the powerful force which had escaped its walls. They didn't have long. Kathryn simply gazed into his eyes, tears forming in the corners of her own, and he knew the choice was made.

The water cascaded over the fall and the incredibly surreal feeling of floating through the air encompassed Kathryn. She could not help but smile both at the beauty of what she was seeing, but at the hilarious spectacle of a woman so heavily pregnant seeming to float without issue. Even Jack could not hide a smile at this place.

Chapter 12

They knew they couldn't stay, but it was a strong pull. A warm breeze caught their parachutes and lifted them further into the air, their trajectory moving further away from where they entered. As they sailed over the purple leaves of the enormous trees of the forest, in the distance, a large black castle loomed into view. Kathryn shouted over the sound of the breeze.

"Look at that! Who do you suppose lives there?"

Jack shook his head.

"No idea! Nice gothic looking place though!"

They began their descent towards the ground as the breeze subsided, and giving several subtle tugs on their guide ropes, they managed to direct themselves towards a large clearing ahead. As they dipped below the edge of the trees, they heard what sounded like a sonic boom. Kathryn's feet touched down first, and she fell to her knees, the weight she was carrying seeming to double with the return of gravity. Jack touched down alongside her, and almost immediately headed towards her to make sure she was alright.

"I'm fine but… didn't you hear that?" she asked.

Jack looked around nodding.

"I heard it."

There were no more words uttered before the rush of wind came from all sides. A giant whooshing sound came from directly above, and a transparent column slammed into the dirt, approximately twenty feet high. Jack dropped to his knees, and immediately extracted a gun from a rear holster, searching for something to lock onto. A second pillar struck the ground six feet from the first, and they continued to drop around them in a circular motion, until a shadow could be seen against the light of the sun. A figure emerged from those shadows and somersaulted downwards, landing in the centre of the circle with a thud, sending dirt up in a cloud around them. The figure was carrying a large staff, and slammed the base of it into the ground once, sending a shaft of light into the air to the mid-point. As it reached level with the top of the pillars, it exploded like a firework, and a net of light sprinkled downwards until it met the top of every pillar, and then it too became transparent.

"You do like a dramatic entrance, Nybor," Kathryn said, a smile spreading across her face.

"One can never be too careful my friends."

The two of them embraced for a moment, although the concern in Nybor was clear. She nodded in Jack's direction, and he holstered his gun and nodded back.

"You should not be here."

The words were sharp and heavy to Kathryn's ears.

"We don't have much choice. There is a threat that we cannot avoid. And we now have others to consider."

She glanced down at her stomach, and Nybor followed her gaze. She reached forward to touch the bump but retracted her hand.

"What is it you are seeking here Kathryn? It has been a decade since we last met after all."

Kathryn looked startlingly at Jack, before she remembered that time passed differently here. It was another part of the reason she wanted to come here.

"Something is coming for us Nybor. Something big. And I can't protect everybody."

Nybor began to understand what was being asked of her.

"I am sorry Kathryn, but I cannot help you."

Kathryn's stomach sank, and her eyes began to well up with tears once more. But Nybor was not done.

"However, I know someone who can."

Chapter 12

The walk was long and tedious, especially for a woman who was eight and a half months pregnant and accelerating by the minute. Given the time difference here, it would surely only be a matter of hours at most before she gave birth. The small hut began to peer between the trees, however, and then Jack saw a couple of people milling about in the garden surrounding the building. Once they had a good view of the place, Kathryn stopped dead in her tracks. One of the people appeared to be *inhuman*. The woman was fairly tall, and well built. Tanned skin and defined muscles beneath a cloth woven into a dress in a beautiful and intricate way. But her head was that of a wolf. It was a truly peculiar sight, despite the horrors and entities that Kathryn had faced, this set her back. Nybor strolled forwards with purpose, and Kathryn began to feel a contraction. It was almost time.

"Nybor! It is so good to see you my friend!"

The wolfwoman jogged half-heartedly towards Nybor, and surprisingly, launched an attack at the Falcon, sliding under her legs, and striking her in the back. Nybor swivelled and snapped her staff in two directly along the mid-point, something Kathryn had not seen her do at Crossroads. She twirled the ends in her hands as if they were batons. Her and the wolf exchanged blows and strikes, each dodging the other, before she leapt onto Nybor's back and in a display of pure beauty, Nybor extended her wings with a burst that sent the woman sailing through the trees hitting the trunk of one with a sickening thud. Bones crunching seemed to be shrugged off by the wolf, who sniggered, and cracked her joints back into place without pain, before running towards Nybor again. She didn't get far however, as Nybor began twirling the sticks in a particular fashion. A whining noise began to emanate from them, and a visible ripple appeared in the air, and the noise got louder. The wolf stopped in her tracks and covered her ears, Jack and Kathryn doing the same.

"Okay, okay! I yield!"

Nybor stopped, the sound ceased, and she slammed the two halves of her staff back together.

"Come inside. Iona will be happy to see you too."

The strange display of aggression was now a forgotten event as the talks continued about Kathryn and Jack's situation, and what they were proposing. They learned that the wolfwoman was called Valdore. She was a creature Nybor referred to as an Omega. The humanoid wolf hybrid was something Kathryn was familiar with in terms of a werewolf but had never encountered a balance in this form before. Her partner, Iona, was a humanoid, but chose to wear a headpiece displaying horns on either side of the head. Her hair was short, just touching her shoulders, and was a shade of blue that seemed to glow regardless of whether light touched it or not. Her clothing was certainly unique. A cropped piece of armour covered her shoulders and chest but left her midriff exposed. More of the same armour began at her waist and ran to the top of her thighs, before breaking and then rejoining at her knee. A loincloth type design covered the front and rear of her legs and appeared to be made from leather.

Valdore's attire was much more basic. One piece of flexible armour covered her entire upper body, a red scarf wrapped around her neck, and deep purple leather-like trousers covered her lower half. The armour on both women looked heavy and cumbersome, but they moved as if it were simply tissue paper. Valdore's dress had been replaced with this outfit when Nybor told them she had a task for them. It was always better to be cautious in Valdore's opinion.

Chapter 12

"There are dangers of our own in Beyond, Nybor, you know this."

Iona's voice was stern, but thoughtful. The idea of them raising a human baby in Beyond was not without its perils. The only other human to even exist in this world was Tommy, who now lived in isolation when not accompanying Nybor. A Green Dragon, who had supposedly masked the doorway he guarded from view upon their return from Crossroads. She made a mental note to have a word with him when this was all over.

"I am aware. But the dangers the child faces in the human world are far greater. All the realms are at a far greater risk than they once were. I cannot leave Beyond to help the humans any more than they can stay to help us."

Kathryn held Jack's hand tightly, as the contractions began to ramp up. He looked towards the three women.

"I think we may have to continue this conversation later. It's time."

The smile on the baby's face was something Kathryn had not been prepared for. Valdore had wrapped him in a beautiful woven blanket, and her son stared up at her. Jack was sat beside her, the strings tugging at his heart. He knew they had to leave soon. The time difference in this realm meant several days or weeks may have passed since they left. But the parental bond was beginning to strengthen. He steeled himself and spoke to the others.

"He cannot know anything of us, or his own world. When he is old enough, I ask that you use your powers or magic or whatever abilities you must to give him new memories. Teach him your ways. Keep him safe and love him."

He glanced down at the baby who was now gripping his pinky

finger with his entire miniature hand. Jack smiled back and he allowed a tear to fall. Valdore leaned forwards.

"Do you have a name for your son?"

Kathryn smiled and spoke one word.

"Joshua."

Jack chuckled at the name choice. They had discussed it several times, but the one they kept coming back to was Joshua.

"Any reason?" asked Iona, who was now using some kind of magic to conjure some milk.

"Jack's favourite album when he was a kid was The Joshua Tree by U2. I used to laugh at him when we were at college, and he would turn up in his dad's car blasting it out the windows."

The three women of Beyond exchanged confused glances, before Nybor spoke.

"I assume this U2… they are a band?"

Jack and Kathryn laughed and nodded.

"There is one more request I have to make," said Kathryn, her smile now fading, knowing it was soon time to say goodbye to their son.

"Of course," replied Iona.

"If Joshua ever grows up to discover where he truly comes from, of his real home, if he makes that choice to cross the threshold… do not let him know about us. If we are still around if that ever happens, and he seeks us out, he is going to be placed in the same dangers we are trying to protect him from now. Give him new memories, new identities, whatever you must do."

All three women nodded, and against her better judgement, Kathryn handed the baby over to Valdore, and immediately began to sob. Nybor stepped forward with a voice full of calm and spoke with the softness of silk.

"Come now you two, you both need rest. You may stay here and get some sleep, regenerate. I will accompany you back to the

Chapter 12

doorway tomorrow. Not too much time will have passed in your world. Those curiosities seem to be in flux of late"

Jack and Kathryn both looked over their shoulder at their newborn son as they stood in the doorway to the bedroom. They absorbed the sight of the baby and memorised his face. For in the morning, they would leave, never to see him again.

13

Josh's world fell silent, and was enveloped by absolute stillness. He had listened to Nybor's story intensely, but it had now left him reeling, slumped on the ground, encircled by mist and grappling with a void in his chest. Nybor's tale had shattered his perception of reality. Those he had despised turned out to be his real parents, and the people he thought he had lost were nothing but implanted memories. His sense of self had been completely unravelled.

"When did I return to Wealdstone?" Josh questioned, with cold detachment, unable to fathom how such a short time had passed for him on Earth, while years had gone by in Beyond.

"Here, it was twenty six years ago, but in human terms, just twelve months."

Josh shot her a look, eyes wide.

"You said they only left me here twelve months ago? How is that possible?"

Nybor held out a hand for him to calm down. Tommy watched on, himself trying to take all this in.

"Something here is beginning to destabilise our realm. The

occurrences on the border of our world are affecting everything. Time is fluctuating here. Previously it was constant, approximately a hundred years here was just a week or so on Earth. But now it is beyond measure. Sometimes it speeds up, sometimes it slows down, but if one of us leaves to go to another realm, particularly your realm, it begins to notice more."

So, there it was. The truth about Josh's heritage. He had been conceived, born, grown up, and moved back to Wealdstone all in the space of a year. He had never actually been present when Jasmine attacked Wealdstone. Neither when Monarch had escaped and terrorised the world from Crossroads. All false memories. He now wondered if his friendship with Chantel was even real. And Dalton. It was now Tommy's turn for some clarification.

"Your comic book. The character in it, you drew him stood at the waterfall. It must have been memories trying to force their way through. You actually had been here before. You even knew of the cat."

Nybor nodded her head. Her reaction to the mention of the changeling indicated that the feline held significance beyond a coincidental appearance. Those memories, however, had not yet returned to Josh, but Tommy decided to fill in the blanks.

"Spiner," he said with a sigh that indicated previous dealings with the creature.

Josh looked around now more confused than angry. It almost felt comfortable to return to a state he was familiar with.

"Who, or what is Spiner?"

The crack of a twig was heard behind them, causing all three of them to jump slightly, even Nybor was caught off guard given the intensity of their conversation. This breaking piece of wood, however, was then accompanied by an image… and a voice.

"If you must know, I am a friend."

The voice was deep and seemed to come from a small creature strolling towards them. As the mist moved away, the small ginger

Chapter 13

cat which had led Josh here in the first place entered the clearing. The cat spoke again.

"I would have thought you'd remember me, Joshua. Apparently not."

With disbelief in his eyes, Josh found himself face to face with a talking cat. He had seen some shit in his time... well perhaps not. He wasn't sure what was real and what was illusion anymore. He thought of Moriarty Hospital and how if he ever made it back, he would likely end up there. Spiner seemed amused by Josh's astonishment.

"What did you think you were doing bringing him back here, Spiner?" accused Nybor, gripping her staff hard, turning her knuckles as white as her hair.

The cat looked back over its shoulder, and then began to grow, stretching out, the features and fur beginning to melt away until the beast was now six foot tall. The eyes and mouth of the cat stretched and altered until they became human-sized. In a few moments, the cat was now a young man, perhaps twenty years old. The eyes remained feline and yellow, but everything else was human in appearance.

"I decided it was worth the risk. You never should have sent him back to the humans anyway. This is his home."

Spiner spoke to Nybor as if she was an irritant rather than a figure of authority. He glanced past her to Tommy and gave a snarl in his direction.

"And this one hasn't exactly proven useful since he arrived either. Sleeping on the job when his parents came through? Surprised the King didn't have you executed for that."

Tommy felt his eyes burn green, and reached for his sword before Nybor held a hand up signalling him to stand down.

"His powers grew beyond our charms, and he discovered who he truly was. We were not his jailors, Spiner, we were his protectors. He asked to return to humanity, and we obliged. We also kept our promise to his parents. We gave him new memories. Had you not brought him back here, then those memories would have remained intact. What you have done is careless."

Spiner laughed, and strolled towards Josh, kneeling in front of his still shocked, apparent former best friend, his yellow eyes burrowing into Josh's very soul, searching for remnants of familiarity.

"Nothing? You don't remember any of it? The training, the sorcery classes? Running supplies between the kingdoms? Building a treehouse in the Forest of Music?"

Josh's face remained blank. Spiner shook his head, and there was a tinge of sadness in those cat-like eyes as he moved away.

"And why on Earth would you give him the last name from the prophecy? What was the thinking behind that?"

For the first time, Nybor appeared embarrassed, and looked down at the floor.

"You gave him *that* name?" Tommy asked astonished. "You took an ancient prophecy, stole the name of the supposed mythical beast that is said to live within the Void, and then just gave it to a human and sent him on his way?"

Nybor slammed her staff on the ground, and the noise echoed all around them.

"The prophecy isn't real!" she shouted.

More silence. This was becoming somewhat of a confessional. More details were emerging than Tommy ever thought possible. And despite this, he still felt things were being held back.

"I'm sorry, what?" he asked in astonishment.

Nybor sighed. The prophecy in question, was a tapestry that hung in the castle near to the throne. It was another lie created to distract the people of Beyond from any hope of recalling their memories from the days before. It pictured a monstrous being made from black silhouettes and dripping in blood. At the time, those who had tried to hide the truth had simply taken random letters from whoever was present at the time and put them together to form the name 'Shaw.' Nybor was forced to convey the importance of such measures to the others.

"There are things far worse and shameful about this land that neither you, Tommy, nor anyone else knows about. That anyone remembers. It was a failsafe. A threat for them to focus on should they start to discover the truth."

Tommy stormed over towards her.

"And just what is that truth?" he asked through gritted teeth.

"You are not capable of processing what had to be done. The truth would burn you from the inside out. It is a secret which must remain buried. You were never even meant to be here!"

Nybor walked away, but Tommy grabbed her arm.

"Do not walk away from me, Falcon!" he shouted.

She gripped his hand with her own, twisted it round until she heard his wrist snap, and spun around kicking him square in the chest. He flew backwards and landed against a boulder with a thud.

"Do not overstep your boundaries, Green Dragon. You have no idea the sacrifices made to keep this realm safe."

Tommy dragged himself to his feet. He considered using his powers to retaliate against his friend, but something told him to simply walk away.

"I clearly do not mean as much to you as I thought I did. And seeing as you can clearly make decisions for this realm alone, I will take my leave of you."

Tommy turned to walk back through the portal and out of the Shadowlands. He paused and looked back.

"But know this, Nybor. The next time we meet, if you don't speak the truth, I will consider you an enemy."

And with that, he walked through the portal and was gone.

14

LeVar's promotion to the leadership of the revered Order of White Falcons had transpired without the grandeur he had expected. Instead, a sense of unease gnawed at him as he assumed the mantle of command. Now in charge during Nybor's unplanned absence, he felt an unprecedented surge of power coursing through him at all times. He wondered how his predecessor managed to carry out her daily tasks with such feelings. However, beneath the surface, something unnatural lurked. The unfamiliar presence place within him during the ceremony by Largox squirmed within him, causing feelings of resentment and darkness that were not his own. Resentment against Nybor. He retained enough control to know these were not his thoughts, his feelings, but one word from either Largox or King Eralf, and he obeyed without question. He was made aware of Zumo's alleged treachery and treason shortly after his execution, and although the foreign part of his brain felt justice was served, the front of his mind suspected this would not be the last sacrifice on this journey.

The journey in question was still mostly unknown to him. He

knew only that he was to return to the Fifth Kingdom, inform Skye, Eva and Gregor of the change of command, and remove the protective bubble around the city. The part that made him uncomfortable, was that he was not to permit any citizen of the Fifth Kingdom to leave the walls of the city. When he questioned why he should remove the bubble of protection if people were still effectively under house arrest, he found himself staring down the business end of King Eralf's broadsword. His foreign presence then snapped back into action, and he agreed to do the bidding of his king, no further questions asked. He was worried that this new part of him would cost him dearly. That at some point, the king would task him with hunting down Nybor. But what really worried him, was the fact that the darkness placed in him by the mage would force him to agree to it.

It had been a two-day flight back to the royal castle. LeVar had refused to stop for sleep, such was the urgency he felt about the unfolding situation at the Void. This time, he was returning with others, and so encouraged them to rest often. They had stopped for respite in the Third Kingdom the previous night, and now as the night closed in once again, they stopped at a small camp outside of the Fourth Kingdom, on the edges of the Sea of Eternity. The scenery was breathtaking, provided you didn't look in the direction of the Void. Even at such a distance, the advanced eyesight of the White Falcons meant they could make out the swirling shapes and monsters on the other side of the barrier. If the cracks were becoming more widespread, LeVar wasn't entirely sure what they could do to stop it. The magic used to contain the Void in the first place no longer existed, and King Eralf had given no indication that he had a plan to stop it either. His orders were simply to contain the citizens of the Fifth Kingdom and await further instructions.

In the distance far off to the south, the faint notes of melodies

Chapter 14

floated on the breeze. The Forest of Music was perhaps Beyond's most breathtaking lands. Once a place of war and famine, the forest was now home to the oldest trees in Beyond, travelled there from near and far to live in peace and harmony. They sang notes between each leaf on each branch, the vibrations sending their melodies out on the wind, carrying as far as The Islands in the sea itself.

As LeVar sparked a fire into life with his new staff, one of the younger members of the White Falcons approached, concern etched on his face.

"My Lord?" he asked, with trepidation.

"Yes young Falcon?" LeVar replied.

"May I ask a rather silly question? Forgive me if I am out of turn in doing so. I am simply curious."

LeVar smiled for the first time in a week, and one of the few gestures he felt was truly one of his own.

"What troubles you my young friend?"

The boy seemed to ease slightly, and LeVar gestured for him to sit on the other side of the fire, which he obliged.

"My knowledge of this area is quite limited. I have never ventured beyond the Second Kingdom where I was born. I'd like to know why they call this ocean the Sea of Eternity."

LeVar smiled and stoked the fire with a stray stick. He had asked the very same question when he was first sent out this way. He himself was of the Third Kingdom. Nicely in the middle. Not born into poverty, but neither born into riches. Nybor had found him when his curiosity got the better of him and he wandered into the gates of the First Kingdom. His parents had died of old age, and there was nobody to look after him, so he began exploring. She had told him the story of the only ocean in Beyond, and so he repeated it to the boy.

"Eons ago, Beyond was in turmoil. War raged in every corner, long before the five kingdoms existed. The black castle was the only constant in this world and was ruled by a vicious overlord. His name is unspoken by those who remember, and so his deeds are forgotten. However, when peace finally came to this realm, the dead numbered in their trillions. Blood soaked the land, and fire reigned down from the sky, and the rivers and oceans ran red. The peacemakers decided to offer the bodies of those that had fallen to the waters so they may sail into the afterlife peacefully.

They were floated out into the ocean on small rafts, and the waters did indeed turn blue once more. But it was soon noticed that the bodies veered off to the north, despite the tide moving south. When they reached the horizon, they would vanish. Sailors tried to journey to the point of disappearance, but no ship could reach it. It was believed that the dead had entered the afterlife. From that day, it was known as The Sea of Eternity. Some called it the Sea of Eternal Rest, but that never really caught on."

The young Falcon was in awe of the story. He had heard similar stories about the rivers running red in the days before, but he had never known why. It was deemed beyond the essential information for a child. He pressed for more information, feeling he could confide in his leader.

"My Lord, why are we travelling to the Fifth Kingdom, if it is not to rescue the people there? Is it not our task to protect those of the realm?"

LeVar stiffened up slightly. The truth of course was that he didn't know either. But leadership was scarcely an easy task. Nybor had shown him that on many occasions.

"The King has decreed we are to contain the kingdom until we know more. So that is what we intend to do."

"But Sir, the people will be frightened. Do we do nothing?"

"On the contrary young one, we will reassure them. We will provide them with provisions and supplies to keep them fed, warm and comfortable. And we will protect them from any dangers."

Chapter 14

It was the last part which sparked fear into the inexperienced warrior.

"And if the Void does collapse, my lord?"

LeVar glanced up and toward the danger in question.

"Then may all the Gods save us."

15

Nybor, Josh and Spiner had travelled for ten hours without so much as a word to each other. Spiner kept scratching the back of his ears much like a cat does. He appeared to have spent less time in his usual form than his feline one. Josh had spent that time trying to digest his true origins. Process the lies he had been fed. Establish what he knew to be fact from fiction. Sadly, he had not been able to regenerate these apparent powers he had developed. The calming effect he had provided to Nybor, and the metamorphic abilities he had displayed in the rocks had not returned to him as of yet, no matter how hard he concentrated.

The Shadowlands, despite its foreboding reputation, appeared to be nothing more than an ancient woodland, wrapped in a shroud of dust and mist. No dangers had made themselves known, and the passage of time remained elusive, the chill in the air suggesting perpetual nightfall. Nybor stopped ahead of them and held up her arm for them to do the same. Bristling with discomfort and impatience, Spiner grew back into his humanoid form, ignored her and barged past.

"I live here, Falcon, I think I know what I'm doi-"

Spiner was cut off abruptly as a bolt of energy fired from the left hand side striking him in his ribs and sending him sprawling across the ground. Nybor did not move, and Josh couldn't help but feel as if the energy beam was not a form of magic or wizardry, but something more artificial. Spiner scrambled to his feet and let out a feline roar in the direction of the beam, but Nybor leaned her staff in his direction to keep him where he was.

"Do not fear, old friend. I simply wish to speak to you."

Nybor's voice carried on the low breeze and in the swirls of mist, Josh could see shimmering, like that of a precious jewel. The he saw more and more points glimmering in the dull light of the Shadowlands. The glinting seemed to merge and then part spreading over a large mass. It began to move towards them, and Josh was able to make out the shape of a person, swallowed by these shining pieces. No, not swallowed.

They *were* the person.

"It would seem you have made many enemies, Falcon. Friends are becoming a luxury for you."

The voice from the mass now approaching the group was soft and cushioned. Josh found his tones very relaxing, considering the appearance of his skin. The figure fully emerged from the mist and Josh attempted to take in what he saw. A man, roughly seven feet tall stood before them. His entire face, lower arms and his chest that was visible below his clothing, was encrusted with diamonds. Josh had been correct in his assumption of the energy fire. The man carried what looked like an assault rifle, only much more advanced than any weapon he had ever seen before. A power cell glowed within it, and he began to suspect that the man was not of this world.

"Spying on me again Syl'Va?" asked Nybor with a hint of amusement in her face.

The man simply nodded.

"It is in my interests to keep tabs on my friends and allies. In

Chapter 15

case of danger. I suspect that is the true reason you are here. Am I wrong?"

Nybor stepped forward and placed her arm on Syl'Va's diamond forearm.

"I am afraid you are correct my Deltarian friend. Enemies mass in our own ranks. The King is planning something, and he means to keep me, and my allies out of the inner circle."

Syl'Va nodded and grunted in agreement. He stepped away and began stalking the ground around them as he spoke.

"Whispers between the people here inform me that the King has replaced you with your friend LeVar and executed his protector."

The words almost floored Nybor. LeVar *promoted*? He would surely never take that offer unless coerced. She knew there were many things uncertain in Beyond, but the loyalty of LeVar was not one of them. Her mind then settled on the words at the end of Syl'Va's statement. *Executed his protector*. Zumo was dead. Likely because of the discovery of the King's treachery. He always had been inquisitive by nature.

"What more do you know?"

Nybor's voice cracked as she spoke, fearing what would come next.

"Your Falcons, the ones named Soren and Lursa are dead. Executed on sight when attempting to break through the ward you came up against. The mage was the one to give the order and the King's Guard carried it out. I fear they have been given magic to strengthen the King's position."

King's Guard with magic? Executing White Falcons? What possible power could Largox have given them to enable them to take down White Falcons?

"Syl'Va, you are correct. I need your help, but it appears you already know the situation we face."

The Deltarian nodded.

"When I first arrived here, I was uncertain. Confused. Unsure of what time or universe I had fallen into. A far cry from the depths of space."

That was another confirmation of Josh's suspicions. Syl'Va was an alien. Based on his statement, Josh surmised he had come through a doorway like the one that took him from Wealdstone. Syl'Va continued.

"It was you who found me and reassured me that I was safe here. For the most part, you were right. However, after several decades, I fear that time is coming to an end. The witches, Blue Spirits and surviving Yellow Demons, are all seeking out the remaining doorways. They are afraid. Terrified of what is coming."

He pointed his weapon at Spiner.

"Even the majority of his kind have deserted this place. Only a few dozen remain."

Spiner's skin tingled with fear, and goosebumps appeared on his arms. His cockiness and bluster were a distant memory now. He moved back towards Josh. Although his friend did not yet remember him, he certainly remembered the shared childhood they had, and felt an air of safety around him. Josh felt the same, despite his lost memories.

"I suspect that I know what Eralf is planning. He has always sought out conquest. Battle. Fights he felt he could win. His ego is beyond that of mortal men. I fear he now considers himself a god in the form of a man."

Syl'Va nodded.

"I felt as much when he murdered his predecessor."

Again, a fact that had escaped Nybor. She suspected that the ascension of her brother to the throne was not one of conventional means, but it had never been fully disclosed. After the corruption of the royal position when her family were rulers of Beyond, and her Aunt was killed in a skirmish, it was decided that the current leader of the Order of White Falcons would become the new King.

Chapter 15

Everyone agreed. Except Eralf. He wanted the throne, and he believed he was the rightful heir. The power of the people, and Nybor, had overruled him. King Kurn ruled for centuries unopposed, and he was a benevolent ruler. Beyond prospered under his rule, and all was well. Even those in the Fifth Kingdom enjoyed prosperity.

Eralf claimed he had died of natural causes, but as a White Falcon, Kurn should have been near to immortal. Nevertheless, a decree was found on Kurn's deathbed declaring Eralf as the new King. Nybor always suspected that it had been forced at the end of a blade or through a magical curse. Now she knew. Syl'Va's advanced technology allowed him to see things others couldn't.

Josh decided to speak up.

"Uh, excuse me, Mr Syl'Va?"

The Deltarian turned in his direction and tipped his head gesturing him to continue with his inquiry.

"If you came through a doorway, why did you not go back? What happened to make you stay?"

The question was not the one Josh had wanted to ask, but his writer's mind came to the fore, and he was envisaging a potential comic book storyline, even in the current scenario. Syl'Va let out a laugh, raspy but loud.

"My human friend, I had no desire to go back even if the doorway which led me here had remained open. I came from a universe where annihilation was coming fast and swiftly. Your race was gone, and the only surviving human was battling my former commander to reach a forbidden piece of technology they thought could bring them power and resurrection. I was a dead man if I stayed. My human friend came up with a plan to transport me to safety on a distant moon. I found the doorway, it led me here, and closed behind me. I decided to make a home for myself here and make myself of service when needed to the protectors of this place. Namely, Nybor."

Nybor now added to the story before making her request.

"Syl'Va's technology can sometimes bypass the magical wards and restrictions imposed here. It is not of this world and so there are no guards against it. A couple of machines he calls drones can scout the land under a cloak. But Syl'Va, I must ask you now. Will you aid me in my quest once again? We must stop the Void from opening and prevent my brother from allowing it to swallow the people of the Fifth Kingdom."

Syl'Va glanced at each one of them in turn, returning to Josh. He stared at him intensely but directed his inquiry to Nybor.

"Does he remember how to utilise his powers yet?"

Both Nybor and Spiner shook their heads.

"Well, my young human, you should probably take this then."

He detached a smaller pistol from the body of his rifle and tossed it towards Josh, who just about managed to catch it. He fumbled it around his hands, and a bolt of energy shot from it, narrowly missing Spiner and burning a hole in the nearest tree.

"Watch it!" he screamed.

"Sorry," said Josh. "It's my first ray gun."

16

In terms of energy barriers, this one was certainly unique both in its design and effectiveness. It clearly bore the markings of a powerful mage. Tommy watched as residents of the First Kingdom walked through the barrier without any issue, and seemingly unaware of its presence at all. Tommy however, felt a ripple of magnetic force the closer he moved to it. With no gateway to guard anymore, he wasn't even sure where he could go, where he could be of use. The simple fact was that he no longer had a purpose here. Ironically, having destroyed the gateway to the human world, he had also eliminated any possibility of returning there. He did not have to wait long to attract the attention of someone in authority.

"You're playing a dangerous game, Green Dragon."

The words of the White Falcon drifted over his head, unimportant as this person seemed. Tommy knew that only Nybor and LeVar held any weight in the ranks of the protectors, and this was likely a lackey with a power complex.

"Oh, and why is that... whoever you are?"

The lack of respect the Falcon expected caused his face to turn sour and his cocky smile to fade.

"Because the time where people could walk around as if they owned this land are gone. King Eralf is seeing to that. You've become... obsolete."

Tommy chuckled, which seemed to infuriate the Falcon even more. He thought of one of his favourite movie quotes from his time in the human world. He looked up at the Falcon, feeling every one of his six hundred years of age.

"Old... not obsolete."

The Falcon moved right up to the edge of the barrier, gritted his teeth, and spoke through flecks of spittle which moved through the surface and landed on Tommy's face.

"Aligning yourself with the betrayer was a mistake, Dragon. It'll see you killed."

Tommy made a show of wiping the spit off his skin and pretended to dust down his armour.

"Well, whoever you are, maybe it would interest you to know that I left her far behind. That bridge is burned."

The Falcon recoiled slightly at this statement. The cocky smile began to return.

"So, she has made enemies amongst her friends as well?" He pondered for a moment. "Is that why you are here? To beg forgiveness from our King?"

Clearly, whoever this soldier was, he wanted to feel superior, and so Tommy played along to a point. But inside, he really was looking for a new purpose. Perhaps he could find that here, or in one of the lower Kingdoms.

"I am a Green Dragon without a doorway. I simply wish to serve in whatever way I can to protect this realm and all within it. A goal we share, I am sure."

Again, the smile faded. It was a fact that the Falcon could not deny. Whilst he had seen the address from King Eralf informing

Chapter 16

the Order of Nybor's so called betrayal, he had felt a tinge of hurt that his former leader and someone he looked up to was capable of treason. And whilst King Eralf was rather vague on the details, he was of course their King. They were bound to serve him. And serve him they would.

"I can arrange for you to pass this barrier, Dragon. But you understand what will happen if you do? Your gateway is gone. You understand?"

Tommy sighed, knowing it would never have been a case of simply stepping through, and he was more than aware of the consequences of destroying his own gateway.

"I understand." he spoke, a hint of fear in his voice, knowing what he was about to go through.

The Falcon reached for a small pouch attached to his waist. He pulled it free and tugged the drawstring open. Within the cloth bag was a dark blue powder, shimmering in the light, as there were fragments of crystal buried within it. Tommy shuddered. He knew what this was. He had seen it before, and he had witnessed its power. Despite the task the Falcon was about to set in motion, he did not appear cocky any longer. He knew what this powder would do, and he did not envy those exposed to it.

"Does it hurt?" asked Tommy, already knowing the answer.

The Falcon simply nodded.

"What's your name, White Falcon?"

"Manor. Yours?"

"Tommy."

The pair exchanged a nervous nod. Each understood what happened next. There was a brief flicker in Tommy's mind of whether he should return to the Shadowlands and help his friends, but in truth, he was tired. He had fought enough. And he just wanted rest. He wasn't sure of the entire repercussions of this action, but he felt it was time, and a whole new adventure may be on the other side.

Manor tossed the bag through the barrier, and it landed at Tommy's feet. He had learned the ritual during his initiation. This was it. There was no going back. He unsheathed his sword and placed it on the ground. As he stood back up, he collected the pouch in his right hand, and pinched the powder with his left. He closed his eyes and tossed the powder into the air. As the shimmering powder fell back down from the sky, it expanded into a cloud of dark blue glitter and fully encompassed Tommy's body. As it did so, he began to tremble. The powder seemed to enter his ears, nose, and mouth like a mist.

Manor looked on, shifting uncomfortably at the sight before him. He had immense respect for those who underwent this process voluntarily. It did not often end well. Tommy's mouth burst open and the scream which left his lips was shattering. Each piece of his armour began to shrivel and contract until it was as small as coin, before it fell to the ground. Upon contact with the sweet and dewy grass, it began to morph into a liquid and surged towards the other pieces as they dropped. Once merged together like liquid metal, they solidified once more in the shape of a dragon's head. The solid object was as if carved from green crystal. But this was when the true pain would strike.

As Manor and several others who had gathered nearby watched on, Tommy began to age. He had been forty-two upon his arrival in Beyond, but with a young face. Now, however, his hair began to turn silver, and his beard shifted to a stone grey. The lines around his eyes began to deepen and were joined by deep furrows in his forehead. When the aging process ceased, Tommy fell to his knees. Manor moved through the barrier, collected the dragon head crystal, and used his free arm to help Tommy to his feet. As he looked at him, he saw the toll the pain had taken on him. Tommy was now displaying the features and appearance of an eighty-year old human. Being born in the human realm, meant he was not subjected to the same aging process as Zumo had been. Only those

Chapter 16

born in Beyond, would age their full years of life upon being stripped of their powers. For a human, it was somewhere in between.

"H-h-how do I look?" Tommy asked in laboured breath.

Manor could not help but smile.

"Not a day over three hundred."

Tommy forced a smile, although he was now experiencing the rigours of old age all at once. Joint pain, knee inflammation, creaking bones. Manor placed the dragon head into the now empty satchel, returned it to his waist, and slung Tommy over his shoulders.

"Come, former Dragon. Let's go find you something to do."

17

It had been six hours since Josh had accidentally nearly shot everyone in his immediate vicinity, and the early morning light was peeking through the smallest gaps in the tree canopy far above. Spiner, however, no longer felt comfortable around his former best friend. He kept alongside the diamond encrusted man from outer space, a spring in his step, and his back still arched as if he wanted to return to his feline shape. Josh had tried to conjure some kind of magical ability during their second night in the dank Shadowlands, but had failed to do so. It seemed his emotions had to be running high before anything even started to happen.

Nybor had told Josh just how vast the Shadowlands were. They began parallel to the waterfall he had entered through and ran all the way to the edge of the Third Kingdom, before meeting a place called the Forest of Music. He didn't ask how far away that was, but he guessed given the previous answer of crossing the entirety of Beyond, he didn't think it was gonna be a quick trip. Something else he had noticed too, was various rippling pockets of air as they walked a very specific path through the woodlands. He had felt they were not anything good, and Syl'Va, the diamond man, had warned him to stay away from them. They were portals into other parts of the Shadowlands containing creatures and beings he would not care to encounter.

The diamond man was a curiosity to Josh. He had heard about the doorways converging in Wealdstone but that had been a large number. And yet Tommy apparently destroyed the only doorway to the human realm. Was he telling the truth and the other doorways led to other places, or was he lying? He hadn't exactly been furnished with the truth since Nybor had revealed his identity to him.

Josh did not wish to spend a third night in the middle of this fantasy haunted forest, and hoped today they would make good progress, although he still didn't know their exact destination. As if reading his mind, Nybor held up her hand and the group stopped.

"Whilst I am able to proceed a while longer, I suggest we stop here, and eat, before venturing further. We need to be always at our most alert."

Spiner sighed and dropped to his haunches. Josh then noticed that his hands were slightly charred, almost like he had dipped them in charcoal. Spiner caught him looking at them and hid them away.

"I'm sorry, Spiner. I didn't mean to stare."

"It's fine."

It most definitely wasn't fine. Spiner had clearly been subjected to something that he was ashamed of, and without remembering who he even was, Josh did not feel able to comfort him. His thoughts, however, were disrupted when the large diamond man slumped down next to him on the ground. Josh shrank back slightly, unsure of how to behave around him. However, it was Syl'Va who started the conversation.

"Have you remembered anything yet, Joshua?"

Josh shook his head.

Chapter 17

"I understand what that is like," he said. "I suffered with the same issue once. In these very Shadowlands."

Okay, I'll bite he thought.

"Really?"

Syl'Va nodded and stretched out an enormous leg.

"When I first arrived here, the effects of the doorway I came through were more intense than the others. I was unaware of this until taught by our mutual friend with the wings over there."

He gestured to Nybor, who made a feigned attempt at a curtsey, before gathering elements to make a fire. Syl'Va continued.

"Apparently, the doorway I came through linked to a world which was abandoned by its inhabitants after the planet itself decided to take the world back. They had spoiled it, corrupted its beauty, and poisoned its atmosphere. The living beings on the planet began to fight back. The plants changed to emit poisonous air. The animals began to attack wilfully. Eventually, the species left, and the planet thrived once more. However, when the Guardian on this side of that doorway ventured through to examine what had happened, the planet killed him, and as a precaution, an enchantment was placed over it. That gave me a stunning bout of amnesia."

Josh thought back to Tommy, and how quickly he had destroyed the gateway, without the promise of even half of that threat.

"Why was it not destroyed? If the threat was that great?"

Syl'Va let out what Nybor's look said was an uncommon laugh.

"You cannot destroy a gateway, my young human friend. It simply destroys that access point. The doorways are always open."

Nybor cleared her throat and held up her hand. Syl'Va gestured for her to proceed.

"That's not strictly true," she said. "Green Dragons are the

Guardians of the gateways. If they die, and a replacement is not selected, the doorways vanish."

Syl'Va's time to interrupt.

"Ah, but they are not destroyed!"

Nybor smiled in the corner of her mouth. Next to her, Spiner could not have been more uninterested if he had tried.

"Not in their entirety, but they are never as strong as they once were, and they move to a location we cannot find them. The enchantment on this doorway held it in place despite lack of a guardian. It was however, patrolled by the White Falcons."

Josh sighed and rubbed his hands over his eyes.

"Are you okay?" asked Spiner, now back in the conversation, and worried his old friend may be suffering a sensory overload of information.

"Yeah. I feel better when I'm talking to somebody. I spent a lot of time bottling up feelings and stuff. I used to talk to people in this awesome group I was a part of. You know, back in human-land."

Spiner moved slightly closer, sensing his friend beginning to open up. He remembered they had used to chat during his training when Josh was only a teenager. He missed those days.

"It helps to talk to people, even if you don't really know what to say," Spiner replied.

"Yeah. I didn't know at the time that all the trauma in my mind was a false memory, and so I found this peer support group on Discord called Flare. They were great. We used to have a games night on a Sunday, and talk-it-out sessions on Thursdays. It really helped."

Spiner felt a tinge of guilt at the revelation that Josh had needed people to talk to. He used to be that person for Josh. When he made the decision to return to the human world, Spiner had argued with him, and the last words he had spoken to him were in anger. He snuck through the doorway once before in his

Chapter 17

feline disguise, but on return was caught by Tommy, interrogated, and then told to get back to the Shadowlands with the other mimics.

Mimics.

Spiner had never liked that name. Mimics always seemed insincere. Like his people were simply copies of something else. It betrayed the work and the effort it took to not only transform into another creature, but the physical and emotional toll it took to keep the new form. He much preferred the term his people had adopted.

Changelings.

It was a much more representative terms, and more literal if you broke it down. Change, as in change into something else, and lings. Things. Change into things. That's how Spiner chose to think of it. Obviously that wasn't the true meaning of the word, but mimics sounded like an insult. He had never been a fan of Tommy, but he was surprised when he left the group alone. Apparently at least he was a man of integrity. They were hard to come by these days.

"This Flame group..." Syl'Va began.

"Flare," Josh corrected.

"Ah yes, apologies. This Flare group... were they comrades?"

Josh thought about that for a moment. Then he nodded.

"Yeah, I guess they were, in a way. Comrades in life. In experiences. In trauma. It was a safe space. Something I had sorely needed."

This time it was Nybor's turn to feel extreme guilt. She had been the one to send him back at his request. She had arranged for Valdore to insert the false memories and for Iona to place the memory block so he couldn't utilise his powers. It had killed them both inside to let the person they now saw as their son, return to another realm. They had however honoured his wish. They had disappeared soon afterwards.

Spiner had moved so quickly and quietly, that Josh didn't

notice he was beside him until he heard the crinkle of his comic book being opened.

"You drew this?" he asked.

Josh nodded.

"Yeah, I thought I'd have a go at drawing my own superhero. Didn't realise I was secretly drawing my past though."

The two former friends shared a laugh. It felt good. In truth, Josh's initial fears that he was some kind of prophet, were explained away. It was simply memories seeping through the block that Iona put in place, and Josh interpreting them as best as he could. The waterfall was accurate, he had been there before of course on his way back to Wealdstone, but the rest was simply coincidental.

"Well in fairness, your book there, is as fictional as the prophecy hanging in the castle," Nybor pointed out.

"Yeah, why exactly did you do that?" Josh asked, still perplexed. "Make up a false prophecy, let alone name me after it."

Nybor thought for a moment. Back to the moment she decided to utilise her artistic talents to create it. Told Valdore and Iona that by giving Josh the last name of Shaw, at least there would always be a memory of Josh in Beyond for them to see, albeit a warped one.

"Your adopted parents. Valdore and Iona didn't want to give you up. They had loved you, trained you, and moulded you into a strong and wise young man. I wanted them to have something to remember you by, even if it wasn't exactly... conventional. That, and getting one up on my brother. He of course wasn't king at that point, but even he is afraid of the prophecy. I hoped if you ever returned and he learned of your name, he would fear you and leave you alone. Guess that isn't going to work now."

Another twinge of guilt, but this time it also speared through Josh. Although he had not caused any of this himself, he was effectively the poster boy for the apocalypse, fake or not. He knew

Chapter 17

it would not only be the King who feared the prophecy, but those in the kingdoms who were taught such scripture. He questioned Nybor's choices in that matter.

The fire which Nybor had lit with her staff using discarded chunks of wood, was now glowing brightly, casting even more shadows into the surrounding forest, and she hauled a large dead mammal up and over the flames, propped on strong twigs either side. Josh had no idea what it was she had found and slain but he was starving so tried to consider it as a pig rotating on a spit. However, the flames themselves captivated him. The fire was not standard red, yellow or orange, but it burned pure white. Another colour coded benefit of being a White Falcon, he guessed.

As he gazed into the flame, and the meat cooked above it, he began to see flashes in his mind. A quick image of him looking up at the furry wolf-like face of Valdore as she smiled at him. Another image of Spiner leaping into the air and transforming into a bird to catch something he had thrown. A third image then flashed up of a tearful Iona and Valdore watching him walk away from the home he had known for over two decades.

And then another image.

The memory broke, and his head snapped up at Nybor who was now staring deep into his eyes. He could not find any words, but she saw in his eyes that the final flash of recognition was now there. She simply nodded, and he thought he saw a tear in her eye. There it was. Confirmation that he had seen the truth.

Josh and Nybor had been lovers.

18

The first hit obliterated Spiner's left arm completely. The flesh bubbled around his shoulder as the rest of his body flew into a large tree trunk, leaving a trail of green blood behind him. As it dripped into the fire as he soared through the air, the flames crackled. He landed on the floor with a thump. And did not move again.

By the time everyone else was alert to the danger, it was too late. Syl'Va was hit with such force, his entire body broke apart into individual crystals, scattering across the forest floor like shards of glass, or frozen metal. Nybor was next. She raised her staff, but as she went to unfurl her wings, a blast of fire struck her from each side, and burned the wings away completely. Singed feathers floated through the air, and her scream was deafening. She collapsed to the floor and her staff rolled away from her until it met a foot.

Josh had not moved. He was still processing the memories revealed to him by the white flames. This could not be real. Two of his friends were now dead, the third one mutilated, and all in the blink of an eye. Josh felt two hands grab his shoulder and drag him to his feet. His eyes kept flickering between the horrific scenes in front of him, and the memories he had just relived. He could feel the rage and the pain growing at his very core. His fists clenched as he was thrown down onto the ground next to the fire, and an unseen boot kicked their meal away, tumbling through the dirt.

When he finally raised his head, he saw a large primate standing before him, in a purple robe, and his fingertips were glowing with white hot flames of their own. Stood either side of Josh were two smaller primates, clearly of the same species, but perhaps younger in their development. Their muscles, although bare and human like, were not as defined. Their strength, however, was not in question. As Nybor continued to whimper in the background, Josh bore holes into the first primate with his stare.

"So, you are the human bringer of the end of days," he spoke with a deep growl in his voice. "You do not appear to be much of a threat to me. Then again, only a foolish idiot would expect that prophecy to ring true."

The creature emitted a wide and sickening grin, showing off two rows of yellow pointed teeth. Less of a primate, more of a demon. Josh remained quiet. His focus was unwavering. The man continued.

"I am Largox, Supreme Mage of the Council of Magic, Chief confidante of King Eralf, and as of two days ago, Chief Protector of the King himself."

Through her intense pain and suffering, Nybor looked up at her attacker. Zumo was dead. She knew it, and Syl'Va had told her of course, but now she had confirmation. The Chief Protector was a lifelong position. It only concluded upon death. She wanted to rip out Largox's throat, but she could not move. Losing her wings without relinquishing her powers was the equivalent of having your legs broken. Largox was not done tormenting the group just yet.

Chapter 18

"I am sorry about your... colleagues? But I'm sure you can understand, the need to eliminate the immediate threat, however small."

He turned his sickening smile towards Nybor, who was now seething with rage. Largox felt he could now savour the moment. He strolled towards her writhing body, the smile never wavering. Josh looked on, flanked on either side by the other guards. Beneath his fists, the dirt began to swirl.

"And you, former Leader of the Order of White Falcons..."

Nybor let out a new blood-curdling scream as Largox slammed his boot onto her back directly at the open wound that lay in place of her wings. The blood began to pour over her limited armour and seep into the ground.

"I do hope you understand that you were never going to live to see our triumph."

Josh turned his head to see what was going on, but his focus remained unbroken. Instinctively, he reached his fingertips towards each of the guards. They too were watching their leader dole out what he deemed was necessary punishment. He placed the tip of both index fingers onto an exposed patch of skin and closed his eyes.

"Your brother is of course a delusional fool. He truly believes he has rule of this land, and that the mages serve his cause. I will of course obey. Until afterwards."

His boot pressed down harder, more screams coming from Nybor.

"When Beyond falls, and the darkness returns, it is WE who will rule over this land. Even the Dark Lord himself will not stop us."

Dark Lord.

Nybor's screams stopped as her mind focussed on those words. No. This could not be happening. Eralf is going after... *him*. He was going to expose the truth. The truth that Nybor and others like her had forced themselves to keep for so long. The truth would destroy Beyond and all those who resided there. Why would he do this? Thankfully, Largox was in such a believed state of control, he continued to reveal the grand plan.

"It really is a fault of you humans and mortals of this place to never be truly happy with what you have. Always striving for more, always greedy for more. Your deluded brother actually believes that if he defeats the Dark Lord himself, he can have everything."

Largox laughed a deep, guttural guffaw.

"*Fools.*"

Largox, however, was not prepared for what happened next. The sound of his guards bodies thudding to the ground was louder simply due to their size, but it was certainly unexpected. But as he turned to face Josh, he was not met with a human boy cowering on the ground. Josh was now surrounded in blue electricity and was floating several feet off the ground. His eyes were also glowing electric blue. As Largox watched on absolutely bewildered, Josh's arm thrust forward, and lightning flew towards him. But as it moved through the air, *it changed into something else.*

The lightning now separate from Josh's body morphed into a huge boulder, solid as any in the forest, and slammed into the giant primate, sending him hurtling away from Nybor. She in turn, swung her head towards him just as another two lightning bolts flew in her direction. She smiled. She knew what was coming next.

Josh was remembering. Remembering everything.

The bolts of lightning hit Nybor's back like a direct jolt of electricity, and as a groggy Largox watched on, Nybor's wings began to grow upwards as if they were materialising from fresh air. Seconds later, the White Falcon was stood in all her glory as she was before the attack, only this time, she was angry.

Josh smiled an electric blue smile and turned his focus towards the other two. Still drawing power from the two bodies beside him,

Chapter 18

Josh sent lightning strikes in both directions, surrounding Spiner first, who had his bones reconstructed, the cracks echoing through the air, and as he regained consciousness, he saw his arm returning to his body. Syl'Va's fragmented pieces began to knit themselves back together as if drawn by a magnetic force until the great diamond coated hulk of a man was once again stood alongside his new found friends.

And with that, Josh collapsed to the floor, all the energy drained from the two bodies beside him. He gasped wildly for breath and held his hand to his chest. Grey hairs now sprouted in his long curly beard, and at the sides of his temples. Nybor rushed towards him and knelt at his side.

"Nice to have you back," she said, her voice cracking slightly.

"Nice to *be* back," he replied between wheezes.

Syl'Va's heavy footsteps approached slowly, followed by light paw taps as Spiner, now in feline form once more, gathered around him. Syl'Va nodded his appreciation to Josh, and then turned to Nybor.

"The mage has gone. Likely scarpered when Joshua showed his true self."

Nybor's eyes returned to a hateful glow, and she helped Josh to his feet. Syl'Va leaned down and stroked Spiner's head gently, the cat purring at the touch.

"You know, I can see why cats like this so much," the cat spoke. "I think I'll spend more time in this form."

"I can't believe that Eralf wants to break the Void open. After everything we have fought for, everything we have sacrificed!"

She instinctively brought her hand up to squeeze around her necklace. Josh had remembered almost everything of his existence, but he had never known the significance of the pendant around her neck. He had also remembered another memory, not unlocked by the fire's initial burning.

He glanced towards Spiner, who was now once more in

humanoid form. His friend smiled at him and waved with a now unburnt hand on the side that had been recreated by Josh's touch.

Josh and Spiner had been lovers too.

19

6 (human) years earlier

"Well that was certainly interesting."
Josh snorted at the very underwhelming description of what had just happened. He had of course been with a few other people, all humanoid, but this was the first time he had been intimate with another being of the realm. It was not a decision he had taken lightly, but his friendship with Spiner had grown so deep that it just felt right leaning in for that first kiss. Luckily nobody had seen them. It was unconventional enough for a banished mimic to reside outside of the Shadowlands, let alone bed a human.

Josh looked down at Spiner's hands. Blackened for his betrayal. He had always felt guilty about what his fellow kind did to him. It was of course Spiner's choice to leave, but Josh could not help but feel responsible. As punishment, the rest of the mimics, or changelings as Spiner preferred to describe themselves, had burnt his hands and cast him out of their territory. The burns remained whatever form he chose to inhabit as a constant reminder of his shame.

Spiner on the other hand, had decided that if he was going to be cast out and marked by his own kind, then he may as well enjoy himself. He had been reluctant to push Joshua to take their friendship further, as he was unsure he felt the same way. But Spiner loved him deeply. He was the one constant in his life that provided him with assurances, safety and comfort. He didn't judge Spiner for anything other than what he was. He didn't care that the changelings had a reputation for deception and betrayal. Spiner wasn't like that. He knew it in his heart. He also knew that his changeling friend had brought out the most progress in terms of harnessing his abilities.

Josh had been told by Valdore at a very young age that being born in this realm would immediately endow him with access to powers that he may not understand.

"It is as if the land chooses what you shall become," she had told him.

He loved his mothers very dearly. They were warriors in truth, but war was far behind them. It left scars on both Valdore and Iona, but they never let it transfer to their adopted son. Josh of course was unaware he was adopted, and believed he was simply another one of the people of Beyond. But Iona had taught him to defend himself, and Valdore showed him how to call upon the magic within him. He was not a witch nor a Blue Spirit. He was something else entirely. It had been difficult in realising what exactly, his power had been.

Josh had the ability to harness any electrical current, or field such as a person's lifeforce, or the growth of a tree or a fruit, and reconstitute it into any other form of matter. It took a lot of practice, but he was becoming adept at such a thing. Nybor was becoming prouder of him every month. She did not reveal that there was a human living in Beyond of course, she was not without common sense. She visited him, usually at the end of the final week, making the excuse of checking on any possible inductees for

Chapter 19

the White Falcons, but he knew she had grown fond of him, and her visits were more personal than business. Nybor had never acted on those feelings though, and this had saddened him. Spiner had filled that gap, but there was the inevitable worry that their friendship would not survive a relationship. And he could not help but feel that undeniable pull to the White Falcon.

It had been a relatively straight forward morning. Josh and Spiner had dressed and begun agility training. Josh would drain the electrical force from a nearby tree, generate an object and launch it into the air. Spiner would then change form into a bird or a tall creature, and then launch the object back at Josh, who would have to use his powers to dodge the danger. His nimble ways had taken a while, but they were coming along nicely. However, when he saw Nybor coming over the hill and down towards the hut, in the middle of the month, he knew all was not well. Spiner sensed drama approaching, and knowing that Josh still harboured feelings for her, and the way he had spent his morning, he made a swift exit.

"Something tells me this isn't the usual house call," he said attempting to put some levity into what would undoubtably be an uncomfortable discussion.

"Eralf has taken the throne."

Josh's face drained of all enthusiasm. In the house, Valdore, Iona and Spiner stopped what they were doing, hearing this through the window, and sidled up to try and hear more.

"What does this mean for the people in the Fifth?" Josh asked, already knowing the answer.

"I suspect that if there were not the Sea of Eternity between us and them, he would sacrifice them for the 'greater good' and other rancid excuses."

King Eralf. That sound was bitter on their tongues. Eralf was Nybor's adopted brother, although he did not act like it. He was also a selfish man and desperate for power. He had been furious when Nybor was inducted into the White Falcons, and completely livid when she was chosen to become Leader. He had sworn for a long time that the more useful members of society would suffer when resources were being used up by those who did not contribute or provide income for those in the other kingdoms. Although in truth, Josh suspected if it were up to him, there would be only one kingdom. The First Kingdom.

"Surely he cannot do that, can he? I mean the people would lose faith in him as King."

Nybor snorted as she sat down on a log near to Josh. He sat down next to her, and instinctively placed a hand on her shoulder. She immediately felt calmed, if a little sleepy. She knew the effect of Josh's powers, and long exposure could harm her, but right now all she wanted to feel was peace, and not be at odds with herself. She tilted her head towards him and smiled. He wanted so badly to kiss her right then, but how could he? He had shared a bed with Spiner, not two hours before. Josh was not the sort of person who could cast aside one lover for another, no matter the feelings he may have had. Sadly, he had no choice but to remain faithful in that vein. At least for now.

"I should get back there," Nybor said as she moved away from Josh's touch and stood up. "How are your mothers?"

Josh cleared his throat and felt Spiner's eyes on the back of his neck.

"They are well. Although Valdore seems to think I need to work on my speed at conjuring the electricity. She says in an emergency, if I was too slow, the fight could be lost."

Nybor looked at him, concerned once more.

"She may be right."

"Is there a fight coming, Nybor?"

Her eyes were stern, but Josh could see beyond that to her fear. White Falcons were required to be fearless in the face of danger.

Chapter 19

Plough into whatever threats came at them. But at the end of the day, they were still people. And people feel things.

"I do not know. I fear that this realm is no longer the haven it has become. The actions of Monarch in the human realm, the reappearance of not only a Fire Demon, but a Blue Spirit as well has set the nerves of our people on edge. There is more conflict, and more people are closing themselves off from the community. Now my brother is in charge, I fear things will quickly escalate. He has a mage with him."

This brought Valdore and Iona out from the house and into the conversation.

"A mage?" Valdore asked, panic in her voice. "Who?"

Nybor shifted her feet and looked at the dirt before returning her gaze to her wolf-like friend.

"Largox."

"Shit."

The profanity came as a surprise to all as the word left Iona's mouth. She felt all the eyes of the group fall upon her.

"Sorry. I heard one of the hum-"

Nybor and Valdore shot her a look.

"One of the villagers say it. Not sure where it came from."

Josh's eyes narrowed. This was not the first time one of his mothers had almost spoken of humans. He suspected they had been in contact with them more than they let on. In truth, he had been having visions of late. Memories which were not his, and thoughts of being a baby surrounded by people he could not make out. He shook his head and returned himself to the conversation.

"So what are we to do? Largox is the most powerful mage of all. With his power, your brother may already have a death grip on Beyond."

Nybor nodded.

"I want to increase your training. I'm going to take over your lessons personally."

Valdore and Iona seemed to reluctantly agree with this, but Spiner's face became a mass of twisted hatred. Josh and Nybor would be spending insurmountable time together, in close quarters. He did not like this one bit.

"I don't think that's necessary, Falcon. My training with Joshua is progressing well."

Valdore and Iona shot him a look that said 'mind your business' and he backed down. Never cross a wolf and a soldier. Especially together.

Nybor ignored Spiner's comments and spoke directly to Josh, not breaking his gaze for a second.

"You will report to the garden of the church in the First Kingdom tonight at sunset. We will train then."

Josh was confused.

"Why so late?" he asked.

Nybor took a step closer to him. He could feel her breath on his face, and it made him shudder. He forced himself not to smile.

"Because nobody must know. They may already be plotting against us. Eralf knows we will side with the people of Beyond no matter what kingdom they belong to. That, to him, is an enemy."

The conversation ended, and Nybor disappeared over the top of the hill again. Valdore and Iona returned to the house, and Spiner glared at Josh. He tried to give Spiner a look of reassurance, but his changeling friend turned and walked off into the woods.

Little did Josh know that the exact thing that Spiner was worried about, would happen the very next night.

20

The waves crashed against the shore with such force, that they left deep and expansive craters in the sand. The ocean water would run for another two hours along the coastline of the Fifth Kingdom before it began to turn red. Certainly the grass surrounding the city was no longer green. Patches of black, charred and violated ground no longer sang with the beauty of this place. Death had arrived at the gates of the Fifth Kingdom, and it had taken its people with it.

LeVar did not move from his place at the top of the beach. The water sprayed him as the droplets swam in the breeze, striking his face with fury. But his skin was numb to its touch. His eyes were permanently welled with tears and his gaze was distant. The horror that had played out before him was one of untold stories, one that no imagination could have conjured. He had seen the initial attack as he flew over the channel of the Sea of Eternity, unable to intervene. By the time he had landed at the water's edge, it was all over. The deafening crack had pierced the air, seemingly a shot from a million cannons, before dark smoke had erupted from the barrier to the Void. Swarming in every direction like a flood, a parasite, seeking out its next prey without discrimination. But this attack was unlike the others.

The creatures, demons, evil inside the Void had burst into Beyond as individuals hazed in the smoke. LeVar had watched as creatures made of ash and teeth tore heads from the bodies of men, women and children. The blood spraying the cobbled stone streets. Visceral, despicable and murderous millions poured forth tearing at limbs and flesh as they charged through every street, and every alley, burning every home they touched. Bolts of black fury rose up into the sky like arrows and tore down the other White Falcons. They dropped like flies, cascading into the sea, where they were lost. The Falcons on the ground were the first to fall.

Skye.

Gregor.

Eva.

All gone.

LeVar blinked for the first time since his arrival. The sting of the wind, salty sea air and pain made him grimace, and grit his teeth. Once the darkness had consumed the city, it was retracted as if on a leash, and every single one of the creatures and manifestations was withdrawn at speed until they flew back into the Void. The crack seemingly healed to a point, but was now clearly visible, and the pounding at its surface had increased to the booming of a million drums. It was as if an entire population had been locked in one room in a small house, and they were all clambering to get out. But of course, the damage was now done.

Feasting on the people of the Fifth Kingdom had given the inhabitants of the Void new strength. New power. The protective barrier had fallen almost immediately after the initial onslaught. They were growing stronger, but still not strong enough to reach the ocean.

For now.

As he managed to move one foot forward, LeVar spotted

Chapter 20

something in his peripheral vision snaking its way along the sand dune, between the blades of stray grass. The sheer black shininess of the substance cutting its way through the blood soaked sand made it stand out to anyone's eye, and yet it made no effort to hide. This was of course the strand of evil which had leapt through the energy barrier the last time LeVar left this place, but the Falcon was not to know that. Witnessing the horror that he had just seen had broken his mind into fragments. Even the forced notion of deception input into his consciousness by Largox to ensure his compliance had fallen away like the droplets of ocean water streaking his face.

And yet still, he felt a sense of duty to investigate. This globular piece of the Void seemed to be in pain. It pushed through the sand, but would then spasm, and writhe around for a moment before striving towards the water once more. LeVar held his staff tight as he approached it, fully aware that it was a creature of the darkness. As he got within the length of his staff from the creature, it stopped its advance and lay still. Silent. Unmoving. Before his bloodshot eyes, LeVar saw the thing crust over as if drying out under a heat of immense power. Twenty seconds later, he was looking at a black rock. No longer shining, no longer moving.

He prodded it with the end of his staff, but it did not move. Against every fibre in his being, he strode forth, knelt down and collected the object in his hands. He studied it for a moment, turning it between his fingers. It had almost no weight to speak of, and its surface was smooth and rigid. If one were to describe the creature's current state to an onlooker, it would be described as little more than a dead worm. It seemed almost cocoon like in its...

Before the thought had time to process in his mind as to the truth of the form now in his hands, the chrysalis split open, and the renewed creature within launched itself into LeVar's open mouth. His eyes became wider than they seemed able to bulge, he pulled at his mouth with his hands, unable to prevent the invasion of this malevolent entity. He dropped his staff to the blood red sand where it rolled away down to the waters edge. Black veins began to trace their way down LeVar's neck and beneath his armour. His mouth showed that he was screaming, but no sound emerged. His body fell to the ground where it lurched and convulsed violently, the blood within the sand staining his white cloth and armour crimson.

Then nothing.

LeVar's motionless body lay on the sand, his long hair whipping over his face in the breeze. Then his left hand twitched. Then his right. His eyes snapped shut, and when they opened, they were black as the night. An effect which began to replicate itself throughout his entire makeup. His pure white hair began to turn the deepest darkest black. The white cloth that made up the clothing beneath his armour joined it in darkness. As LeVar stood to his feet, to anyone watching, he would have become a different person. The White Falcon was gone. LeVar was gone. The person who now stood on the bloody dunes of the Fifth Kingdom was something entirely different. When he spoke, his voice was deeper than the ocean, vibrating the land with each word.

"WHERE... IS... MY... *CASTLE*?"

21

The glass crunched under Eralf's feet as he stomped around either side of his throne, his paces quickening with every minute that passed as he absorbed what Largox had told him.

"You're certain about this?" he asked for the fifth time.

Largox nodded.

"Then this boy is of no use to us? And to think that I considered him the gateway to bringing down the Dark Lord of the Void. And you're sure about what my sister spoke of the prophecy?"

He stabbed a stubby finger in the direction of the cloth hanging behind the throne of fire and death, and a picture sewn into the centre which he now knew to be lies.

Again Largox nodded.

"Clever... very clever. My sister is... *clever*."

He spoke the last word in a hiss, before the anger started to overtake his confusion and absorption of this new knowledge.

"But if he is of no use to us in opening the Void, then why did you not simply kill him?!?!"

Largox rolled his eyes, but he stood at such a height that the

King did not see. He spoke carefully chosen words as to not reveal his true nature.

"The boy may not be the key to the Void, sire, but he is powerful. Very... powerful. He has certain abilities. I have never seen them before."

King Eralf now had a new peak to his curiosity. One eyebrow raised in intrigue, he wanted to know more. He had known of Joshua all along, and knew his name was Shaw. He foolishly deciphered that the boy would help him break down the security of the barrier and allow him access. Largox now told his King about Josh's powers which could seemingly extract the life force from other beings and use it to create or recreate other objects. Even genetic regeneration. He did play down the boy's power to a certain degree. Even though the King could not dream to defeat Largox if it should come to it, he did not wish to create unnecessary hassle by suggesting Largox may have an equal.

"Do you believe the boy can be utilised, or do you consider him more of a threat?"

Largox considered this for a moment. The boy's spirit had appeared weak upon first glance, but his fury, his *power* seemed to come from seeing his loved ones in danger. He did not see a way to bypass these feelings. There would always be the hint of betrayal. Even the small amount of influence Largox had sent into LeVar to ensure his compliance would be dissipated soon.

"The individual must be sterilised from the land. He is dangerous and cannot be trusted."

Eralf almost seemed disappointed by this. He had hoped he may have a new ally or at least another pledge to his cause should the right incentive be found. However, it seemed he had another target to take care of. He knew it would be only a matter of time before the Void fell and the Fifth Kingdom was gone. That would give him two to three days at most to send his forces to the edge of the Sea of Eternity to meet them. Whilst he was fully prepared to

Chapter 21

sacrifice the Fourth Kingdom to the darkness to attain his goals, he preferred to be on the front foot.

"Very well. Take as many as you need and... cleanse... the Shadowlands. Burn it to the ground if you must. I want no place left for them to hide. Do you understand me?"

Largox, for the first time felt troubled by the words of his King. The Shadowlands were an enormous part of the realm, holding many doorways and species, many of whom had no quarrel with anyone, and some who the mages were aligned with.

"Sire, I don't think..."

"YOU ARE NOT HERE TO THINK, MAGE! YOU ARE HERE TO ABIDE BY YOUR KING'S RULE! Or have you forgotten?"

The audacity of this puny mortal always grated on Largox. The tension within him manifested in the form of goosebumps, which Eralf always took to mean the huge magical primate was in fear of his safety from his King. It was in fact the opposite. It was how Largox prevented himself from ripping Eralf into many small pieces. The atmosphere, however, was then shattered when a deafening crack erupted from outside, and the entire castle shook, the King barely keeping his footing as fixtures collapsed from the walls and nearby tables.

"What in the Five Kingdoms was that?" spoke Eralf with a hint of fear himself.

Largox suspected he knew the answer, but shook his head in ignorance, and followed his King as he burst through the doors ahead of him and charged through the castle until he found himself outside at the stone balcony where he had a clear view over the First Kingdom, and a distant view all the way to the ocean.

Whilst Eralf could not see the Void or the Fifth Kingdom from his position on this hill, Largox could. He saw all too well that their plans were now irrelevant. The cracks had appeared, and the Void was now open, at least in part. On the wind, Largox heard the screams of the millions who lived within the walls of the Fifth Kingdom, and then as abruptly as it had started, it ended. Silence.

Visually, King Eralf could see the sky was darker and more overcast above, and suspected something was not right. He had planned his attack as precisely as he possibly could. The level of detail was as intricate as a serial killer plotting his next victim years in advance. And yet he couldn't help but feel as he gazed upon the land which he presided over that it was now all for nothing. Beside him, his mage said nothing. He did not move other than his jaw clenching occasionally. Eralf had no intention of asking him what he saw. He was through with trusting actions to others that failed him repeatedly. If the truth was revealed to the people of the kingdoms of what their King had planned, they would turn on him.

For now, they believed their King had their interests at heart. They did not question why neither the kingdoms themselves or the towns or villages within them had no true names. Villages with numbers for names, and districts with the same numerical monikers did not perturb those within as long as they could live their lives happily. They did not know the true reason why Beyond's residencies were nameless. Why Beyond itself was called Beyond. They had no inclination why the Void, whilst fixed in one location, was where it was.

Only King Eralf knew.

And Largox.

And Nybor.

Nybor.

Still alive, and a threat to his plans. He knew her tenacity, devotion, and ability to fuck up everything he had created here. He span on his heels to face Largox and spoke through gritted teeth.

"Seal off this part of the city. I want guards surrounding the castle at all times. Kings Guard, not White Falcons. I don't trust them anymore. Return to the Shadowlands. Burn it to the ground.

Chapter 21

No excuses. Find my sister, the boy, and all those who shelter or guard her. Tear them apart limb from limb. And bring me back evidence."

He glanced back at the horizon. Four more booms echoed across the land, the ground vibrating with each one. If he didn't know better, Eralf could have sworn he heard words within those vibrations. Largox reacted as if he too heard something, but this was no time for a conversation or debate. Eralf jabbed Largox in the side, causing him to glare at his King.

"GO!" Eralf bellowed.

Reluctantly, Largox nodded and turned away, stomping his way down the pathway and out of sight. Under his breath he muttered one short sentence, out of reach of his King's ears.

"You have just sealed your fate, coward."

22

The panic in the streets was evident, and confused both the now elderly Tommy, and his White Falcon comrade, Manor. The latter was now seething with rage at a nearby member of the King's Guard who refused to let him pass.

"My home is in this district you piece of rectal sputum!" he screamed, to no avail.

He was simply pushed back and ordered to disperse. He could easily tear this guard to pieces, but there was something different about them. The armour they were wearing seemed to have a deeper shine to it than normal. Manor suspected it had been enchanted. He thought back to the whispers of Nybor's betrayal, and suspected his King may have misled the Order after all. He turned back towards Tommy, who was propped up against a wooden barrel.

"What's wrong?" he asked through laboured breath.

"The King's Guards will not allow us entry into this part of the kingdom. I suspect they have been provided with magic based assistance, and it would be unwise to challenge them. Particularly in the condition you are in."

Tommy attempted a laugh at this statement, but stopped short when he received a rather sharp pain in his lungs. He doubled over and began wheezing, until he coughed up a small amount of blood. The concern on Manor's face was clear. It appeared the former Green Dragon was now falling victim to many of the issues faced by older humans. Namely, disease, but at an accelerated rate.

"We need to find you your next job, my friend before you aren't fit for duty."

This time, Tommy did manage a small chuckle. He nodded in an exaggerated way as if his head was so heavy that he had trouble keeping it upright. To Manor's eyes, Tommy had aged another few years since crossing the barrier. While it had been the only way for him to cross the barrier, and inevitable whether there had even been a barrier or not, he felt regret at aiding the man to go through such pain and torment. He of course knew of many ways that Tommy could be returned to a pillar of strength, but all of them required someone in authority, or someone of higher power.

Like Nybor.

The question was, would Tommy survive a journey into the heart of the Shadowlands long enough to be restored by the friend he had so willingly left behind? Clearly, something was going on here that even the Order was being kept from, and everyone in the world had heard the booming and the loud crack that echoed across the entire realm. Perhaps it was time to gather the remaining Falcons and formulate a plan. He felt the pouch on his belt and fumbled his fingers over the bumps and features of the dragon statue within it. He knew once removed from a person, it could not be given back to the same individual. Whatever the solution to Tommy's inevitable death, it did not lie here.

"Dragon, I need to know why you left Nybor in the Shadowlands, and I need to know now. Did she betray us?"

Tommy shook his head as his eyes opened and closed with

Chapter 22

weariness. A small piece of dried blood now hung in the corner of his mouth. It dislodged itself as he spoke as best he could.

"Eralf is up to something. When she came to investigate Joshua's arrival, he had his mage put up the ward. She went to the Shadowlands looking for help. Nothing more."

Manor nodded. He now suspected as much. The secrecy surrounding the castle, the King, his mage and the whereabouts of LeVar were all forming together to create some kind of conspiracy that was being held not only from the protectors of the realm but from the people within it also.

"Then we will need help. And we need to find Nybor."

Tommy groaned at the suggestion, but Manor shook his head.

"You will not survive without her, Dragon. I may have taken your powers, but I am not prepared to see you die. Unless it is in the heat of battle of course."

Manor's lips curled into a wry smile, and despite the obvious effort it took for him to do so, Tommy did the same.

"How far can you fly with me?" Tommy asked, knowing he would never be able to walk back to the Shadowlands.

Manor tilted his head side to side in a so-so motion.

"Long enough. I'll do my best not to drop you."

Tommy sighed sarcastically.

"Excellent. Sign me up, I'm won over by your confident enthusiasm."

The two shared a chuckle as they moved off into the crowd. Their actions and conversation had not been missed, however, by one individual. Despite the huge crowd and the chatter surrounding everything, their words had been as clear as day to him. He felt betrayed by Nybor himself and felt he had been lied to. He had been stopped from achieving his true potential and the time for restraining himself was now over.

As Tommy and Manor disappeared into the crowd, Chan followed behind them, rage burned into his eyes.

23

The lack of sleep following the previous night's attack had left the group feeling low and sorely deprived of energy. The only thing keeping them going right now was the discovery of Josh's true abilities, and the flood of memories returning to him. Since that had happened, Spiner had maintained a cautious distance, whilst Nybor had done the opposite. She encouraged him to walk alongside her as much as possible. Josh suspected she was attempting to reinforce their bond that they had lost when Josh returned to Earth. Syl'Va walked at the rear, still paranoid that he would fall apart any minute after being shattered by the power of Largox's magic. Technology did not do much to save him in that particular battle, and now he faced a potentially larger one. Spiner noticed his discomfort, and after boring holes into the back of Josh's head with his staring, he sidled alongside the Deltarian and tried to learn more about their unique accomplice.

"You know it's not some sort of glue that's going to fade. You're you again. As whole as you were before."

Syl'Va nodded in acknowledgement, but still found himself checking every few minutes.

"I have never been in that kind of situation before. I have seen some strange and powerful things in this land since my arrival, but never have I felt so... helpless."

Spiner nodded. He had felt the same the day his kind banished him from their land. If they knew he was here now, they'd probably kill him. He had pledged loyalty to a friend. A lover. And for what? He was cast aside within forty-eight hours. Josh had told him all about his one-night stand with Nybor, and been completely upfront about it, but the damage was done. Spiner retreated from him, and their connection never fully reformed in the years leading up to Josh returning to Earth.

"I understand that. I often feel alone now. I travelled to Earth when Joshua went back in some deluded attempt to make him come back. But he wouldn't have known who I was anyway. I was clutching onto anything to give me purpose or meaning again. I never found it."

Syl'Va gestured towards Josh.

"Even now? Your friend is back. Times are different. Perhaps now he needs you as a friend once again, if nothing more."

Spiner had not even considered this. He desperately wanted to be with Josh once again, like it had been on that first morning they awoke alongside each other. The only morning. But it wouldn't. That was the past, and this was now. In truth he needed all the friends he could find. He had nowhere else to go. This was the main reason for him stalking Beyond and other realms in his feline form. It was his preferred manifestation outside of his usual guise simply because he could blend in. Nobody questioned the appearance of a cat on Earth. Often he had considered remaining there himself, but the pull of his kind was too strong. They no longer wanted him, but *he* wanted *them*. Spiner had spent a long time dwelling on facts such as these, but the truth was, he wouldn't have to for much longer.

Without much in the way of warning, Nybor sprung up into the

Chapter 23

air as she had done so many times before, and she began circling above, her newly regenerated wings swooping behind her, and she attempted her usual performance of creating a safe barrier around them. However, as everyone ducked into a defensive posture, and the second transparent column slammed into the ground, a large eagle with a wingspan of at least ten feet slammed into her side, and the two of them cascaded to the ground below.

Nybor's groans were loud, but she was resilient. She rolled to her side, grabbing her staff as she righted herself, and poised for another attack. But it didn't come. Her white eyes searched every square inch of their surroundings, but nothing appeared. Wait. Nothing? She had been so focussed on her own defence, she had taken her eyes off the ball once again. The forest was *too* quiet.

"Joshua? Syl'Va? Spiner?"

No reply.

She got to her feet, and began stalking the dirt path, emitting a gaze reserved for movie cyborgs scanning their surroundings for their targets. But of course, Nybor did not know such an analogy. All she was concerned with were finding her friends and continuing their mission. *Her* mission. A rustle in the tree canopy above caused her to whip round to her left, and crouch back, aiming her staff at the tree tops. Her head tilted from one side to the other as she tried to take in what she saw. The eagle which had struck her from the sky was now perched on a branch approximately sixty feet up, but it was... altering.

One of the wings dissolved and briefly became a limb. An arm. Then it melted away back into a wing. The head seemed to be in a constant state of flux, shifting from one creature to another and then back again. There was no mistaking what this being now was. It was a changeling. A mimic. The creature seemed to be in some distress and Nybor suspected it was not from striking the White Falcon, but more from some kind of ailment. She reached a hand forward into the air and lowered her staff.

"It is alright. You can come down, I will not harm you."

The changeling seemed to blur into a grey liquid state, its features blurred, and moved to the trunk of the tree where it then slid down all the way to the ground, making no sound upon landing. As Nybor watched on in fascination, the changeling reassembled itself as best as it could into a humanoid shape, but certain parts remained in flux.

"You... you are Spiner's friend?" it asked through laboured breaths.

"Well... I wouldn't go that far, but I am travelling with him, yes."

The creature nodded. It was after all more creature than person at this point. One eye was surrounded by the fur of a primate, one arm was sprouting feathers, and the mouth was off centre slightly as if it were melting. Nybor had sympathies with them, but she needed to know.

"Where are my friends, changeling?" She spoke as kindly as possible, and it did not go unnoticed by the being in front of her that Nybor had chosen to use the word changeling instead of mimic. She was respecting their wishes. "I must know. We are all in grave danger here."

The changeling nodded.

"Grave danger... yes... all of us... all that are left."

Nybor did not like the inference of those words. All that are left? What could they possibly mean by that? As far as Syl'Va had told her, several dozen remained. Had their numbers dwindled further? Were they here to claim Spiner back? She did feel a notable sting of guilt for potentially being the cause of Spiner's unrest, but there was no time to dwell on such matters right now.

An Earth shattering boom... no... a cracking sound burst across the sky. It was as if billions of panes of glass had fractured in a single moment. The air began to smell like copper, and despite her refusal to take in a breath, Nybor had no choice. It was then

Chapter 23

that she tasted it. Copper. Metallic. *Blood*. Her heart dropped into her stomach where it began to enter a tumbling motion along with the little food she had consumed since the start of this journey. In the distance, she heard faint screams. Then silence. She looked back in front of her having been distracted by the sensations surrounding her. But the changeling was gone. She turned around trying to find a trace of her new friend but saw nothing. And then came the four booming words she had long feared. The words she had been terrified of hearing for so very long.

"WHERE... IS... MY... CASTLE..."

She dropped to the floor, and threw her hands over her head, and began to sob. The secrets surrounding the land of Beyond and the steps taken to ensure its safety came at great cost to both her and the others who had been around at the time. There were reasons they knew how to modify people's memories. In some cases, they had done it to themselves to try and escape the horror of the days before. *The days before*. What even was that now? Could Nybor truly remember when the rivers and the Sea of Eternity ran red? When were the lands blackened by fire and death? Or was it a memory created only half way and was now corrupted? No. It was not a distorted memory. She was there. She remembered it all. And now, so would everyone else. The cleverly disguised lies that her, Eralf, and others had created were going to unravel.

Before too much longer, the world of Beyond would understand the truth. The truth that Nybor, LeVar, Eralf and others were not White Falcons at all. They were something far stronger. Far older. And far more dangerous.

24

The noises had shaken the group, but unlike Nybor, they had not been able to hear the distinctive words spoken on the shores of the Fifth Kingdom. And after a brief bout of dizziness, they had all come to realise they were surrounded by others. Standing approximately three feet apart in a complete circle, were changelings. It was evident that they were indeed such creatures as every single one of them was in a state of flux or disarray. Spiner had his eyes locked on each one of them in turn. He had seen this only once before, a long time ago. His mother had fallen ill at the wedding of another changeling couple, and within two weeks her body had completely dissolved into nothing.

"What's happening to them?" Josh asked with a crack in his voice.

"They've been infected," replied Spiner.

"Infected with what?" a confused Syl'Va asked.

Spiner took a moment, before he replied through tears.

"The curse of the Shadows."

After a brief period of silence, Nybor appeared at the edge of the trees, and the changelings parted to allow her to enter the clearing. She saw the one she had already been acquainted with and moved over to speak with them. They seemed to be able to hold their form slightly better around others of their own kind, and upon approach, introduced themselves as Terok. After a few moments of hushed conversation between the two, Nybor nodded, turned and returned to the others.

"So, what is going on?" Josh asked, his voice higher than he would've liked, but also partially acknowledging his own relief to see that Nybor was safe. Those feelings were far from gone.

"It's a fairly long story," she spoke cautiously, "but I'll do my best. It's how you humans say... Shadowlands 101."

For a very brief second, Josh smiled at the reference to basic understanding of a subject, but that soon disappeared. To his knowledge, Nybor had only spent time on Earth for four hours during the battle with Monarch at Crossroads, and a brief chat in the aftermath. She had then returned to Beyond and never left again. So how is it that she was able to recite so many human references and colloquialisms that she could not have absorbed in such a short period of time? Regardless of this, she continued with her lengthy explanation.

"The Shadowlands are vast and are divided up into several micro-realms. This is so that each of the beings within these borders have extra protection. It was decided a long time ago that this was necessary to keep the more powerful species away from harm. The Shadowlands draws its power from the Void."

This hit Josh and Syl'Va like a ton of bricks directly in the centre of the chest. Draws power from the very thing they are trying to keep contained? Josh felt the bile rising in his throat but kept quiet. He already had suspicions that Nybor was keeping secrets from them, and he wanted them all. She continued.

"The barrier put in place around the Void was designed to absorb the energy of those trying to escape and direct it across the world and into the Shadowlands. It helped power the micro-portals

Chapter 24

you've seen and keep that added layer of disguise working. But something we hoped would never happen, and always feared, has begun. The Void has cracked, and as the evil within begins to seep out, the power is dwindling, and the safeguards are failing. And now instead of energy seeping into the Shadowlands... it's evil. Evil which is now targeting those who were using its power for protection."

Josh grew beyond the bile in his stomach, beyond the terror that they faced personally, and began to seethe with rage. His fists clenched, and his face contorted deepening more and more red as it built.

"You used countless innocent people and creatures to act as, what, a failsafe? You placed them in harm's way as... as... a burglar alarm?!?!"

The fire within him was now beginning to manifest, and the few plants around him began to wither and die, lightning sparking on Josh's fingertips as the electricity within them transferred to him. Nybor held her hands up to try and calm him but knew she would fail. They had done exactly what he had accused them of. They kept the more dangerous beings at bay with the promise of infinite power to sustain them. What they hadn't told the dwellers of the Shadowlands was that if the Void ever did break, they'd be the first among the dead. After failing to construct a solid sentence, Nybor ducked as the small amount of power he had drawn from the foliage morphed into a small spear and hurtled towards her. The point skewered itself into a nearby tree, and Josh fell calmer, unprepared, however angry, to take life force from his other companions.

"ANY MORE SECRETS?!" Josh bellowed. He spun around, arms wide at his side, staring everyone down. He had had enough of all of this. He thought recovering his memory was the only true hurdle, but he was wrong. That was only the beginning. And even now, he sensed there was more. He saw Nybor clutching at her necklace again, and once more the fact came to him that even when he was fighting alongside her in training all those years ago, she had never revealed to him the purpose of the pendant.

"Or is that something that helps you hide them?" he said pointing at it from a distance.

Nybor looked at him, her eyes hurting. Josh's mind told him he had gone too far, but he was over the precipice and heading to the base of the cliff now. He was all in.

"Every time you fondle that stupid necklace, I asked you why you revered it so. You told me, it was too complicated. Always too complicated, never the time for me. Well guess what Falcon? NOW IS THE TIME!"

Even Syl'Va was staggered at the level of anger coming from Josh. He felt like he should intervene, but despite the length of time he had been in these lands, this was not his home. He thought back to Deltaria, and all its flaws. Many times, he had fought to escape his homeworld as it mined itself a little closer to oblivion each day. But right now, the politics of home didn't seem so bad. He had remembered when he had been hiding between alleyways in the slums waiting for a trolley of food to glide by so he could grab some fruit or bread to sustain himself with as a child. He thought back to the first time Lu'Thar, his future Captain, had apprehended him. Something he had seen in Lu'Thar's eyes told him that he had nothing to fear from this man. The penalty for stealing was death on Deltaria. But Syl'Va never faced such a penalty. Instead, he was recruited into the military and became the first slum dweller to rise to the rank of Commander and became the First Officer of the flagship Challenger. Those days of course did not end well either. Syl'Va now contemplated if he was ever meant for a simple straightforward existence. Somehow, he suspected not. You must play with the hand that fate deals you. A typically militaristic phrase Lu'Thar had told him once. He never really understood it until now. His colleagues were tearing themselves

Chapter 24

apart. They had already lost one, they had told him, in Tommy. Now it seemed there was darkness not only in the Void, but within the strongest of his compatriots. He sat alongside a very silent Spiner, and watched as Josh did the one thing he should never have done. He reached for Nybor's necklace.

As everyone else watched on, Josh's hand was held in place by an invisible field surrounding the gem at the centre of the pendant. Unable to move, he tried to wriggle free, but he was fixed in place. Nybor's eyes began to well up with tears, for she knew what was about to happen. As Josh watched on, her face changed. It became older, wrinkles appeared under her eyes and in the corner of her mouth. And then her eyes. Her eyes glazed over from white to black. The staggered and now fearful face of Josh reflected in the pits that now stood in her eye sockets. The motion was sudden, but also played out in Nybor's mind in slow motion. She saw every single millisecond of movement. She watched as the centre of her gemstone morphed and erupted with spears of darkest obsidian glass. She watched as each of the five tips that sprung forward skewered Josh's hand. She gazed into his eyes as he screamed a cry of immense pain. And she watched on helplessly as the shards embedded in his hand then shattered in every direction, bursting his hand apart in an explosion of flesh, blood and bone leaving only the stump of his forearm behind.

And then it was over.

Nybor's appearance returned back to normal, the gem appeared as it had done previously, and her eyes returned to a dim white glow. Josh, however, was not the same. The pool of blood now darkening the dirt surrounding his arm was increasing, sweat now pierced his brow, and he began to convulse.

"STAY THE FUCK AWAY FROM ME!" he screamed between sharp breaths.

Nybor did not stay away. She had unfortunately seen this happen several times. They had however been genuine targets of her aggression, and Joshua Shaw was not one of them. She leaned down towards him and placed his remaining hand on her chest. The cool metal of her breastplate soothed his breathing.

"Take what you need."

She spoke no other words, but simply closed her eyes. Josh did the same, and his breathing became more regulated as the tiny sparks of lightning tingled in his fingertips. Sparks surrounded Nybor, and she began to lean to the side slightly as she grew weaker, and Josh grew stronger. As Syl'Va and Spiner, and all of the other changelings watched on, Josh's hand grew from the jagged stump piece by piece, until he once again had two complete hands, and there was no evidence of any injury. He opened his eyes and contemplated draining the rest of Nybor's life force. He felt powerful. Her energy was something on a scale he had never experienced. It brought with it a certain kind of euphoria that he was reluctant to relinquish. But the small part of him that still shared love for her, that desired to return to those nights of training and togetherness forced him to let go. She slumped to the ground unconscious, but alive. Josh stood up, and simply walked away until he was lost in the trees. Terok walked forward to the remainder of the group and spoke directly to Spiner.

"You were wise to leave. Our selfishness cast you out, but in the end condemned us. You are safe because you were exiled. A cruel irony perhaps."

Spiner's heart leapt into his mouth. Was it true? Was he only alive and immune of this curse because he had been cast aside by his fellow changelings? His mother had endured the wrath of a witch in order to suffer from this condition. She had directly cursed the woman. But he was now the only changeling left without this ailment. And very soon, could be the only changeling left in existence. He did not know what to say, and so simply nodded. Terok walked away in the direction the group had come initially, and moments later, the rest of them had gone. They had simply

Chapter 24

wanted to speak to their former brother. To make peace with him. They already knew they were dying. Perhaps there was a place in his family for him after all. At least in their dying moments. They had absolved him of any sin. The torture he had put himself through all these years was now gone. But as with all moments of deep thought on their journey so far, Spiner did not have time to deliberate these ramifications. More rustling came from the west, twigs snapping underfoot. Syl'Va stood and aimed his weapon into the distance, but soon lowered it when several white glows came through the mist.

Manor, and five other White Falcons emerged into the clearing, behind them, on a makeshift stretcher, was an old man. An old man that upon opening her eyes briefly, Nybor recognised. She sighed and rolled back into slumber. Manor looked down at his former commander, and then back down at Tommy.

"Well, I guess she's not gonna be as much use as we thought she was."

25

Despite the fight that churned in Eralf's stomach, he had never actually successfully won a battle. There had of course been many to choose from in the centuries of his life, and he had indeed been involved in them, but always in a supporting or reserve role. While he had taken countless lives, all of them had been in cowardly or insincere fashion. A blade through the back, drugging someone and suffocating them in their sleep. And of course the latest death at his hands was that of Zumo, having Largox remove his power before stabbing an old man to death.

Perhaps then it was this reason that was primary and most at the front of his mind when he decided to take on the one known as the Dark Lord of the Void. There had been whispers across time and all over Beyond about what lay within the Void. However, in reality there were only a handful of people left alive who knew the truth. That knew what Beyond grew from. The sacrifices made to change this realm forever. Eralf had made no such sacrifices. He was a selfish and greedy bastard who cared for no one but himself. Sending his mage to kill his only sibling was a good example of such brutality. The brutality of a coward.

Despite giving the order to prepare the army of soldiers at his disposal, Eralf was still housed within the castle walls. He looked around, his eyes cascading over every blackened and uneven surface, up at the red stained glass that stood in the window frames, all the way up to the giant blood coloured glass adorning the dome in the castle roof. He lowered his head and looked at his throne. The throne that had once belonged to *him*. Eralf had always spoken that he should have been killed rather than locked up with his monsters. He told the Order, and the royal family in no uncertain terms that unless they slayed the beast, he would one day return and offer them no quarter. But the desire of the people of Beyond, and the humanity that still remained in them could not bring themselves to do it. They offered him the chance to go quietly or die and he had chosen death himself. The Dark Lord of the Void *asked* for death. But Nybor and the others were too kind... too *weak* to grant him his only wish. They imprisoned him with his soldiers, his demons, his disciples, whatever you wanted to call them.

The castle doors creaked open, and King Eralf heard approaching footsteps in the entrance hall. As the large blackened stone doors parted in front of him, he saw his General, the one man who obeyed orders without question. He did not sit with the King at lunch, he did not speak to him as a friend. He was a loyal and singular servant. Vidic was oathbound to serve the reigning monarch whatever the cost, whatever the order. His soul was owned by the throne, and he was unaware of any other way of life. He stopped before the King and knelt, his armour rustling as he did so.

"The soldiers have reached the Second Kingdom, sire. They report no unusual behaviour. On your order they will march on the Third tomorrow at dawn."

Eralf nodded and pondered his thoughts. If the Dark Lord of the Void had not reached the other side of the Sea of Eternity yet it

Chapter 25

could only mean one thing. His followers were not strong enough. They had no energy left to consume. If they had not reached the Second Kingdom then they had not crossed the sea. This he was certain of because without the ocean as a barrier, the darkness would have swept across the land. It is why the Fifth Kingdom was built on the other side. They were always meant to be sacrifices. The first warning of danger. Nybor and the others chose to deny this of course, but he knew the truth. He also suspected that LeVar and the others were long dead, but that was of no matter. If Nybor ever returned, they would swear allegiance to her once more and he would have to have them destroyed anyway. This was cleaner. To have them die in the heat of battle was both honourable and lacked suspicion.

"Send word, Vidic. They are to march on the Third immediately."

Had any other soldier been given that order, to send exhausted men onward without rest into a potentially fatal battle, they may have questioned it. But Vidic did not have his own mind to ponder. He simply nodded and gestured to a nearby squire to send the message. Eralf turned back towards his General.

"Did the enchantments that Largox gave your men adhere suitably?"

Vidic stood and nodded.

"Yes my King. The armour seems to be tripled in strength and the ward surrounding the castle and the immediate buildings has proven to only be passable by Kings Guard. One person attempted to cross to their home and was vapourised upon contact."

King Eralf smiled. He truly did have Largox in his pocket. For such a powerful beast, the mage really did not show much of a spine. He did what he was told and knew that if he did not, Eralf would dispose of him. He had seen the mages in battle during the war between the Yellow Demons and Blue Spirits. They fought so vehemently for evil and yet the second the Demons lost, the mages switched sides. The fear of defeat swamped them. Eralf saw it, and he knew he could exploit it. And exploit it he had. There was only one reason why Eralf had ordered the mage to burn down the Shadowlands. He knew of its powers. He knew as well as Nybor that the Shadowlands siphoned the energy of the Void to prevent it becoming too powerful. And he knew that now the cracks were opening and the Dark Lord free that power would begin to return and threaten to make the darkness more powerful. He cared not for the beings who dwelled there. They were oddities, the freaks, the people who could not live amongst normal society. And of course, there were the powerful in hiding. The Blue Spirits, the remaining Yellow Demons still imprisoned in a micro-realm within the forest. Wiping them all out would be a cleansing of the realm. He had planned when he won the great battle ahead to rebuild the world in his image. Those who did not fit in were to be exterminated.

Arrogance was certainly the way of this King. But he did not pick battles he did not expect to win. He had considered invading the Earth realm given the trouble it had spewed into his own, but luckily the gateway had been destroyed and he did not need to know any more about it. The human wizard however, proved a problem. Being born of Beyond had given him this extraordinary power, but being human limited his uses to the crown. When Eralf believed him to be the key to unlocking the Void, he had wanted him very much alive, but after learning the prophecy was a deliberate forgery, he had had it torn down and burned and made the decision to call for Joshua's head as well as Nybor's.

"I will leave for the battle once our forces reach the Third Kingdom, Vidic. Arrange for my transport. I have no intention of walking there for days at a time."

A notable flicker in Vidic's eyes suggested he wasn't quite sure how he would achieve this. He did not question his orders, of course, but he was at that time unsure how to secure such transport. The only way he knew of was through assistance from White

Chapter 25

Falcons. However, reports had seen the remaining Falcons leaving the city gates almost eight hours previously.

"I will arrange the most suitable transport possible, sire."

He spoke, and a wave of Eralf's hand provided him with his exit. As the doors closed once more behind him, and the second set at the entrance clicked shut behind them, Eralf wandered over to where the prophecy had been displayed before its removal. He had noticed this earlier, but it was so slight, he had felt no desire to mention it to anyone else, even Largox. But carved into the black stone where the cloth had once been, was a symbol.

The image in question was of a serpent. There was slight colouring in the body of the snake, a dark hue of red, just enough to stand out against the black of the wall itself. But the snake was in a perfect circle, the tail of the creature swallowed by the mouth of it. A perfect serpentine circle. He had never laid eyes on this particular carving before, but he of course knew it to be an ouroboros marking.

"And round and round we go," he spoke quietly to himself. "Cleanse the land and secure the evil, the evil is released and cleanses the land in a different way, and again and again we go round in circles."

There were other carvings of the same symbol around the room, hidden under paintings and other trinkets. They were old, and clearly worn so were not a recent addition, but until the removal of the false prophecy, they had been unknown to him. However, now was not the time to dwell on the potential futility of the fight ahead. This was the line of no return.

He had a battle to prepare for.

26

Frustration was the order of the day today. Nybor, now fully recovered from her draining at the hands of Josh, was stalking around another, bigger campfire in the exact same clearing they had been in for two days now. Her recovery had taken much longer than she anticipated given her level of power and abilities, and the arrival of Tommy did not help matters. She was glad to see her friend, of course she was, but he had provided her with yet another obstacle to overcome. While Manor had informed her of the situation back in the First Kingdom, she was more preoccupied with the lack of progress in their journey. Along with that, Josh had not returned to them after stalking off into the trees. Spiner offered to go look for him, but she ordered everyone to stay put. Nobody else would be lost today.

"He's probably only got a few hours left," Manor spoke, loudly enough for Nybor to hear. There was also a tinge of annoyance in his tone that landed in her ears like a hammer.

"I will not do it, Manor," she retorted with as much venom as she could muster. "He is not ready for it, he has not been trained, he does not know…" She stopped herself from saying anything more.

"Know what, Nybor?" Syl'Va spoke in a deep gravelly voice. His tone too suggested he was fed up of all the secrecy. "He does not know the secrets you keep? The ones that are so clearly important to the fight ahead? The secrets that nearly cost Joshua his hand? Well, I'm afraid to tell you my friend, that we don't either. So, you either have to trust and save your friend, or reveal all to us and do it anyway."

Nybor tensed up so much, Spiner thought she was going to explode. Her tunic surrounding her arms tore along one bicep revealing muscles much larger than Nybor's outfit had suggested. Her strength was not only in her powers but in a physical sense too. It often frustrated her that during combat, attackers would subdue her with magic or enchantments before she had time to utilise her physical prowess. But here, she knew she was out of options. No more guarding secrets around her friends and her companions. Those she trusted had given their lives to her, and she could no longer keep them in the dark. But the anger at what she now had to do grew so great that before she could stop herself, she grabbed her staff and snapped it clean in half with her rage. The wood at the centre of the staff splintered. She had sheared it completely in two broken pieces, not the nice neat divide which allowed her to deliberately separate it during combat.

The others looked on in shock. The staff had been Nybor's way to channel her power more effectively, and she had wilfully destroyed it. The effect was immediate. Her head was thrown back, and her eyes began to burn with white flame. Her hands began to display literal white flame, and her mouth now agape was illuminated by a fire burning from within her throat. Despite the scene playing out in front of them looking like an unprepared consequence of an angry outburst, Nybor knew exactly what she was doing. She thrust her right hand *into* Tommy's chest. The

Chapter 26

crunching of bone was sickening, and Spiner turned away in disgust. The others continued to watch the incredible spectacle unfolding before their eyes. The arm now submerged in Tommy's torso began to burn with the same literal white flame that previously encompassed Nybor's hand. Despite his friend being elbow deep inside of his chest, Tommy felt no pain. No discomfort. His eyes closed peacefully, and the flame now travelled down Nybor's arm and along Tommy's entire body until he was nothing but a burning mass of white fire. One final scream later, an eruption of white light accompanied by a shockwave blew through the forest, knocking everyone to the ground.

As the light began to clear, and people's vision returned, there were audible gasps. Now standing before them was Nybor, slightly hunched over and trying to catch her breath. And Tommy. Only not the Tommy they had known previously. He was now stood upright, his muscles dense and shoulders broad. His face was young once more, and his beard previously peppered with grey was now pure white. His hair now matched his regenerated look and although not as long as Nybor's, it did reach his shoulders, straight and unwavering as opposed to his wavy brown hair of the Green Dragon days. His eyes snapped open and for a moment they glowed as white as his friend's had moments before, before dissipating back to normal.

"Holy shit," he exclaimed with his first words. "Like... holy shit!"

Syl'Va approached Tommy, the others following just a step behind, using the giant diamond encrusted man as protection. He spoke kindly, and in hushed tones.

"How do you feel?"

Tommy's eyes widened and narrowed repeatedly like he was trying to adjust to something.

"Like I've been injected with a million Red Bulls!" he blurted out.

"Red... Bulls?" Syl'Va asked quizzically.

Tommy smiled wide, his teeth gleaming as brightly as the rest of his new features.

"Don't worry about it."

Movement in the tree line went unnoticed for a moment or two until the figure fully emerged into the clearing.

"Good to see you back Tommy. And nice upgrade."

Josh stumbled over a rock, and appeared to be a little dazed and confused, but soon sat down next to Spiner, giving him a little jab in the arm.

"You okay?" asked his changeling friend.

"I'm good. I heard we were sharing secrets, so I came back. I want to hear everything. I think we all deserve to hear everything."

Nybor glared at him for a moment, but not for his calling her out, but for leaving in the first place, if only for a day. He could've been killed or mauled or captured. She knew in his now restored state that all of those things were unlikely, but nevertheless her feelings were real, and so was her concern. She also noticed he appeared almost drunk and unsteady on his feet. Her questioning would have to wait though, as she knew if she didn't reveal the truth now, she never would.

"I will tell you what you ask of me, but I must remind you that you will know things about me, about this realm, and about people you lost long ago that will make you want to run to the nearest gateway and jump through. But I must ask that you trust me and listen to every word I'm about to tell you."

Syl'Va, Spiner, Josh, Tommy, Manor and the other Falcons all moved into a semi-circle and sat on the ground, Nybor sitting in front of them. They knew the next words were going to weigh heavy on them, but they were completely unprepared for Nybor's first sentence.

"I will begin by revealing my true name. Something I have hidden for millennia."

Chapter 26

But the answer was not what Josh and Tommy were expecting. It was something that shook them to their very core. Something that instilled fear and aimed to destroy any hope they may have, and a name that was inherently designed to frighten all humans.

"My name… is Lucifer."

27

The shouting and arguing was now at a point where no individual voices could be discerned, and it took an enormous blast of fire into a nearby wall to silence the room once more. Small bits of blackened bone rolled from the hole in the wall onto the floor where several of them collided with the hooves of Eralf's form.

"Enough," Lucifer protested. "We must all be in agreement. No questions, no arguments, all on one side."

The Queen of the Underworld was truly a magnificent sight to behold. She stood eleven feet tall, her skin was a dark olive colour, and her hair long, straight and jet black. Her eyes burned golden fire, and the two horns protruding from her forehead were darkest black ringed bone. There was a permanent heat surrounding her, enough to make the other demons sweat, a remarkable feat considering the temperature in Hell was a steady thousand degrees Celsius at all times. The table before her was surrounded by her closest allies and those she considered family. But the reason they were all gathered here was not one of a reunion or enjoyment. It was because of a threat to their very existence.

"As you know, my brother Gabriel has fallen from grace. Our father cast him out and gave him one condition on which he could return. To destroy hell and everyone within it. Our realm is crucial not only to our own existence, but to those of humanity and all the other realms who rely on us to free them of their evil. Gabriel has already attacked the northern face of our world, and the casualties were heavy. The Realm of Screams have been severed from this place, and we can no longer house their dead. The one they call Jasmine is now running rampant across time and space and I fear there may be no stopping her. In addition to this, we no longer have a connection to the Horizon. As you know that is a huge hinderance for us. The Horizon connected us with not only many worlds, but also many realities. The more powerful Gabriel becomes, the more it threatens existence itself."

The crowd fell silent, and after a few moments, the first to speak was Eralf. He had grown up alongside Lucifer in Heaven before they were both cast out. He had been given the form of a human-goat hybrid, a design which often hindered his movement and had given him deep rooted anxiety at being an easy target for torture by the other evil creatures residing here.

"But Gabriel isn't only destroying parts of Hell, he is beginning to assimilate them somehow. The last reports I heard was that he was drawing from their power."

Lucifer nodded. She sighed deeply and continued to reveal more.

"It appears Gabriel is on a quest not to destroy Hell, but to become its new ruler. We believe when our father cast him out, rather than attempt to return, he decided to retaliate. Which is why we are here today. I have a plan and I need you to follow me as you have done so unreservedly in the past."

Again, the group was silent. This time, it was a younger demon who asked the question.

"My Queen, we suffer on a daily basis as is the nature of our

Chapter 27

punishment. We are here to be condemned for our actions in life. We accept that. But what Gabriel is doing is beyond damnation. He is drawing our life forces. He is absorbing power the likes of which we have never seen. Forgive me for asking this but... are we going to die?"

Lucifer was not a heartless demon. A fallen angel, yes, but not heartless. She had attempted to rule Hell efficiently but had never lost sight of her conscience. The people who came here were here to be punished, as decreed by her father. But she believed in rehabilitation, and on multiple occasions successfully lobbied for those she deemed worthy to ascend to Heaven. Others believed her foolish. A benevolent Queen ruling Hell? Ridiculous. Impossible. Gabriel tended to agree. He had always been a thorn in her side long before her descent. He had tormented her and ridiculed her, and it was effectively Gabriel who tricked her into her banishment. But this was time for all that to end. To stop him from taking over Hell. There was only one option. She looked down at the young boy and smiled, her blackened lips cracking from the dry air.

"Not if I can help it Petri."

The next few hours were a tumultuous time. Lucifer unveiled her plans to the council and her allies in great detail. No stone must be left unturned, and every eventuality must be covered. The plan was to enlist the help of the mages, witches, and most powerful demons to create an enchantment beyond the likes of which the universe had ever known. The casting would collect all of the purest evil and condense it, compress it into a single plain of existence separate from Hell, and contain it for the rest of time. The power required to do such a thing was almost unfathomable. But Lucifer was certain it could be done.

"But what becomes of us if we succeed?" Eralf pleaded, unsure he wanted to be part of such a plan if it were to go awry.

"We will live in peace in lush forests, and green kingdoms, and we can finally be at rest. Our own haven. No fear of pain or torture. We will be free."

Murmurs of acceptance and appeal travelled around the table, but one thing had not yet been discussed. The price of this plan. A question that Lucifer's adopted father, Dorn, was only too happy to ask.

"And what is this going to cost, daughter of mine?"

Dorn was another angel who had fallen but was a great deal older than Lucifer. He had been one of the few who had stood up for her when faced with the wrath of the Almighty, but his banishment had come with an extra punishment for his defiance. God had endowed him with a hunger for power. It was something he had been able to keep at bay to this point, but without demonic creatures surrounding him, he was unsure if he could do the same.

"The cost is high."

She glanced around the room until her eyes fell upon her daughter. The only person she truly loved in all this world and the next. She had been informed of the requirements of this strength of magic and had already agreed to it. She knew the cost of failure. Gabriel would consume hell and all of its inhabitants. Then it was likely he'd go after Earth. Whatever the cost, he must be stopped.

"How high?" asked Eralf.

"Higher than any of us could imagine."

Lucifer's voice began to break as she once again looked over at her daughter. While Lucifer had not taken a mate, Lucy had been born directly from her mother. The name had been a conscious choice, because she knew at some point her daughter would leave this realm. She wanted her to have a familiarity of her mother but also a name humans would not fear. This meeting was not for everyone's approval. It was for Lucifer. She had already made the call, and the gathering powers were already beginning to cast the spell. She had called this meeting to see her friends, family, and allies one last time. She knew that most would not remember who

Chapter 27

they were when this was done. She would of course remember. Her daughter Lucy would be sent to the human realm and be reborn to a human couple and raised as a human child. The part of the spell she had insisted on was that whomever she was born to on Earth, would name her the same so she could potentially visit her at some point.

Lucifer herself would renounce her name and adopt a more modest life. No longer would she rule over the lands. She would name the place Beyond, a vague and unknown name across the realms. Each kingdom would be numbered, each town and village similarly so. Each step taken to prevent anyone from remembering the days before the spell. The entirety of evil, and Gabriel along with it would be contained in a place known as the Void. To help restrict the power within from growing and someday breaking free, some of the lower demons would reside in an isolated location. The Shadowlands. Each would be protected in micro-realms of their own, shielded by the power siphoned from the creatures in the Void.

But blood magic requires a blood sacrifice. Lucy aside, countless souls would be lost forever. She looked around the room. Abaddon. Azazel. Dantanian. Enepsigos. Lahash. Naberius. Saleos. They would soon perish. A slight breeze penetrated the room. Lucifer knew what was happening. And not a moment too soon, as above them in the main body of the castle, she could hear screams. Gabriel was here. And he was in the throne room. The others sensed his presence, and as Gabriel slaughtered the only guards surrounding the throne itself, he lowered himself into the seat, and the ground began to rumble and shift.

Everyone began to look around in panic, and it was Dorn who spoke first.

"Daughter, what do we do? Is it too late?"

His eyes were pleading, and it took every ounce of her strength to look back at him.

"It is already done."

Dorn's face seemed to fall at the words. As the breeze intensified around them, the ground stopped rumbling, and the bellowing voice of Gabriel echoed around every space in the realm.

"NO! I WILL NOT BE BANISHED FROM MY CASTLE! THIS PLACE IS MINE! FATHER WILL PAY! I WILL MAKE HIM PAY!"

A bright white light rushed over the room, and the terror, the screams, the shouting, and the panicked cries vanished. Lucifer looked over at her daughter just in time to see her figure melt away and shoot upwards towards the Earth. Lucifer closed her eyes and allowed herself to be swallowed by the light.

As the realm of Hell began to contort and change around her, she spoke only one sentence.

"May my father forgive me."

28

S ilence. Nobody spoke a word as they tried to absorb everything they had just been told. Many things still did not make sense to them, and they had many questions, but they just couldn't formulate the words. Nybor continued to finish her story.

"Beyond was formed and for a while those who remained did not know who they were, what their purpose was. But of course, they no longer had one. Only Eralf and a handful of others remembered the days before and were sworn to secrecy for the protection of the realm. A battery was constructed across the Sea of Eternity to guard the Void and was manned by those who knew of its existence. Over time, others became aware of it and simply knew of it as the darkness from every realm sent to live for all eternity. Lucy would only learn of her abilities upon her death which I hope she has not yet reached. I have been unable to see her. Eralf became too ambitious and the opposite of the man I knew growing up, developing into what you see now.

The more of a backseat I took to things, the more typical politics grew throughout Beyond. Dominant forces grew, Kings sprouted forward and turned the battery into the Fifth Kingdom, where they sent the poorest and most destitute to live in effective exile. Wars came and went, and Beyond became much like the Earth. Violent. Unstable. Awash with a darkness albeit an invisible one. Hell, no longer existed for the humans. Those who died often remained as spirits or entities. Once they had completed their time as such, their energy simply dissipated. Demons however, once exorcised, still travelled to the Void. That was another condition of the spell."

The first one to speak was Manor.

"What of Heaven?" he asked.

Nybor shrugged.

"Once my true father could no longer sense Hell's existence or that of Gabriel, he feared the worst, and closed the gates to Heaven indefinitely. Since then, to my knowledge, no souls have crossed over. They are simply... lost."

Tommy was next to find words.

"So, all of the beings here, the Blue Spirits, the Yellow Demons, the Green Dragons? You... the White Falcons, were other things before?"

Nybor nodded.

"The Blue Spirits were the sorcerers damned to Hell upon their death for daring to practice white magic, healing magic, the spells which would benefit humanity. Yellow Demons were those who practiced Satanism, the Occult, and dark magic. Something that despite how it is perceived on Earth, is not something I endorsed. The Green Dragons have always been. They are not a creation of mine. They have always guarded the doorways between realms all over existence, not just this one. Here, they are called Green Dragons, but they have different names throughout time. The White Falcons are simply what we already were before banishment."

"Angels," Josh said, acceptance in his voice.

Chapter 28

"Yes Joshua, I'm sorry I belittled you when you called that out on your return. For a moment I feared the spell was failing. But yes, we returned to our angel forms, sworn to protect our new home from attack. One day, I feared the Void would fail and we would be needed. Gabriel had asked for death at the hands of the witches and sorcerers and they had prepared to provide it to him. But I said no. I fear now that my choice was the wrong one."

Everyone now realised the stakes, and exactly what Eralf was planning. He planned to break open the Void, defeat Gabriel, and be the definitive ruler over all of Hell and Beyond. If he failed, all of Beyond would be lost. There were no longer any questions. There was nothing left to say. Except for one thing. And Josh was the one to volunteer it.

"We're through running from these bastards."

29

The Islands as they were now known were once the location for punishment. In the days before when the Sea of Eternity was known as the River Styx and ran red, these islands were used to house those who refused to accept their fate, those who refused to acknowledge their crimes. They would be marooned here until they either broke or redeemed themselves. They knew they could not swim for it, as the water of the river was the temperature of molten lava and they'd burn for all eternity, so their only option was to accept their fate, when they would then return to the mainland to take up their eternal duties.

However, in the time following the transformation into Beyond, the Islands were a refuge from those seeking to live a life of tranquillity and non-interference from whatever ruling body sat on the throne. Usually, the people here came from the Fourth or Fifth Kingdoms. Those who felt oppressed or did not have much to call their own on the mainland. Usually, anything they had was taxed and then lost to the King or Queen. More often it was a King. Men in power just seemed to have a need to grasp for more and take from those they deemed weaker like the women and children.

But the women and children of these Islands were far from weak. They were strong not just in mind, but in body. Any man who dared challenge them were likely to find themselves hurled into the sea or torn apart with the exquisite weaponry from their forge.

There were three islands in total and two were connected by an iron bridge, curved in the middle with a golden sand surface on the top. The railings running along the sides of the bridge were painted in gold, and a small guard booth sat at one end to ensure those passing across came to no harm. But in truth, there was nothing here to harm the people at all. They often became a stopover point for those sailing trade or supplies between the main land and the Fifth Kingdom, and those who visited did so with respect and courteousness. And of course, if they didn't, they answered to the Enforcer.

There was only one person on any of the three Islands to fear, and the people loved her for it. She had come to them several years ago in refuge after she lost her son and her wife had been taken whilst in the First Kingdom. She had rage and pain swirling throughout her mind, and she was found by a trade ship docking for respite in a storm. Since then, she had become an integral part of society, often teaching self-defence classes to the younger members of the community. They were lucky that at this point in the ocean, they did not have to worry about the pirates. Vicious and violent creatures, so the stories said. Raiding multiple ships, a week of their supplies and docking at a point at the north shore of the Fifth Kingdom, where nobody dared to tread.

But today was no ordinary day. And these were no ordinary circumstances. They had all seen the White Falcons struck from the skies overhead. They had all heard the venomous crack and thundering voice of the Dark Lord booming across the entire realm. They knew even their safety was at risk.

The boats had been prepared almost immediately, but many citizens of the Islands refused to board, wanting to help to fortify

Chapter 29

their home, but the Enforcer was having none of it. She had ensured the children were ferried away to safety first and ordered them to take shelter in the Forest of Music.

"The trees will protect you," she had told them all.

In truth, she did not know if anything could protect them. But at least they would be near a gateway as a last resort. Few knew of the gateway in the Forest of Music, as the trees that resided within made it their mission to disguise it. The trees themselves were magnificent beasts, at least sixty feet in height with roots stretching over two miles in all directions. It was one of the few safe havens on the mainland left unless you happened to be King. It took a full three hours to load each boat and as the last one sailed off towards the shores nearest the Fourth Kingdom, the few remaining elders stood alongside the Enforcer, who was now no longer watching her people sail away from their home, but turned towards the Fifth Kingdom, where in the distance, gigantic booms rang out across the sky as Gabriel now inhabiting LeVar's form began hammering his incredible strength against the Void attempting to crack the surface and allow his minions out into the open air. Whilst he was plenty strong enough after taking the powerful form of a White Falcon, he was still bound by the sea and would need to draw more strength from those on the other side of the barrier to cross the water. Having a host who can fly is one thing, but the will and ability to use them is another. Alongside the Enforcer, a concerned elder turned to face the same direction.

"How long do you think we have?" they asked with trepidation in their voice.

"I am unsure. But if he succeeds in breaking down that barrier, the Fifth and these Islands will be lost within the hour."

Another elder joined the pair, and behind them they could sense the others joining their viewing party. The second, Malia, tapped the Enforcer on the shoulder, and attempted to relax her tension a little.

"There is nothing you can do to prevent this, Iona. It is beyond our capabilities."

But the words rang hollow in the ears of the Enforcer. She had lost everything in recent years due to greed of the royals, and the ever increasing skirmishes between the people of each kingdom. She felt she finally found a home on the Islands, and while she was not powerful enough to take on anything that Gabriel would throw at them, she refused to entertain either leaving, or going down without a fight. She knew there were those out on the open ocean who could help them, but there was a trust issue. The pirates who stalked the Sea of Eternity were often vicious and violent in their attacks and pillaging, but they held some of the strongest fighters in all of Beyond. The question was, if they received word from the Enforcer, would they realise a treaty is in the best interests of everyone, or would they take advantage of the opportunity to raid an almost empty trio of Islands?

That was a question she would soon find out the answer to because as the booming intensified, the tip of a mast and the faint outline of sails could be seen in the distance. As a large, hulking ship emerged from the horizon, a quick burst of anxiety traversed Iona's spine. This was happening. But then her anxiety began to turn into something much more intense. As everyone remaining on the Islands watched on, now ignoring the drum roll of death against the barrier of the Void, behind the first ship, fifty more emerged from the sea mist and honed into view.

It was the entire pirate army.

30

The faces of those surrounding him did not appear to move for almost five minutes. Josh's eyes darted to each one in turn, but nobody spoke. He had felt that the plan was a worthwhile one, and slight nausea was a minimal price to pay for the advantages of traversing the land in such a quick time. The others, however, were unreadable. After an eternity of silence, it was Syl'Va who spoke first.

"Please go over that again."

Josh sighed and lowered his head. He did not have time to detail the whole process again. After the revelations of Nybor's true identity and that of Beyond, Josh had been asked as to his whereabouts for the past day. He detailed how he had stormed off into the forest in anger, and stumbled upon another person. A witch named Braddock had been collecting the rock fruit Tommy had introduced him to, when she tripped down a small embankment. Josh had helped her back to the path and in return, she offered to show him a shortcut. In his blind rage he sheathed his suspicion and uncertainty and accepted the offer wholeheartedly. The small portal was hidden between the entrance to a cave and a twisted tree. He ventured through and found himself on the edge of an even larger forest, the air filled with the sound of music. In the near distance, he could hear the sound of waves crashing on the shore. When he realised how much distance had been covered, he turned back through the portal, where he told Braddock all about the King, and his mage. Witches and mages were sworn enemies, and Josh could see that Braddock was greatly disturbed by the presence of such a powerful one as Largox. She wished him well, and disappeared through her own portal to speak with her elders. Josh then wandered back to the clearing to find his friends.

After detailing this tale for the second time, Tommy stepped forward, his new glow taking some getting used to, and Josh could not help but admire his new white mane of hair.

"It is true that the witches and mages have fought previously. Even as recently as my tenure here, I have seen skirmishes on the border between the Shadowlands and the First Kingdom. Witches practice their magic in secret, and provide healing and magic of wellbeing. They were the ones who helped the trees of the Forest of Music to lay root there. This will frighten them. And anger them also."

Nybor nodded.

"If Largox truly does have his own plans, then it is imperative we speed up our journey. Joshua, do you remember where this portal is located?"

Josh nodded enthusiastically, but his newly spread smile began to waver, as the smell of smoke began drifting between them.

"What is that?" he asked, turning to try and find the source of the burning scent now within his nostrils.

Spiner and Manor walked in opposite directions to try and locate it, but it was Nybor who leapt into the sky. When she returned to the ground, her face was solemn.

"The Shadowlands are burning."

Spiner's face became a vision of pain and fear. He knew where

Chapter 30

his people resided, and it was near to the Shadowlands entrance. He looked directly into Josh's eyes, and Josh simply offered an understanding nod. With a quick smile, Spiner raced off into the trees, transforming as he went into a beast not too dissimilar to a cheetah. Seconds later, he was gone.

"If Largox burns the Shadowlands, then all of the power being siphoned from the Void will return, its power will grow, and it will give Gabriel all he needs to break the darkness free."

Manor's words drilled themselves into each of them. Nybor stood firm, and gripped the two splintered pieces of her staff. She now had two options. The first was to turn tail and run back where they had come from in an effort to stop Largox from destroying this place. The second, was to head towards this portal and attempt to stop the Void from failing, and perhaps take down Gabriel himself. The decision was tearing her mind apart. Could they prevent the Void from collapsing if the Shadowlands were to fall? Which was the bigger risk? Now that everything was out in the open, the truth revealed, she no longer knew what to do with any degree of certainty. She was beginning to second guess every decision, every question, every order. The element of blame hung over her heart, and she could not help but feel as if this entire situation was her fault. Should she truly have killed Gabriel all those years ago? She was the Queen of Hell, and she was meant to lead the damnation of the souls within this realm. Except she wasn't. She was leader of this place at one time, but despite the circumstances which threw her here in the first place, she was not a cruel and evil person. Her father saw ignorance, disloyalty and stupidity. He was not a benevolent deity, nor the wonderous creator which the humans worshipped. He was a tyrant. It was *he* that was in fact a devil. Part of her wondered if she should let her brother take Hell back and target the man who shunned them both. But the lives that would be lost meant too much to her. She needed to stop them from losing their lives. She owed them that. Leaving the ruling of this place to another had only brought war, death and destruction. Now it was time to fix her mistakes, and reclaim the throne herself. To do that, she needed to stop Largox, Eralf and Gabriel. As she was beginning to formulate the question in her mind of just how exactly she was to achieve that, it was answered from a voice in the treeline, and the sound of dozens of approaching footsteps.

"Do not fear, angel. We will tackle Largox and his mage forces. They will not survive."

Josh looked up and saw a familiar face.

"Braddock?"

The witch nodded. She had warned her elders of the dangers, and they had seen the smoke rising in the distance.

"This is our home. And we will not let it be defiled by those demons. We will stop them."

Nybor was a little unsteady. She called her angel. How could she know?

"Because it is my gift, child."

Braddock smiled, and nodded as the truth became clear. She could read her mind. Nybor had heard stories of the witches having such power since they cast the initial spell over Hell. It was said that they acquired the gift as part of the ritual so that they may watch over the land ensuring the spell stayed true. That part was now evidenced.

"You must follow the portal that I showed to young Joshua, and stop Gabriel. He has broken free and taken one of your own, angel."

Nybor did not even need to ask. The tone of Braddock's voice told her everything she needed to know.

"LeVar."

Again, Braddock nodded.

"He is now using your friend's powers to damage the barrier.

Chapter 30

Even without the power being drawn from this place, he will soon break the evil free. You must stop him. Whatever the cost."

Nybor walked forward and placed a hand on Braddock's shoulder.

"How will you stop them, there are but two dozen of you?"

"They won't be alone."

A second voice, deeper, more masculine, came from behind them, and as they turned to look, they saw the Changelings walking back into the clearing, Spiner at their lead.

"And we will assist the Changelings and the Witches."

A third voice, female, echoed from above as bright blue swirls of gas seemed to float down from the canopies of the trees, before forming into fully fledged people.

"Blue Spirits."

The shock in Nybor's voice was expressed in the faces of everyone else. They had all come from the shadows. All of those she thought hidden in the forest, now stepped forward, hundreds of them. It was the army of the Shadowlands. And it was beautiful.

As each section turned and took to running or flight in the direction of the fires, Nybor surveyed her group and took a deep breath.

"Manor, take the remaining Falcons and Joshua, and scout the way ahead, clearing any obstacles you may find. We still don't know what's out there. Tommy, if you can stomach it, take flight and check the aerial perimeter. Syl'Va, we go on foot. Let's stop this."

Each and every member of the mismatched group stood tall, and burst forward in whatever instruction they had been given. Pride swelled through Nybor's heart, the loyalty she had earned still embedded into each and every one of them, despite their arguments or differences. But as she strolled forwards with her Deltarian friend, she could not help but fear her true confidante was lost. And she wanted to weep for LeVar, but she had to remain strong. With all of Beyond at stake, she must make the decision to kill him if necessary. Their course set, their goal in sight, they vanished towards the mystical portal in the forest.

However, as the army of the Shadowlands converged on the fire at its entrance, what they would soon find would not be Largox burning down their home, stripping it of its magic and security. They would find a fire demon.

31

Eralf looked over the empty streets of the Third Kingdom as he descended from the sky to land in the courtyard of the Kings Guard campus. The people had been ordered to remain indoors and offer any item or service demanded of them by the crown. The transportation had not been precisely what he had in mind, but the winged horses known as Panax had gotten him to his first destination. Here he would make his base of operations, and his fallback position should he need it. He intended to use the people as cannon fodder if necessary. These were not the people he knew, those that had been sacrificed by Nybor's enchantment. They were simply newly bred creatures who drained the lifeblood of the kingdom, offering nothing in return. It would bring him pleasure to cleanse the area if the time came. And if not, he would smite them upon his victorious return. Vidic was already in the courtyard, and approached Eralf, bowing to acknowledge his presence.

"Speak Vidic."

"My liege, scouts report that your new Leader of the White

Falcons has been corrupted by the Dark Lord. He is seen and heard to be pounding on the walls of the barrier day and night. What is more, the effects of the darkness are beginning to reach into the sea. There are sections which show red colour along the shore of the Fifth."

Eralf swallowed hard. He had simply figured LeVar would be a casualty of the mission and a quick fix to a problem he had not anticipated originally. Now he feared he had given his enemy a powerful weapon. Some of his bravado was now lost, and he had wondered if sending Largox away was the correct decision after all.

"How many troops do we have in number?" he asked, trying his hardest not to allow his concern into his voice. He failed.

"One-hundred-twenty-thousand my King."

Vidic did not acknowledge his King's loss of total dominance, such was his duty, but some of the soldiers around him did and they began nodding and gesturing to each other.

"You there!" Eralf shouted at them. "I suggest you focus on the task at hand or I will have my mage tear you to pieces, slowly. Do not forget your places here!"

As he spoke in such a derisory manner, the soldiers began to smile. Their grins got wider, and their eyes began to bulge as they slowly stepped forwards, inching their way towards the King. As Eralf watched, their eyes seemed to glaze over.

"Vidic, order your men to return to their post!" he bellowed.

Vidic did nothing.

"Vidic! I gave you an order!"

Still, no movement from Vidic. Eralf walked right up to his face and spat words to him, saliva trickling into his dense beard, but he stopped quickly when he saw Vidic's eyes glaze over in the same way as the soldiers around him. Moments later, every soldier in the courtyard was walking in a trance, smiling, eyes bulging, all heading towards the King.

Chapter 31

"What is this?" Eralf spat. He spoke with poison but also with extreme fear.

Over a thousand soldiers were in this space and they were all encircling him. It was then that Vidic finally turned to his King and spoke.

"You thought me a fool, Eralf?"

The voice was not that belonging to Vidic. But it was one that he recognised.

"Largox?!" he exclaimed.

A frightening and deep laugh echoed in Vidic's throat and soon spread throughout the thousand mouths around him, and every single one of them spoke in unison, and all portraying the voice of the mage.

"Did you really think you were in control? That I would let you live, and rule over all?"

Eralf began to back away but found himself surrounded whichever way he went.

"Largox, how are you doing this?"

More laughter, deeper, more echoey. Vidic placed his hand on Eralf's shoulder, and span him around to face him.

"You are just a blundering old fool. And your usefulness has come to an end."

Vidic thrust his broadsword straight through Eralf's stomach, the sound of flesh being seared along the metal, drowned out only by the sharp exhale of breath from Eralf's own lips. His eyes bulged so wide that they threatened to explode. Then, a second blade penetrated his back, causing him to wrench his body forward, further impaling it on Vidic's weapon. As blood began to dribble down from his mouth, a third and then a fourth blade sliced into him. The crowd closed in, and one by one, a thousand blades found themselves burying their lengths within the body of their now murdered King. Each one withdrew their blade, and plunged it a second time. And a third. Meticulous and devastating. As Largox watched on from atop the campus walls, his smile mimicked those on the shoulders now blood-soaked faces.

32

The sheer volume of vomit now cascading down the small hill on the other side of the portal was becoming a stream. The only ones unaffected by the extreme shortcut from the Shadowlands were Josh and Nybor. Every single Falcon, and even Syl'Va were disorientated to the point of sickness. The Deltarian's involvement drew humour from Nybor, who took a brief moment to simply relax in the natural light shining through the canopy above.

"You have travelled on starships at many times the speed of light, and yet you cannot hold your stomach contents after stepping through a tunnel?"

Syl'Va wiped his shiny chin and turned to face his friend.

"I was the same when I once travelled through a wormhole. The sheer compression of distance versus time it should have taken to travel that far simply... did not agree with me."

As everyone recovered, they began to take stock of where they were. Surrounding them on all sides were the largest and most beautiful trees any of them had ever witnessed. They were traditional, in the sense that they simply appeared as just that.

Trees. Brown and weathered bark gave way higher up to green foliage, leaves the width of a dinner plate, but just regular, stereotypical trees. And yet the beauty in that image was enhanced, not just by the fact they were no longer shrouded in grey and mist and seemingly dampened daylight, but by the sounds now flowing through their ears. Having never been here before, Tommy had to be the one to ask.

"What... what is that?"

He was unable to hide a smile as it began to filter into his mind, and almost wrap itself around his inner most thoughts like a soft and welcoming blanket. Nybor smiled. It had been many years since she was last here.

"The trees, my friend. It is their song."

Tommy and the other Falcons could not help but spin around, trying to find some kind of ultimate source for the music, but soon they just seemed to realise that Nybor was correct. It was the trees themselves emitting the notes and chords. As they watched even closer with their superior eyesight, they could see the branches and leaves vibrating with each note. Small tremors, and intermittent waves moving down the branches as if they were a conductor's baton, orchestrating the whole forest. It was stunningly beautiful. The story behind such wonder, however, was not so enchanting.

During the war between the Blue Spirits and the Yellow Demons, no part of Beyond was untouched. Every faction and group waded in to try and stop the atrocities, including the trees. They did not just sing, they *moved*. Often, they attempted to move into the centre of a battle to divide the warring factions, and emit high concentrations of their song in order to try and ease the fighters on both sides, and end the battles. But the greed and the violent nature of the Yellow Demons, and the resilience of the Blue Spirits meant that millions of the trees were burned, hacked down, or lost in some other way. They had waded into a war that was not their own and were butchered for their efforts of peace. Knowing

Chapter 32

this made Nybor feel sadness. While the song was beautiful, she knew its true meaning. It was a song of sadness and lost for all those trees who perished in the war. The trees were one of the more beautiful things to come out of repressing Hell into the Void. Nobody knew where they came from, but they showed the best of the realm, the true potential of what Beyond could be. Sadly, like many other similar elements, they were beaten, and forced into submission. Hell had not been contained. Merely the idea and the true demonic evil lay within the Void. The arrogance of man still remained.

The sound of waves crashing nearby startled them all into realising their true location. They were not simply at the mouth of the Forest of Music, but they were almost at the exit on the other side. Nybor gasped as she realised this portal had cut almost a fortnight off their journey. Whilst White Falcons ordinarily could traverse the distance in a mere three days without stopping, on foot, the time was much longer. While it was true that the weakening barrier to the Void had affected how time passed here, their journey was now cut down by over seventy-five percent. She made a mental note to thank Braddock... if they ever saw her again. Even the former ruler of Hell did not know all the secrets of the realm, and that made her smile. Mystery was part of the excitement that was life. Something she had sorely missed when Hell was at its highest peak.

And then they heard it.

The cracking sound echoed louder than before, but this time it was accompanied by a distant whooshing sound, as if someone had let the air out of a tyre and it was slowly deflating. The smile vanished from everyone's faces, and the trees seemingly noticing the shift in tone, altered their music. The notes were less frequent, and took on minor keys. There was almost *fear* within the new notes being played, and the trees themselves began to shrink inward slightly, almost imperceptible to the naked eye, but the movement was there, it was not an illusion.

"What are they doing?" Josh asked fearfully, his own dread rising within his chest.

Nybor simply turned to look at him with sad eyes.

"They're singing their funeral march."

Josh's heart contracted. These beautiful things were scared. They had faced battle before and now they faced extinction. As he looked around him, the branches began to wilt slightly, and small thin lines of sap began to drip down the bark to the ground. He squinted as he examined this phenomenon. He glanced over at Nybor, and she simply nodded.

"They're crying."

The tenderness of the moment was once again broken by a voice ahead of them. Everyone dropped to a defensive posture, but there was no need. The voice ahead of them was friendly, and as its owner stepped into their line of sight. She was older than she was when Josh had last seen her, at least twenty to thirty years by human standards. And her face was whiter than he remembered, the lines of fur now tinged with age. But as the memories came flooding back, he ran forward, and Valdore embraced him in a tight and loving hug. He felt a tear drop or two land on his head, but he had buried his face into the warm leather of her vest, and only after several tightened squeezes of affection, did he back away. Valdore held him at arms length, and examined her adopted son.

"You've gotten a bit chubby, my boy," she said through a smile. "The human world still makes cheeseburgers I see."

Josh burst out laughing, happy tears falling from his eyes. He tapped his barely there paunch and nodded affectionately.

"The cheeseburgers are fine, mother. It's the triple cheeseburgers that get you."

Valdore released a belly laugh that was barely an octave away from turning into a full on howl. It was only now that both Josh

Chapter 32

and Nybor took in Valdore's appearance. She was indeed different to the day they returned Josh to Wealdstone. Her fur was whiter around her face, but her outfit told a different story. She wore a maroon leather vest, and beneath was a white flowing shirt. That was coupled with a sword attached to a belt around her waist, and she sported black trousers with high boots of a mocha coloured shade. But the head was what Tommy was focussed on. Atop Valdore's figure, sat a tricorn. A Captain's tricorn.

"She's a pirate," Tommy said defiantly, gritting his teeth.

Valdore looked at him and nodded.

"I'm a pirate Captain, actually."

Almost as if on cue, the forest rustled with the sound of footsteps, as a dozen other pirates moved in behind Valdore. Instinctively, Josh and the others backed away, but his mother held her hands up for understanding.

"It is not what you think," she said pleading. "This is my crew. And we are not the pirates that you have heard about. We do not pillage, or plunder, or attack anyone. Well that's not entirely true."

Nybor gripped the two broken pieces of her staff, preparing for the possibility of taking on her old friend, and hoping this was indeed a misunderstanding. Valdore glanced down at Nybor's staff, and back up at her friend.

"Here, let me help you with that, Nybor."

She stepped forward, and placed her hands around Nybor's staff, and while every fibre in her being told her to move away, she was transfixed with what was happening in front of her own eyes. As she watched, a similar set of lightning to Josh's began to wrap itself around the two pieces of her staff, and it was then she noticed that only one hand was wrapped around the object, and Valdore's free hand was pressed against another person. The staff began to knit back together, and Valdore released both it, and her crewmember. Both slumped to the ground, but she looked at the other pirate, and he nodded and smiled that he was alright. Nybor examined her repaired channelling device, and gave it a swift twirl in the air. She smiled. It was as if she had never broken it. Valdore's more ancient magic certainly had its uses, and she had missed her greatly. But the pirates could not just be dismissed. Thankfully, Valdore offered her explanation.

"After Joshua had left us, me and Iona decided to try and prepare ourselves for the arrival of trouble. We suspected it would only be a matter of time before Eralf knew of our involvement with a human and he would sent forces to take us. What we didn't expect was Largox himself."

The name of the mage sent a shudder down Syl'Va's spine. He still had not fully recovered from being so easily defeated in their last encounter. Valdore continued.

"Iona was out collecting firewood, she did always like to do things the old fashioned way, when she saw him entering the Shadowlands threshold. She followed him in, and saw him talking to a changeling. Whoever it was, was in the form of a large feline, and she could not hear what they were discussing, but when he spotted her, he chased her out into the open. He attempted to take her down with beams of flame, but she was able to counteract him enough to get home. I tried to gather our belongings, but he was too fast, too powerful. He blew the house to pieces. When I came around, it was nightfall and the house and Iona were gone. I had hoped that she may have been captured or escaped, but I dared not risk going to track Largox down. I am powerful, as is Iona, but he is something else.

I wandered through the Shadowlands for what seemed like an eternity, and then through this very forest until I met the ocean shore. There was a boat docked at the jetty. It was pirates. They were stealing grain and food bound for the Fifth Kingdom. I was in such a rage and all of the turmoil within me had reached a precipice and I just... leapt. I took down their captain, and first mate. I took out anyone who opposed me and then told those who

Chapter 32

remained that if they followed me, and helped me to liberate our land from this infestation, then I would let them live, and they would become family. And here we are."

The group took in her story, and all apprehension around her pirate status soon vanished. Josh was thinking back to his other mother. It had been Iona who had taught them to fight, to defend themselves. He missed her strength. But then a thought struck him.

"Why are you here now?"

Valdore opened her mouth to answer, but it was not her voice which spoke next. Behind her, a new presence emerged.

"Because I asked her here."

Josh had not yet recovered from seeing his adoptive mother return to him, and now behind her... was Iona.

The emotions were almost palpable, almost touchable in the air. No words were exchanged for a moment, and Iona just stared into the eyes of Valdore. There was no animosity, no hatred for the long absence. There was only love. Having had no idea that it was Valdore she had sent word to, the surprise was akin to that of being reunited with a long lost family member. Iona spoke next.

"I always thought you were dead. I should have known better. I'm sorry I did not look for you either, Valdore."

Her wife simply smiled between tears, and the two of them shared a loving embrace of a family reunited. Iona had listened to the tale spoken by Valdore from the shadows. When Josh had joined the hug of his mothers, he had asked what had happened to Iona. She told them that she too was thrown clear of the structure, but unlike Valdore, she remained conscious and attempted to re-enter the burning remains to find her wife. When she saw Largox had not yet left, she felt no option but to vanish into the woods. She had taken the direct route to the ocean, through each kingdom in disguise, seeking out a place she could stay and be of use. When she found passage to the Islands, she helped defeat a small group of pirates herself, and from then on remained on the Islands as the Enforcer.

"The Enforcer? Nice title."

Valdore spoke with a voice that suggested more sensuality than just being impressed. "I'll have to remember that." She winked as she spoke, and although usually resilient in displaying too much emotion, Iona's cheeks flushed a little.

The entire pirate fleet that had moored at the shore, was under Valdore's command. They had found a new way to survive, and to help. But she warned there were still dangerous pirates in the ocean and that it would be best if they avoided them. After another two hours of relaying stories between each other, everyone was fully up to date on the situation. It was universally agreed that the clear breach of the Void that they had all heard earlier, meant the Shadowlands must have fallen, or at least enough to allow some of the darkness to escape. They shared a silent prayer for those who had rallied to fight. For Spiner, who had gone to help his people even after they shunned him. Josh thought about that a lot. He had always been a wonderful friend to him, but he had never truly been what Spiner had been looking for. He would always carry a guilt about that. But right now, the threat was near, and very real, and becoming more pronounced with every passing second.

"We have to go. We have to do this now, and we have no more time to waste. Gabriel must be stopped."

Nybor, Iona and Valdore stood on top of a small mound looking down towards the docks, Josh and Syl'Va just behind them, and the Falcons either side in a long formation. This was the dawn of the battle which would either save Beyond or return it to Hell.

33

Gabriel stood at the edge of the Void, the gigantic fissure directly in front of him. As he held his arms wide, and closed the eyes of his host body, a thick, black swirl of fog began to seep through and curl around his feet. A fainter, silvery-grey mist was coursing into his back, carried on the breeze all the way from the now depleted Shadowlands. Gabriel may not have been the master of Hell when it was supressed, but in the countless years he had spent locked up in the darkness within the Void, he had become their leader, their messiah. Every inch of ground that the fog swept over turned to ash, blades of grass crisping before it even touched them. But this was not a burn caused by an intense heat. This was ice cold.

The fires of Hell were not yet reignited.

Nature was being consumed by the darkness one inch at a time. As demons slowly began manifesting around him, now with the power to do so, Gabriel considered how he had arrived here. His father had cast him out of Heaven for the smallest infringement. He had dared to side with his sister, Lucifer, on the issue of standing up for what was right. He had no real affinity or love for her, of course. He always envied her being able to host her own realm, even if it was in damnation of those it served. But Hell was a powerful weapon. The magic, energy, and resources that filled those hills and caverns and fires, were an untapped source of revenge. Whilst his father had offered him salvation if he were to destroy Hell, Gabriel had decided to remain fallen and instead, take Hell from Lucifer, and launch a full scale attack on Heaven, taking rule over both realms.

Then came the day of the invasion.

Everything was in place. He had arrived in the fires of Hell through a celestial gateway unguarded by the now Green Dragons, and he brought with him an army of the undead, risen up from the very depths of Hell itself. He cut down any and all in his path, and the more land he occupied, the more realms were cut off from Hell. No souls were flowing into damnation, but the battle caused the Creator himself to seal off the heavens. The longer the war raged on, the more species like humans came to realise and believe that there was no Heaven and Hell. How very wrong they were. Souls of the dead and their energy would simply either dissipate, or remain trapped as spirits, lost without guidance, and beyond saving or damning. Eventually, they were simply lost to the nothing.

The Void, however, was still a functioning part of Hell. Whilst true it was only a small vacuum, reserved for the darkest of demons and the most vile of evil creatures, it maintained its connection as a somewhat separate realm. If a demon was exorcised on Earth for example, it would be cast to the Void. Only extreme incantations could briefly drag it from its confinement. Then came the Phantom Wraiths. They were a creature born from the darkness at the very dawn of creation. They were able to hop from one realm to another simply by thought. If any other means of traversing the worlds was found, they hunted it down and destroyed it. The advantage must remain theirs, and they were prepared to kill for it. When they too began to vanish, without

Chapter 33

Hell's presence, they were cast into the Void, only allowed their freedom through ancient rituals. Some merged with humans, some with alien species. But without Hell to feed them power, they were weak, and could not manifest for long.

Gabriel, however, would hold no prisoner captive. As soon as he discovered that all he had to do was sit on the throne in the Black Castle to claim the realm, he freed them all. The Void was broken, and death swamped the already dead. He had been just moments from lowering himself into the ruling chair itself, when Lucifer had unleashed the full power of her witches and sorcerers, wiping the entirety of Hell clean, and forcing everything in its path into a new, endless version of The Void.

Beyond. Pah.

The last realm before the Void. How quaint a choice. His sister had never been one for taking charge or having a back bone for dishing out punishment. He had learned through invading the body of her friend LeVar, that she now called herself Nybor, and was leader of the White Falcons. She did not rule, but kept a watchful eye over proceedings and intervened when necessary. But all that had happened was that the land had found its own way to corruption and poverty. Segregation of the rich and poor, the ruling monarchy, whoever it had been had simply chosen to profit on the backs of others. The multiple gateways between worlds had been left open for the most part.

A foolish mistake.

Having a presence in skirmishes on Earth was bound to lead to more interference. In an effort to free themselves from the damnation of Hell, they had created it again regardless, simply in a different image. No matter though, Gabriel thought. Beyond would fall and Hell would rise once again. He and the others now had enough power to cross the Sea of Eternity, a name Gabriel found ironic considering Lucifer's attempts at creating time in this new realm.

Three nearby demons were now fully formed, jet black and shimmering as if moulded from some kind of oily substance. Two of them sported curled horns of jet black bone. Their eyes were fiery red, and their jagged teeth yellowed but glistening with drool the consistency of blood. Every other feature one would expect to find on a human, however, was non-existent. It was as if someone had drawn the outline of a demon, coloured the shape in black, and only added minimal facial features. One approached Gabriel, who turned to acknowledge the creature.

"My Lord," the creature bowed and spoke with a rasp in its voice. "Our eternal gratitude for granting us our freedom."

Gabriel tilted his head as he examined his addresser.

"Your name, demon child?" he inquired directly.

"I was no simple demon, my Lord. I was a deity. My name is Baphomet. I was worshipped by the human Knights Templar, and revered for my existence to bring about balance. But foolish mortals sought to cast me from their realms, and after several attempted possessions to cling to my stature, I was cast out by a powerful sorceress during an attack on the human world."

Gabriel could feel the anger and hatred coming from this fallen deity. It was as if the fires of Hell itself were burning within this now demon creature. Gabriel could relate to this one. Having fallen himself, he knew the anger that accompanied it.

"What is the last thing you remember about your existence on Earth?" Gabriel asked, curious to find how long he had been held within the Void.

"I became attached to a human, Hector. His form allowed me to leave my confined surroundings. I had been summoned and then left in a dwelling. Other spirits resided there but I was the only demon. I kept myself isolated, waiting for the right moment. I joined with this Hector, and found my freedom. It was too brief, however. Hector's body was weak. My presence drained him, and he was killed. I latched onto another, a person who travelled to a

Chapter 33

place called... Montana. But another human, a powerful one, with magic I had never experienced before, cast me out and I was banished to the Void. I, am what you see now."

The emergence of Baphomet's story seemed to bring small relief to the creature. He had been in the Void for the equivalent of just five human years, and yet it had changed him, altered him. He was now constructed from the darkness, and whilst a potential servant, he was now too weak to be a threat to Gabriel.

"Very well Baphomet, you shall serve at my side. We will take this place and return Hell to all of its glory. And then? We shall take Earth."

34

The Islands were certainly a busy place, and Josh thought back to a scene from an *Assassin's Creed* video game where he had boarded a similar ship. Whilst he now knew his time on Earth had been very short, he still thought fondly of the distractions it had provided. As he watched Iona, Valdore, Tommy, Nybor and the others load the vessels with supplies, he thought back to the destruction of the gateway right at the start of his journey, and how it likely meant he would never be able to return to Earth, whatever the outcome here. He knew of Kathryn Silverton, and the others, but he had only recently learned they were his true family. The concept of the time difference still did little to assuage his confusion. What would they do if he knew he had been in Wealdstone this whole time? If he had known they were truly his parents, would he have in fact gone back at all? After all, he had only found out about Earth's existence by mistake. He travelled there out of curiosity, and as he now knew, with false memories. They had certainly felt real.

The levels of confusion, deceit and effort that had gone into rewriting who he was not once, but twice, had him concerned. He looked around at his new allies, his mothers who had raised him, and while he knew he was in safe company, he could not help but feel an uneasiness. He had fallen for the Queen of Hell. No amount of comic book storylines could have prepared him for that realisation. He placed his left palm onto a nearby plant, and watched it wilt as he drew its electrical life force, and then he conjured a dagger into his right. Whilst he had been taught how to reconstitute electricity or life force into physical objects, he still did not know how this ability managed to create mass from current. Only that he could do it. And that he was human. A child of two homes, the best of both worlds, surely? And yet in a matter of hours, he may be left with no home at all. The idea of living in Hell, ruled by a demonic fallen angel with his own ironic God complex, did not appeal. And of course, if Gabriel won, he would go after Earth next.

Tommy sauntered over to him, and tapped him on the shoulder.

"You okay there, Josh?" he asked as reassuringly as he could.

Josh simply nodded, and twirled the dagger around in his hands. It was an unusual creation. The blade was ice white, and the wider part of the blade was matched by the top of the handle, which then narrowed to the same width as the tip of the blade at the opposite end. The handle itself was a blend of deep purple and a white stripe. It was a design Josh had seen in an army surplus shop window one night was he was walking home. Given his agility training and the top up lessons he had received from Manor as the moved from the Forest of Music to the shoreline, and on the brief crossing to the Islands, he figured he should have a close quarters weapon that allowed him to utilise it.

"Just trying to figure out which realm I actually belong in. Beyond, Earth, and I suppose technically Beyond is two realms if you count Hell. Just feels weird that in a few hours, if we survive but lose, we could literally be in Hell. Does that make sense?"

"Nope. Not one bit. Not even slightly."

Chapter 34

The pair of them shared a laugh to mask the fear they were both feeling. In truth, Tommy wasn't sure how this was going to play out either. Unlike Josh, he no longer had the option of simply walking back into Earth. Being gifted the powers of the White Falcons meant he was tied to the realm forever. Although not being as he put it, one of the OG angels, he wasn't sure what being present in any version of Hell would mean for him either. Tommy had spent so long in Beyond, that he knew nothing else. And that was what he was going to fight for. But he still wasn't sure that he *belonged* here. Even now. Similarly to Josh, he felt somewhat displaced.

"When you came here, did you ever feel like you'd wanna go back?" Josh asked him.

"For a very short period of time. I was on my way back to the gateway, and this whole place felt like a fever dream. Knowing what I would be going back to, however much of this wonky time had passed."

Josh could not help but laugh at the phrase 'wonky time' because that's exactly what it felt like. One moment they were being told twenty years had passed in a matter of days, then it was a few years had passed in the space of a week. Josh's mind floated back to *Doctor Who* and mentions of 'timey-wimey stuff.'

"So why didn't you?" Josh prodded.

"When I'd saved those people from being robbed, people here looked at me like I was some kind of hero. That I mattered, and I had a purpose here. Back in Wealdstone, I had nothing and nobody. Just a nutjob trying to bring down every realm in existence. The choice kinda made itself."

Josh understood. He had often felt out of place in Wealdstone. He had his minor friendship with Chantel and Dalton, but in reality that was all he had. Even his house was rented. The only thing that was truly his, was his comic book. And even that turned out to be memories of his abilities trying to poke their way through the mind-block. Here, he felt different. He had people around him, caring for him, fighting for him. And they wanted him to be a part of this place. Right then, both Josh and Tommy nodded at each other, as they realised that this was a fight worth winning.

Tommy reached down and helped Josh to his feet, and together they climbed onto Valdore's flagship, Iona close behind, and began the crossing to The Void.

35

There was still very much an elephant in the room, albeit that the room was a huge pirate ship. Nybor paced along the deck by the wheel behind Valdore back and forth. The elephant in question, of course, was just how they were going to win this battle. Nobody had asked questions thus far, which staggered Nybor to her very core, but Iona had tried to tell her that it was because of the affection and loyalty her comrades had for her. Despite being a statement of warmth towards a friend, Nybor had felt a huge package of guilt land on her shoulders from that, as it reminded her that it was loyalty and love that got her into this mess in the first place.

"I would prefer it if you didn't try and wear out my floor before we get there."

Valdore's silky smooth voice penetrated right through Nybor's all consuming thoughts. Valdore was born purely of Beyond. She had not known the days before, neither had Iona. There was something to be said about the female creatures and beings of this new paradise she had attempted to create. They were far more stoic and stronger than their male counterparts. This was not a commentary on all males, but throughout the history of Beyond, however long that had now been, it had been the men who had waged the wars and started the battles, and sought out glory.

"Sorry, I just cannot seem to fathom why you are all following me when I haven't even told you how we are going to win this battle."

Valdore flickered her fingers over the oak-like wood of the ship's wheel and strands of electricity wrapped around the spokes, and began steering the ship as Valdore stepped away.

"Iona tried to tell you why. What you created here came at great cost to not just you, but all those who remained afterward. It is our home. Without you, Nybor, we would not have even been born. We are of Beyond, and it is a part of us. If we do not fight for it, then who will?"

Nybor had not thought of it like that before. She felt the guilt for commanding people to their potential demise, but had not even considered the fact that Beyond was what they were actually fighting for. Not her. This was their home.

"There are few things in life worth truly fighting for. One of them is love. One is your home."

A raised eyebrow from Valdore elicited elaboration from Nybor.

"Something my adoptive father said to me just before the Yellow Demon and Blue Spirit War. I often think that was the last shred of the true Dorn that I ever saw. But he was right."

She reached up and touched her necklace once more. Valdore looked at it, and smiled before looking back up to meet Nybor's gaze.

"So have you told them what that thing actually does yet, or is it just me that knows about the mind-bending power of that thing?"

Nybor smiled in a way that answered the question without saying a word. Valdore nodded, and a wry smile crept over her own face.

Chapter 35

"Just me then," she whispered. "You know you always said that you felt silly creating something for a worst case scenario. You never felt truly comfortable here did you?"

Nybor shook her head.

"I was one of the few who knew the true cost of getting this world into existence. I had to have a failsafe, a contingency. It would not have been possible to contain such power without your help Valdore."

"Well if anything, it proves you were right. We need that pendant now more than ever. But are you prepared to unleash it? For people to look at you in your true form?"

Nybor had considered that at length. The guise she and the other White Falcons now donned was of course an idyllic cover. Whilst the only true remaining angels currently in Beyond were Nybor and Gabriel, the transfer of her powers to create the Falcons gave them the same true appearance. How would they react when this change occurred in battle?

"Perhaps I should speak to them to prepare them for what will happen once the battle begins."

"A wise choice. We only have two hours before we make land, and it would not help us if we were fighting our own surprises as well as an immortal enemy."

Nybor gave her friend a warm hug, and walked down the steep wooden steps to the main deck area. The others saw her approach and moved towards her. She held up a hand to stop their advance, and kept a good distance.

"It is time I told you how this is going to work. Everything I am about to tell you is our key to winning this battle, and we need a contingency ready to go. We have two hours, so listen very carefully."

36

The stench of the burning bodies beneath his feet had not wavered his feelings of immense power or superiority at all, however Chan's inability to take down the White Falcons had certainly angered him greatly. There had been direct orders from Largox to burn the Shadowlands to a crisp and then head for the Fifth Kingdom, but Chan had decided he had no intentions of obeying yet another constraint on his development. He stepped over the charred remains of dozens of Changelings, witches, and even a stray White Falcon who had come looking for Nybor. As the flames encompassing his entire body subsided, he heard laboured breathing coming from just in front of him somewhere. As he approached, he saw the charred legs of the strongest fighter of the group he had just incinerated. Spiner was trying to drag himself to the nearest pile of rocks. He was not done yet. At least, that's what he thought.

Chan watched on as Spiner's left hand tried to morph into come kind of extended animal limb to reach the rocks faster. His thought process was clearly impaired, the blood covering his face, and the burns over his other arm rendered him virtually disabled.

Chan stopped and watched as the metamorphosis failed to take hold, and his victim screamed as loud as he could, before collapsing onto his back. He raised his head slightly, and looked Chan directly in the eyes.

"Largox won't win this war, Fire Demon. You're just cannon fodder to him!"

Spiner spat all the saliva he could muster at Chan's feet, which sizzled the liquid away in less than a second leaving just a tiny white mark. He knelt down in front of Spiner, showing no emotion other than rage.

"I am not Largox's puppet, or anybody else's. I abandoned the notion of living under anyone else's rule the second these dormant powers came to me. And if I have to take down the entire realm to come out of this free, then so be it."

Spiner's face filled with fear, as he realised that Chan had given him the unfiltered truth. He was genuinely insane. Nybor had stunted his development, and this being was not about to allow Largox to do the same thing. The last thing the Changeling known as Spiner ever saw, was a double stream of red flame burst forth from Chan's eyes as his skin sizzled and he melted away into nothingness.

37

The vibrations of each boat beaching on the shore amassed until the combined sensation rippled through the ground to Gabriel's feet. Having swallowed the Fifth Kingdom entirely, buildings, fortifications and all, he had watched the ships arrive from a short distance away, and had carefully counted the number of the fleet. There were forty-eight vessels in total. He needed only one. His new pet demon Baphomet had attempted to race to the vessels before being sent to do so. Gabriel had sliced his demon throat open from ear to ear in response.

"No creature of the Void is indispensable. You will all obey me, or face my wrath. This is NOT a democracy!"

Gabriel had made a scene of the execution, ensuring the White Falcon blade was super heated, and he leaned Baphomet's body towards the others so they could watch his ink-like blood pour out of the open wound, before his entire being dissolved into ash. The misconception that demons could not be killed was a human invention, designed to invoke fear in those who sought them out. Demons could in fact be killed. With the right weapon. No other demons dared make their own choices after that display. A couple did ask their Dark Lord why they were waiting rather than attacking them at sea.

"Their most powerful allies and weapons are on those ships. Once they are all ashore, we will wipe them from existence all at once. After that, Hell is ours."

That seemed to keep the demons in line, and they were satisfied with the logic of that notion. Gabriel, however was still hiding a fact. Whilst they were now incredibly powerful, they still required a physical ship to traverse the ocean. While the Void had indeed been breached, it still stood tall. Eons worth of evil and darkness were still contained inside, the crack not large enough to accommodate their exit. Besides, there was another problem. The creature that Gabriel was now inhabiting was resisting him. He thought LeVar long dead, and yet for whatever reason, Gabriel was unable to unfurl LeVar's wings to take flight. If he had the entire contents of the Void at his disposal, he would have been able to manifest in his own body once again, but that was not currently an option. No. He had one petty requirement to win this battle that his egotistical self would not allow to pass.

He intended to tear Nybor's wings from her back, peg her to the ground, and make her watch while he killed everyone she ever cared about. And then, and only then, would he use her mangled corpse to break open the Void, and destroy it. That would prove to their father that he was worthy.

38

    Roars from the pirate crews echoed for miles along the shoreline of the Fifth Kingdom as they disembarked the row boats and charged towards the rippling black mass that was the demons and the very essence of evil in physical form. Nybor led the charge overhead with Manor and the other White Falcons, Tommy choosing to remain on the ground unless absolutely necessary. He had not had time to practice his flight and therefore they chose to negate any risk. He led the ground troops alongside Valdore, with Iona far out in front jumping in enormous bounds covering a hundred yards in seconds.

    Her weapon of choice was a double ended weapon constructed of a spiked boulder at each end of a thick chain. The weapon, however, was constructed of pure energy, rendering it virtually indestructible. It had been another one of Valdore's magical creations. Josh, remained on board the flagship for the time being. According to Nybor, he was a crucial part to the success of their plan, and they needed him to remain on board. Nybor suspected Gabriel was not yet as powerful as he would like to be, making now the opportune moment for attack.

Nybor and the Falcons dived from above, sending blasts of hot white energy directly through the centre of the mass, cutting a swathe through the middle, before moving around for another pass. The tactic allowed Iona to burst through the front line, and swing her weapon through the demon flesh from within their lines. The gap in the middle of the crowd began to increase in a circular pattern. Each time the demons attempted to close her down, another barrage of fire would come from above. Moments later, the pirate crews advanced on the front lines that remained on either side. Some of the enemy had turned their backs on them to try and take down Iona, but she was fierce and holding her own, and now Valdore and Tommy were leading the battle on opposite sides of the middle space. As Nybor made her fourth pass, she scanned the scene below, but saw no sign of Gabriel. There was no possibility that they could have been late. She was certain of it. Well, almost certain. She shouted commands to Manor and the others to continue the barrage from above for three more passes, and she broke off from the formation to fly and inspect the Void.

The ruined and blackened walls of the Fifth Kingdom almost broke her heart. These had been good people. Their only crime was living on the poverty line. She thought back to the young boy, Berg and how when he lost his friend Petri, he thought at least he had made it. At least he would live. She suspected a small section of the billowing ash below was whatever was left of the young boy. Her blood ran cold at the thought.

Approaching the barrier of the Void, she gasped and slowly lowered herself to the ground. As her feet moved forward, the grass crunched beneath her, and although blackened, it crunched with consistency of ice. However, she was not interested in the texture or feel of the ground on which she was walking. She was staring not into a crack, but a chasm.

The barrier was now inert, and translucent. There appeared to

Chapter 38

be no black shadows beyond it, and no activity within the Void at all. Nybor stopped about thirty feet away from it, unsure what to do next.

"I always thought it would be me to kill you, little sister."

The raspy, deep voice froze Nybor in place. She slowly turned her head to her right where, propped up against a large mound of disturbed earth, was the mangled body of LeVar. The voice, however, was Gabriel's.

"Oh come now, Lucifer. Don't tell me you're sad to see me like this?" Gabriel spoke, albeit through laboured breaths. "Did you not regret leaving me alive all these centuries?"

Nybor found it within herself to move towards him, but stopped again when she saw the wound which was claiming his life. Seeing her reaction, Gabriel's gaze followed her own, and together they surveyed the entirely hollow hole in his chest. The edges were still glowing, some of the skin bubbling from the immense heat, and it was clear now that it was only Gabriel's power which now kept him alive.

"Who did this to you?" she asked in a whisper.

She was unsure how to feel. Yes, this was her brother, but she had long moved past the family connections and was definitive in her need to stop Gabriel. But the part that was snagging on her emotions, was the fact that he had used her friend, her trusted number one to attempt this invasion. And now they were both dying. But the response Gabriel gave was not the one she expected.

"Of all people, it was a small boy. Me, the great fallen angel Gabriel with all the power of the Void behind me, and I was taken down by a teenager. The shame of that alone should have killed me."

Teenager? Fire. Burning flesh. No, it couldn't possibly be. If she ever needed more confirmation, it came with Gabriel's next words.

235

"I was luckier than your mage friend over there. Not much left of him."

Nybor's head snapped round and she placed a hand over her mouth as her eyes fell upon the severed head of Largox, resting on the dirt ground, blood soaked into the black earth, the flesh around his neck crisp and bubbled in much the same way as Gabriel's chest cavity. His eyes were dark, mouth slightly agape. She suspected it was the element of surprise. Largox had been the most powerful mage she had ever witnessed, and Gabriel one of the original creations. This wasn't possible. Seemingly reading her mind, Gabriel interjected.

"Oh but it is."

She snapped her head away from the sight of Largox's head and back to her brother.

"I had hoped you'd arrive in time to save me, but I guess now you'll just have to save yourself."

"He couldn't have done this. Not him. Not Chan."

"As I said Lucifer, he did. Your little protégé I believe it was he said to me after he burned a whole through my torso. Wonderful little prodigy you have there. Couldn't have done it better myself. Never would have imagined a being so powerful that he could burn the Void itself. Had my minions not already found their way to the beach, there'd be nothing left."

Nybor couldn't process this. It was too much information, and it had shot her plan to pieces. There was no processing this. The very essence of Hell was gone, and it would not return. There was nothing to return it *with*. But Chan? How did he get here? How did he rediscover his powers? How powerful *was* he? Gabriel began coughing, his spiritual energy apparently dissipating.

"Tell me sister, what is he? What lies did you feed him? Was he one of the originals like us, or was he a creation of this... Beyond? Best be honest with your answers little one, before I leave you all alone."

Chapter 38

Nybor grasped her necklace, feeling now more than ever as if she should unleash it, but she resisted as she finally revealed the last truth that she had kept hidden from everyone. The truth that she had never dared speak before. And she suspected the truth which would kill them all.

"He's my son."

39

Iona was not tiring in any way. She continued slinging her energy mace around with devastating force. Her shoes were now squelching in the ink well of the demon blood, and her face was spattered with each impact. Valdore was leaping from target to target on their own shoulders, such was her agility, and burying beams of lightning through their skulls. Tommy had begun to get overwhelmed, but the correct time had come for him to learn how to unfurl his vast wingspan on command, and each time it sent dozens of demons hurtling back or through the air into the waiting weaponry of the pirate crowd. Despite their initial success, the swell of the demon horde was still growing. Each enemy that was not slain in its entirety would then rise up once more, fully rejuvenated from the blood of their kin. And despite the notoriety which followed the pirates around the realm, their actual fighting skills left something to be desired. Several of them swung their blades too late, or caught an arm instead of a head, only to then be cut down by the darkness. It was a scene being played out at distance to Josh as he paced the ship much like Nybor had done hours earlier. She was meant to have put her plan into action by now. Where was she?

He was also wondering when they would have to face the likes of Largox and King Eralf. The dread of their arrival knocked his anxiety up another gear. He of course, did not know that they were already dead. Josh could not do this for too much longer. He remembered his abilities, had retrained some of his skills, and he needed to help his colleagues. If he did not see some kind of improvement soon, he would have no choice but to join the battle.

Almost as if on cue, Josh watched on, a smile spreading across his face as a mystified look came over the demon forces advancing further down the beach. They were sent sprawling in all directions, inky blood spattering through the sky, as some unseen force began carving a path through their number. Despite their viciousness, demons were not stupid and valued self preservation. Several dozen of them began to break away from the invisible attacker, and attempt to target the others instead, but then pulses of energy blasted from out of thin air, striking several demonic heads clean from their bodies. A momentary glitch saw a shining figure appear, before the cloaking shroud failed, and Syl'Va was revealed in all his Deltarian glory. His enormous diamond encrusted figure battered through the crowds of menace as if he were a bowling ball and they were the pins. Creatures scattered left and right, Syl'Va almost relishing the return to battle that he had missed since his days in the Deltarian military. He soon thinned out the masses surrounding him, and turned towards the initial attack. Raising his weapon, his fired a shot at the crowd. A demon's entire form exploded upon contact.

"Surely it can't be this easy?" Syl'Va asked himself.

He had good reason to wonder, as he had yet to see signs of a resistance capable of threatening their prowess. In fact, he was fairly certain that he could wipe these demons out single handedly, should it come to it. They were apparently no match for futuristic

Chapter 39

technology. At least that's what he thought. The demons had begun to catch on to his advantage, and several of them had created a line on a nearby dune, launching rocks at the weapon he carried. As one struck the power cell in the Beresian Disruptor he carried, it exploded, sending the weapon shattering into pieces and Syl'Va several feet back, suffering from facial burns. As he landed heavily on the sand, the demons with the rocks swarmed him. It was similar to watching water washing over rocks. A plague of demonic entities consumed Syl'Va's entire form, and every punch he threw caused apparent splashes in the maelstrom.

The other demons that were previously being kept occupied by Valdore, Iona, Tommy and the others, were also becoming smarter, more agile, more deadly in their attacks. Manor and the other Falcons gave up their aerial attacks, now unable to get clear shots from above, and began attempting to blast away the perimeters. In truth, from above it had looked like a blob of black ink beginning to spread over a white sheet of paper.

Back on the flagship, which Josh had noted was named after him, he watched as his friends began to fall against the immense forces overwhelming them. Where was Nybor? Where for that matter was Gabriel?

GABRIEL!

Josh now feared that Nybor had been cornered by her brother, and every fibre of his being began to consume him with urgency, and he searched the whole deck looking for some kind of power source he could draw from. Nothing below deck, and nothing at the stern. He was about to run back up to check the bow, when two feet appeared in his eyeline. As he rose the few steps to the ship's wheel, his eyes rose up the person in turn. Burned clothing, and blood spatters came into view, until he was stood level with a very beleaguered and injured Braddock.

"What the fuck! Are you alright?" Josh blurted out.

Braddock coughed and blood trickled down her mouth. Beside

her, Josh noticed a faint ripple in the air as the remnants of a quickly created portal vanished. Braddock lurched forward, and Josh was just able to catch her in time.

"Joshua, you must reach Nybor," she whispered, each breath causing her distinct pain.

"Yes, that's exactly what I was planning on doing! Gabriel must have her-"

"NO!" she bellowed at the expense of a huge amount of her remaining energy. "The boy! The one she trains! It is he who destroyed the Shadowlands, not the mage!"

Josh's eyes flicked back and forth trying to find some memory of who she might be talking about. And then he recalled Chantel telling him the details of the Crossroads incident. When they took on Monarch, Nybor was assisted by Annie, the Blue Spirit, a collection of Pain Wraiths, the Silverton team... and a boy! Chan!

"Chan? You mean, the kid who helped her in Wealdstone?"

Braddock nodded, and then she grabbed Josh's hands and thrust them over her heart and pushed them against her chest.

"Take it, Joshua. Take it before it fades and it's too late!"

Josh was confused.

"Take what? What do you mean?"

She pressed his hands against her harder this time.

"My life force! Take it and use its power to defeat the boy!"

Josh shook his head frantically, and tried to pull his hands away, but Braddock held firm.

"If you don't absorb my life force, it will dissipate into nothingness. I'm dying anyway. Help me find peace rather than die in pain. Please!"

Josh stopped his attempts to get away when he saw the tears amassing in her eyes. She was pleading with him to help her die peacefully. He felt his own tears welling up as he nodded in acceptance. He had barely known this woman, and they had only spent minimal time together, and yet she was dear to him.

Chapter 39

Everyone here was, and if he could help her pass without pain and save his friends, then he had no choice. As he stopped resisting and placed his hands back on Braddock's chest, they began to glow. This was different to the lightning effects that he had previously known. His hands were beginning to become beacons of light as energy moved from Braddock's body up along his arms until it reached his head. The curls of his beard and his wispy hair began fluttering as if caught in a breeze, and he closed his eyes with contentment. He had never experienced such a feeling. It was as if he was being warmed from the exchange, like a comfort blanket was being wrapped around him. When the glow finally ceased, he opened his eyes, and looked down. Braddock was now limp in his arms, but had her eyes closed and a thin smile on her lips. She was at peace now. Josh carefully laid her on the deck, and stood looking over the water to the beach where he now struggled to see any sign of his friends.

He took a deep breath, crouched, and launched into the air, the newfound power within him acting like some mystical rocket booster. As he soared through the air, he could not help but giggle at the irony of *Doctor Strange* being his favourite superhero, but currently resembling *Iron Man*. He narrowed his flight path, and as he approached the beach at high speed he thrust his hands forwards and sent both beams and sparks into the centre of the black mass, blowing hundreds of demons apart, gliding like a knife through butter. Iona was the first to emerge into the open, and Josh landed beside her, still glowing.

She smiled adoringly at her adopted son, and then they turned back to back and began firing energy blasts, flames, and weapon strikes at anything that moved. They shuffled their feet in tandem, always keeping pressed against each other, allowing the demons to come to them. As another section was cleared by Josh, Valdore rose above a small group, battered and her fur matted with ink blood, but with a newfound sense of determination. She smiled at her family wielding powers galore, and found another level herself. One by one, their allies were pulled from under the heaving mass of oily darkness until they were all standing centralised in the middle of the attack, each sending beams of energy against the evil. Josh became overwhelmed with joy. He was of course living his literal superhero team up moment. But then his smile faded. Nybor. He had been so entranced by his increased power levels, he had forgotten why he took the extra energy in the first place.

"Mother!" he shouted to Iona. "I have to go and find Nybor!"

Iona nodded and Valdore joined her side.

"Go get her son."

40

Nybor sat slumped on the ground staring at the now lifeless body of her brother. Her confession had been the last thing she had said to him, and now as she watched, his form began to fall into golden ash. She mourned for him, despite everything. She mourned for LeVar who she had also lost today. But now she must face the task no parent ever should. She must kill her son.

Chan was not her son as the result of a marriage or demonic one night stand, of course. He was as Lucy was, created directly from her. He was the creature that humanity labelled The Devil. The common misconception was that Lucifer and The Devil were the same person. Such ignorance and whispers through time caused inconsistency throughout myth and history. She created Lucy to have a normal life outside of Hell. She chose to create Chan as a way of having an heir of sorts. However, in her efforts to pass over some of her soul and personality to her son, he took the dark and vengeful parts of her psyche along with her rage. It consumed him to the point where she was forced to cast him into the River Styx. She had thought him lost, until one night when she was still a Green Dragon in her youth, or perceived youth, he had manifested outside the castle, flames and all. Shocked, she had concealed him, and used all of her knowledge to suppress his abilities.

He had no memory of who he was, or where he had come from. She had been unsure of whether that was a side effect of creating Beyond, as it had been with most of the others, or if it was her casting him into eternal damnation. Either way, deciding he could never know his true self, she gave him the identity and memories of a simple apprentice sorcerer, and tutored him to draw on the good rather than the negative. The day at Crossroads when he rediscovered his so-called Fire Demon heritage, she feared that her efforts had failed. Thankfully that was not the case, and she had been trying to prevent him from calling upon those powers again ever since.

Nybor had not travelled to Earth when Lucy had died. She knew her daughter was gone. There was an invisible tether between the two even though the child did not know it was there. She could not bring herself to see the broken and battered body of her daughter buried beneath the concrete of some dilapidated asylum. She had failed in all aspects as a mother to her children. But then again, she had been naïve and egotistical to try and create them in her own image. They had been given no say in their lives or their existence, she had pre-planned all of these things out. She had been no better than her father. No more. She would correct this mistake. She would not kill Chan, she would save him. She could fix this.

Josh landed beside her with a thud, just in time to see the last remnants of Gabriel floating away in the breeze. He scouted the area and saw Largox's severed head still where it had fallen. He grabbed Nybor by the shoulders and looked her dead in the eyes.

"Are you okay? Gabriel? Where is Chan?"

This surprised Nybor.

"You know about him?" she asked.

Chapter 40

Josh nodded, but of course did not know the truth about who he was, only that he was the real threat.

"Where is he?" Josh asked, his voice becoming more panicked with every breath.

Nybor shook her head as she spoke.

"I... I... I don't know, he was here, but-"

Their brief conversation was cut off by a distant explosion. The size and enormity of the blast was so immense that the mushroom cloud of smoke could be seen from the edge of the Void. Seconds later, millions of screams could be heard on the wind. Any colour remaining in Josh and Nybor's faces drained away instantly. They each turned to face one another, before both leaping into the air once more, flying until they were once again on the beach, where they found Valdore and Manor slaying the last of the demons. But all other eyes were fixed on the sight across the other side of the narrow sea.

"The Fourth Kingdom," Iona announced, confirming what Nybor and Josh had feared. "It's... gone."

"Oh my god."

"It was all a distraction."

"No this can't be right!"

The various voices of the group landed on the horror of the truth. All of this, the Void, Gabriel, Largox, Eralf, it had all been a distraction. Chan had been the true danger all along. But the horror was not done yet. Just moments later, a second explosion rocked the horizon. This one was much larger, and was accompanied by smaller secondary explosions. From the shoreline, Beyond was a straight line to the naked eye, and despite not being able to see the actual kingdoms or buildings, everyone knew.

The Third Kingdom was under attack.

"We... we have to get over there, we have to do something!"

Valdore was now borderline hysterical. The air was consumed by distant screams and cries of help that were simply too far away.

247

Iona was trying to comfort her, but in truth, she too was trying to stop herself from launching into the ocean, swimming it if necessary to reach the people being slaughtered.

Another explosion.

The Second Kingdom was gone.

Nybor collapsed onto the ground. Josh staggered forward a few steps, but he too fell to his knees. Nybor's head was swimming, the ground was moving, and the sky was spinning so fast she couldn't get a grip on her own reality anymore. All of the feelings of hurt, guilt, betrayal, the lies, and the questions burning her up from the inside. How was Chan doing this? How was he moving so quickly between kingdoms? How was he able to destroy entire kingdoms in a matter of minutes. And then it dawned on her. She had been fighting to save Beyond from being consumed by Hell once again. And in the process, she had lost it anyway. Every kingdom in Beyond was burning. Everyone was dead or dying. Everyone except those in the First Kingdom. She had started to cringe in expectance of the final explosion that would consume her home, but it never came. A thought that Tommy seemed to notice too.

"Why hasn't he attacked the First?"

"Nybor?" Valdore asked as she turned to face her friend. "Could he know? Is that possible?"

The others looked confused, and were still trying to process the grief and scenes on display before them. Their minds were each like a picture reel running on full speed, all the images blurring into one another. But Nybor knew why Chan had stopped at the First Kingdom. It was not to sit on the throne and claim the land for his own. The throne had no power outside of Hell's domain, and Chan had made sure that was never going to be a possibility again.

No.

Chan had stopped at the First Kingdom for a reason. Nybor found her words.

Chapter 40

"If he remembers who he is... who he *truly* is... he knows."

Josh was the next to speak.

"What do you mean, who he truly is? Who is he, Nybor? Please tell me there isn't another secret you've hidden from me?"

Nybor refused to look Josh or anyone else in the eyes. The shame was too much. This was it. The moment everyone turned on her. She had expected it to come much sooner, many millennia ago. But here they were. There was no running, no hiding, no more lying. The truth was now all that was left. She dragged herself to her feet, the toe of her boots dug into the sand, and she almost stumbled, but Josh caught her arm. She reached up and tugged the pendant from her necklace, snapping the chain holding it, the individual links cascading down her front and disappearing into the sand below. Her voice began muttering an ancient language unknown to any of the others, except Valdore. She closed her eyes, and gripped Iona's arms. Then, with one swift movement, Nybor threw the pendant into the air, and blasted a concentrated beam of white light directly at the centre with her staff. The jewel shattered into millions of tiny pieces, but they hung in the air like asteroids in the vastness of space. The individual shards began to vibrate, and a red light began to glow in the centre of them, as if the pieces were pulsing to the rhythm of a heart.

BOOM!

The pieces burst, each one turning into dust, expanding as it did so until it became invisible, so minute that it was undetectable to the naked eye. A red glow bathed everyone but was of such intensity that they all had to slam their eyes shut. When the light vanished, and they opened their eyes, the truth had been revealed. Nybor was now no longer the white of a White Falcon. Her feathered wings were black as the night itself, her skin an off white, two small horns protruded from her forehead, and her attire was a mixture of black and blood red cloth. Her staff was also now gone, replaced with a long silver blade, with a blackened bone handle, and a red jewel at the base. Each of the White Falcons now sported a similar appearance. Black wings, matching attire, horns, and a pale complexion. The only difference was they all appeared more muscular, and their cloaks were red with black detailing as opposed to Nybor's which was the other way around. Valdore and Iona were unchanged in appearance, as were many of the remaining pirates, as they were creatures of Beyond, not Hell. And Josh too, remained unchanged in physical appearance, although his clothing had altered to a more typical Earth look, his clothes of Beyond now gone. Nybor, now once more in her true form of Lucifer, Queen of Hell strode forward to stand at the edge of the water. She addressed them all without turning back to look at any of them. She couldn't. The pain was too much.

"Chan is not his real name. His true name is Mammon. He is my son. The Devil, as humans call him. I created him to be my heir. When he tried to kill me and those I held dear, I cast him into oblivion. But he reappeared here, and I gave him false memories. There is no such thing as a Fire Demon."

The look of abject horror on everyone's faces was almost identical. None of them could believe what they were hearing. But the final nail in the proverbial coffin was yet to come.

"And the reason he has stopped at the First Kingdom... is because there's a hidden gateway in the depths of the castle. A gateway... to Earth."

EPILOGUE

The cut above Grace's left eye was stinging, but it was a mild affliction considering the pain she had just dished out to her opponent. Christian Verne's alter ego was now a battered heap on the floor of the warehouse, whining like an injured child. On the other side of the room, Beth was now pulling herself to her feet, having been thrown across the room by Hyde in the initial attack. She staggered over to her father, who was beaten, but still alive, and tied to a table. Thankfully, they had gotten to him before Hyde had managed to do any experiments on him. But while Hyde was the tool, he was not the instigator of this kidnapping.

Beth's father had been taken as an incentive for her to do the bidding of a more powerful enemy. Someone who had been tracking down those suspected of having supernatural powers, abilities that could be of use. Until now, they had suspected that person to be Hyde, or his human counterpart, the former Henry Jekyll, now Christian Verne. But now they knew the truth. After confiding everything to Grace, Beth Ford and her friend were now trying to track down the kingpin behind all this. Their searches had led to a warehouse thirty miles outside of Trinity Bay.

Above them, on a mezzanine level, was an office. From inside that office, there was a dim purple glow. Grace nodded at Beth, and she returned the gesture. Grace gave one final swift kick to Hyde's head, and he slumped into unconsciousness. His enhanced form had been a tough match for that of Grace's wolf-vampire genetics, but he had seemed distracted and not really in the fight. More indications he wasn't the one in charge here.

As the two of them gradually climbed the rickety staircase on the far wall, both with altered weapons drawn, they reached the doorway. The door itself was open, and Beth stepped through first. As she did so, Grace followed in behind and made an audible gasp. Against her better judgement, she clasped a hand across her mouth. Sat in a swivel chair, hunched over the desk, surrounded in a fading purple halo of light, was Kimberley.

Her face was ragged, and aged, and her facial features seemed to be blurring in and out of reality, almost as if they were phasing. Beth had only heard about the Pain Wraiths recently, but even she knew who Kimberley was. Grace and the others had thought her lost when she was blasted near to one of the gathered doorways at Crossroads. However, she had spent the next couple of years phasing between realities, becoming weaker and weaker. Yet now, here she was.

"I suppose you're surprised to see me?" she whispered through lips which did not quite part enough to speak without a lisp.

"You could say that, Kim." Grace's reply was curt and to the point. "So you gonna tell me why you've been hunting these... specials down? Why you're so interested in Kristin?"

Kimberley attempted a laugh, but it came out as more of a choking sound. Her face glitched again, and seemed to age another few years in that moment before she spoke again.

"The incident at Crossroads destabilised my very existence. I glitched from one world to the next, one realm to the next,

Epilogue

weakening more and more, until I landed in a heap in the middle of the road out there!"

She gestured vaguely out of the window towards the main road, before continuing.

"I came across Christian's research, saw he had been keeping an eye on some unique individuals, some of whom you and your friends had already run into. He seemed to be getting to them too late, and spent too long observing them before they either died or vanished. So last year, I decided to take over the operation. I found Kristin, and I learned about what had happened to her. I knew I could find a way to take the Pain Wraith energy from her, and use it to restore me. I had to kill quite a respectable power in the police to get the release order authorised. Pah. Not that anybody actually did anything with it. Christian fucked it up. Beth fucked it up. And now here I am... dying."

Kimberley coughed so much that her entire body momentarily vanished, before returning, again, several years older.

"But it doesn't matter. I was coming for her. But now she's coming for you."

The forced laugh emanating from Kimberley was almost as blood curdling as a scream, and as it intensified, Kimberley's purple glow flickered and dimmed to almost nothing, and then just like that, she was gone.

"What does she mean, Kristin is coming for us?" Beth asked, a new level of fear ignited.

"Something happened to her in the Realm of Screams. As you know, she's... different now. She's... more."

"Yeah, fucking wonderful. Can this place go five minutes without having some world-ending, apocalypse starting, cataclysmic event?!"

Grace was about to answer that very question, when they heard a car horn beep from outside the building. Rushing back down the stairs, and out the main doors, they found Chantel honking the horn of their car as quickly as she could, Beth's father tucked in the back seat.

"What is it?" Grace shouted to her.

Chantel was simply pointing frantically behind them. As they turned around, they saw a familiar sight. One Grace had hoped to never see again. A thin green outline, shaped like a doorway began to glow in the middle of the street. This one was different, however. At points in the green silhouette, there were traces of ornate decoration, such as you would find on a Victorian picture frame. Grace stepped back and gestured for Beth to do the same.

"Run."

"What?" Beth asked.

"RUN!"

The two of them yanked open the car doors, and dove inside, as Chantel cranked the engine into life, and reversed at high speed. She flipped the car into a J-turn and slammed her foot down on the accelerator, hard. In the rear view mirror, Grace saw a figure emerge from the doorway. A figure she recognised.

"Stop the car," she said softly, coupling it with a hand on Chantel's shoulder.

She did as was asked, and they all got out of the car again. Slowly, Grace began to walk towards him.

"Chan?" she asked cautiously. "Is that you?"

Fire burned in his eyes, and he gritted his teeth tightly. Without warning, a barrage of flames thrust itself forward and hit the car, blowing the vehicle apart with an incredible force. All four previous passengers were launched in opposite directions, the sound of metal piercing flesh the only discernible sound amongst the destruction of the strike.

Striding forward, the now fully aware son of Lucifer marched down the road, oblivious of the destruction he had just caused. He did not find Grace or Chantel, but he did come across two other people. Beth Ford was propped up against the side of the

Epilogue

warehouse. A large piece of sheared metal had punctured her stomach, and was protruding from her back, her shirt soaked with blood, and the same liquid pouring from her mouth. She was barely conscious. Beside her, she was unaware that her father was already dead.

"Y…you… you're a good guy… Chan?"

The fire returned in the eyes of the man.

"My name is Mammon."

With a flick of his wrist, the flames burst forth again, and incinerated what remained of Beth Ford and her father, leaving only scorched outlines of their bodies. He continued to march away, his eyes set on a target that he knew would hurt his mother even more. She had a distinct fondness for the humans, several in particular. He would burn them to pieces and turn them to ash before he set this world on fire. As he disappeared into the distance, Chantel and Grace dragged themselves up to the top of the embankment they had been thrown down. Neither of them had life threatening injuries, but both would need medical treatment. Grace flipped out her phone, and punched in a number.

"Hello? Grace is that you?"

"Annie, we have a problem. Chan, he's here, he's gone rogue. We need help."

"Fuck. His Fire Demon abilities. I can get the next flight back from Montana."

"Annie? One more thing."

"What is it?"

"Chan isn't the only problem. Bring Kathryn and Jack back with you."

"But I don't know where they are, they're in hiding!"

"Then fucking find them! We're gonna need all the help we can get."

ADDITIONAL CONTENT

THE ROAD NOT TAKEN

Petrified Petri. That's what they called him. Always afraid of everything, and brave against nothing. He had been offered a scholarship in the Third Kingdom, which would have provided him with a home, and income and a valuable skill. One day he may even have been designing artwork for King Eralf in the First Kingdom. But Petri had turned it down. He was too afraid to leave his family behind, too scared of being on his own in another city. His father refused to talk to him for two weeks after that. He had told him that he was a selfish boy and had not thought of the benefit the position would bring to his entire family. And here he was doing the same thing again.

"You cannot go through your entire life without taking some kind of risks, my friend."

Berg, Petri's best friend and in truth, only friend, was always trying to get him to come out of his shell a little more. The prime example would be his unyielding efforts to find Petri a companion. He had seen the way Petri had looked at one of the White Falcons, Sky, in particular. But she was way out of his league and probably old enough to be his grandmother, despite only looking in her early twenties.

"What if she says no?" pleaded Petri. "What if she laughs at me and tells all the others in the village. I'll be laughed out of Seven in no time!"

Berg sighed deeply.

"My friend, you must stop all of this conjecture and what ifs you insist on dwelling over. If you never try, then you never know!"

But it was no use. Another wasted five minutes of staring at the girl in question, before she wandered off and the chance was lost.

"Oh well, I suppose that's number twenty-one on the list of missed opportunities for this year."

Berg's sarcasm cut through Petri like a knife. Not because it was demeaning, but because he knew that his friend was right. The notion of fear had come from his grandfather. Harker had been one of the fiercest warriors in all of Beyond. He was one of the few from the Fifth Kingdom who ended up serving in all five kingdoms at one point. He had even been one of those present at the induction of the latest Green Dragon, Tommy. Always deemed as one of the bravest men ever to be born in all of the realm. But it was his bravery which had gotten him killed. He had ventured out one day on a rare break from his duties, when he came across a woman being robbed on the edge of the Shadowlands. The perpetrator appeared to be a changeling, altering its shape to try and throw the woman off. Harker had heard her cries for help and when he discovered her, he saw she was also travelling with a baby. Leaping into action, he took down the changeling and saved the woman. But it had been a trap. The woman was also a changeling, and as her face contorted into a grin, and her shape changed, Harker had known he had fallen for an elaborate trick. Seven changelings assaulted him, and by the time Harker was found, he had been robbed of all his possessions and stabbed thirty-two times in the chest. From that day on, Petri vowed never to take a serious risk, no matter what the cost.

"Fine. I'm going to give you two choices. We're going to break you out of this nonsensical state of mind you have wedged yourself in," began Berg. "Either you come with me to the tavern, and we spend the day talking to people, well women in particular, or…"

Berg trailed off as his mind hesitated on his second choice.

"Or what?" asked Petri, his own curiosity now peaking.

"Or… we walk to the Void."

The shiver that ran through Petri's body was instant, and all encompassing. His skin prickled goosebumps, and his blood ran cold. The Void was not a place people travelled to. It was a place to be avoided at all costs. It was, of course, there for a reason. To keep the darkness of the universe contained. There had been rumors of cracks appearing in the surface of the barrier for months now, but nobody had dared investigate. They left all that kind of thing to the White Falcons, protectors of the realm. But despite all of the fear and worry that dwelled within Petri, he had always been curious as to what the Void actually looked like. Harker had told him that he had been to its perimeter once, and felt as though all of the joy had been sucked out of him. As if the darkness itself seeped out from within like a fog that took a firm grip and refused to let go.

"You know we can't do that," Petri whispered, his eyes already turning toward the edge of the city. "Nobody goes there."

"All the more reason to go and charm some ladies then, wouldn't you say?"

Berg was convinced of victory here. He knew that nobody in their right mind would go to the Void, and certainly not someone as cowardly as his friend. Even Berg wouldn't go to the Void willingly.

"Yes, I suppose so."

Berg was surprised to hear a tone of reluctance in Petri's voice at taking the safer option. This was something he had not seen in his friend before. Actual preference to taking the more dangerous road. For a moment, he thought he had accidentally traversed one of the doorways into another world. He blinked twice and shook his head.

"You aren't actually thinking about going to the Void? Are you?" Berg asked in disbelief.

"I... I don't know. I feel like something is calling me there. You know, I've been a coward all of my life, but there's just something... curiosity. Part of me wants to know how it feels. What it tastes like, to take the most dangerous chance of them all."

Berg shook his head again, and now started to worry about pushing his friend too far.

"Petri, we can't! I was only joking with you to get you to go to the tavern! Why would you of all people try to do something so stupid!" shouted Berg.

But the truth was, Petri simply didn't know. Something was compelling him to do this, to take this walk out of the huge stone gates of the Fifth Kingdom, leaving his village of Seven, and crossing the meadows towards the darkness. He only realised he had made his choice as he realised he was already walking forwards.

"Wait! Wait for me!" cried Berg, still in disbelief at what his friend was doing. "You're not going out there alone!"

Berg may have been terrified of the Void, but he was the most loyal of friends, and was not prepared to let Petri go alone. Finally, Petrified Petri was about to grow a spine, and show the whole city he was as brave as anyone else. As brave as his grandfather. And with Berg running to catch up, Petri exited the gates to the Fifth Kingdom and began the long walk towards the home of eternal darkness.

The irony of this was that in his determination not to make a mistake similar to that of his brave grandfather, he had done

The Road Not Taken

exactly that. Perhaps if Petri had remained his usual fearful self, he would have met the girl of his dreams in the tavern. They may have been married, had children and even moved to one of the better kingdoms. Perhaps if he had listened to his friend, both of them would have come back that day and not just one. Perhaps the tavern really had been the braver option. Alas, as it proved, it was the road not taken.

And Petri paid for it with his life.

AFTERWORD

I have, over the years, thanked many people from all aspects and avenues of my life in the backs of my books. Sometimes, even mentioning famous people who have inspired me, despite I knew all too well that they would never see it. But, it was my book and I could say what I wanted to!

Now the series is coming to an end, I would like to unify my acknowledgements across the board into this one message. Particularly as I have even more people to thank years after the first book hit websites!

First and foremost, I must thank my incredible wife, Charlotte. Without her, I simply do not know where I would be, not just with my writing but in my life. I was starting to give up on almost everything when I met her, and she quickly became my rock, my confidante, and more importantly, my best friend. It is with her that I was able to start a family, and in February 2022, we welcomed little Molly Rose Adams into the world. They are both my world, and entire universe and I simply cannot imagine anywhere in the multiverse where we aren't all together.

Naturally, the next in line for thanks and appreciation would be

Afterword

my parents, Shirley and Vince Adams. Particularly since my introduction to various forms of social media in the last few years, I have come across far too many stories of unhappy childhoods, and lack of support from families of many people in my life. I, fortunately, am certainly not one of them. My mother and father have never once put me down, attempted to dissuade me from doing anything or making any significant life changes. They have shown me nothing but unconditional love, support, and at times, financial help. They continue to be a beacon of light in my life, and are devoted to my little family completely. If there was a blueprint on how to parent a child, these two would have written it.

That support flows down the family chain, and emanates from my sister, Francesca too. When we were younger, we did not get on. Always hitting each other, shouting at each other, and making each other unhappy and angry almost every day. But as we have gotten older, our bond has strengthened, and she has been there for me, Charlotte and Molly every step of the way. It has even reached the point where we left our home in Plymouth, and moved to Dorset, just a matter of streets away from each other! Her other half, Anthony, is a tower of strength for her, and their two children Jack and Isabelle are the jewels in their little family. It is a joy to be in their company, and their unique place on the autistic spectrum makes them extra loveable, and always fun to be around, because they adore companionship. I'm proud to be their uncle.

My grandparents played a vital role in my early life. My grandfather, William Henry Griffiths, for whom the first book is dedicated, was my best friend. I would see him every fortnight growing up, and he would always have a happy and yet powerful aura around him. He was a huge imposing figure in stature, but was as kind as could be. There were always miniature bars of chocolate in a tin waiting for me and Francesca, and a couple of quid pocket money. His death in 2005 devastated me, and in truth, 18 years later, still resonates within me. I miss him dearly.

Afterword

My other grandparents, Marlene and Dave are a force of encouragement and love. Nobody fucks with my Nan. Not if they know what is good for them. I remember distinctly her glaring at my soon to be mother-in-law at our wedding when the registrar spoke the words 'if anyone knows of any reason why these two should not be married, speak now.' It was definitely a 'don't fuck with me' look. And of course my Grandad is nothing but a funny cuddle teddy bear, even now. His humour always cuts through any tension or discomfort, as bad as his jokes are, and I was proud to ask him to be my best man at my wedding, where he made the customary jokes, and I was blessed that he accepted.

I never had a job that I truly loved, until I moved to Ilfracombe in North Devon about a year and a half after my maternal grandfather died. I spent 10 months hunting for a job to no avail, before being told that whole time, the fruit and veg shop next door had been looking for someone! And so in the September of 2008, I began what would turn out to be 8 years working for the Norman family. That family made me feel like one of my own. I owe a debt of gratitude to Pam Norman for being my extra grandmother, Trevor and Sarah Norman for showing me such kindness, support and friendship, and Paula Hobman and her family for being like a crazy aunt and always cheering me up. I miss working for them, and being around them all the time, but they left an everlasting mark on my life that I will always carry with me.

Charlotte's Great Uncle Richard Oliver, and his daughter Nancy, have become two of our strongest connections. They have always backed us with whatever choices we made, and helped us along the way. They exude love and support, and at certain times, I'm not sure what we would have done without them. I simply cannot accurately place into words, what the two of them mean, but I like to think that they know.

And finally, I would like to take a minute or two to mention

Afterword

some of the people I have met in recent years through the wonders of the online community.

I joined Flare in 2023, a peer support group for those dealing with mental health issues and physical disabilities. It is a place to talk together, support others, and build a friendly safe community in the often toxic world of the internet. Founded by Robyn, Josh and Emma, it has gone from strength to strength and in doing so, I gained some very good friends. Like many friends, we have our differences, but the benefit they have given to my life has helped me develop my persona, particularly through their support of my social media presence and helping me to be more outgoing through mentoring and doing my own livestreams. Robyn in particular was instrumental in that, and for someone who has gone through so much in her short life, she gives so much more.

In the same timeframe, I met Chantel. Much like my Nan, you don't fuck with Chantel. She is fierce, devoted and loving in a way that makes her a very treasured individual. I have given her cause to digitally slap me in the face numerous times, but I have never stopped admiring her and the person she has become through the adversity she has battled through. I hope we remain friends for a long time to come.

BookTok's community changed me for the better. I met some wonderful author friends, and not only are they kind and supportive and funny, they are extremely talented writers and designers.

RD Baker is one of my closest author friends. Which is no mean feat considering she lives in Australia! I had never read either a fantasy or spicy book until I was enraptured by her book *Shadow and the Draw*. The world building was so well done and yet I was able to follow it all! I have since joined her ARC team and anticipate every book she writes with rising enthusiasm. She is also an incredible advocate for indie authors, and kindness across

Afterword

the world. If you haven't read her books before, what are you doing with your life?!?!

Next up is someone who I came across during a giveaway she was doing on TikTok. Alexia Mulle-Rushbrook very kindly sent me a free copy of her dystopian sci-fi The Minority Rule, and once I read it, I immediately bought the rest of the trilogy, devouring each book. They were simply wonderful, and I was happy to become part of her ARC team for the more recent release *They Call Me Angel*, which was her best work to date. She is a kind and giving person, and we chat often through direct messages, and always support each other on TikTok.

And no thanks would be complete without the presence of Christian Francis. I came across him when I saw one of his many videos on TikTok offering advice to indie authors like me, and everything the man said made perfect sense, and I followed it often. I particularly enjoyed his video on writing a scary scene which I may have coerced into a particular chapter of *Frame of Mind*, so this is me giving him credit! He also very kindly was the man behind this redesign of *The Dark Corner* series, and I will never forget the time, effort and resources he provided to me for that task. As if that wasn't enough, he designed the covers for my other series *The Frozen Planet Trilogy*, and created the amazing myindiebookshelf.com which champions indie authors, giving them a platform to showcase their work and link people exactly where to find them. And let's not forget that his books are fucking awesome. Disturbing... but fucking awesome.

Well, I have rambled on long enough. It's almost as if I was reciting my life story at times, I know, but with this being the best version of my work out there, I wanted to really get the message across.

Arnold Schwarzenegger says often that people are free to call him many things, but don't ever call him a self-made man. Because he has had help from people all his life, and without them,

Afterword

he wouldn't be who he is today. And that sums up perfectly how I feel. Without all the people I mentioned above, I wouldn't be who I am today.

I have written many books since my debut, and I am proud of most of them. While *The Dark Corner* series comes to an end, other journeys begin, and I am happy to say I don't see me stopping typing away anytime soon. So thank you for joining me on the journey, and I hope we can go on many more adventures together as the years go by.

Oh and one more thing...

It is possible to make no mistakes and still lose. That is not failure, that is life. I feel too many people forget that, particularly in this industry.

Take care, and see you in Sisko's.

David W. Adams
November 2023

ABOUT THE AUTHOR

David was born in 1988 in Wolverhampton, England. He spent most of his youth growing up in nearby Telford, where he attended the prestigious Thomas Telford School. However, unsure of which direction he wished his life to go in, he left higher education during sixth form, in order to get a job and pay his way. He has spent most of his life since, working in retail.

In 2007, following the death of his grandfather William Henry Griffiths a couple of years earlier, David's family relocated to the North Devon coastal town of Ilfracombe, where he got a job in local greengrocers, Normans Fruit & Veg as a general assistant, and spent 8 happy years there. In 2014, David met Charlotte, and in 2016, relocated to Plymouth to live with her as she continued her University studies.

In 2018, the pair were married, and currently reside on the Isle of Portland, Dorset.

The first published works of David's, was *The Dark Corner*. It was a compilation of short haunting stories which he wrote to help him escape the reality of the Coronavirus pandemic in early-mid 2020. However, it was not until January 2021, that he made the decision to publish.

From there... *The Dark Corner Literary Universe* was spawned....

You can follow David on TikTok @davidwadams.author.

ABOUT THE AUTHOR

tiktok.com/@davidwadams.author
amazon.com/stores/author/B08VHD911S

David was born in 1958 in Wolverhampton, England. He spent most of his youth growing up in nearby Telford, where he attended the prestigious Thomas Telford School. However, unsure of which direction he wished his life to go in, he left higher education during sixth form, in order to get a job and pay his way. He has spent most of his life since, working in retail.

In 2007, following the death of his grandfather William Henry Gething a couple of years earlier, David's family relocated to the North Devon coastal town of Ilfracombe, where he got a job in local greengrocers, Normans Fruit & Veg as a general assistant, and spent 8 happy years there. In 2014, David met Charlotte, and in 2016, relocated to Plymouth to live with her as she continued her University studies.

In 2018, the pair were married and currently reside on the Isle of Portland, Dorset.

The first published works of David's, was The Dark Corner. It was a compilation of short haunting stories which he wrote to help him escape the reality of the Coronavirus pandemic in early-mid 2020. However, it was not until January 2021, that he made the decision to publish.

From there, The Dark Corner, Interwoven Everyone, was spawned...

You can follow David on TikTok @davidwadams.author.